D0616999

WINDOM'S WAY

JAMES RAMSEY ULLMAN

WINDOM'S WAY

J. B. LIPPINCOTT COMPANY
PHILADELPHIA AND NEW YORK

PRINTED IN THE
UNITED STATES OF AMERICA

Library of Congress catalog card number 52-5093

To

Lynn and Virginia Carrick

Note

Every work of fiction has its genesis in reality. As most readers will be well aware, there are many living men—some physicians, some in other fields; some obscure, some widely known—who, in the far corners of the earth today, are fighting the battle, not of partisan politics, but of humanity. It is from such men and their lives that the theme of this book is derived.

But anyone who assumes that it depicts specific persons or events will do so in error. Its protagonist, Dr. Windom, is wholly imaginary. So too are all the other characters, as well as the incidents and the locale; and any resemblances to factual reality are inadvertent and coincidental.

In short, this is a work of fiction.

J. R. U.

Acknowledgment

My thanks are due to Dr. Robert E. Kaufman, of New York, and Dr. David Ashdown, of Bermuda, for help with the medical details of this story. I hasten to add, however, that this does not make them responsible for any errors that may have eluded their notice.—J. R. U.

WINDOM'S WAY

ONE

IT WAS STILL DARK WHEN THEY LEFT THE HOSPITAL COMPOUND. The air was almost cool. But ahead of them, over the sea, the stars were paling, and soon now, with the quick magic of the tropics, it would be bright flaming day.

The man and the boy walked quickly down the village street.

Usually, at this time, the man was alone, but today the boy had been waiting for him as he came from his bungalow and had asked to go along.

The man had hesitated.

"Please, my doctor."

And he had said, "All right. Come on."

Now, passing through the village, the man walked with a long loose-jointed stride and the boy trotted to keep pace with him. Behind a mud wall a cock crowed. Then a mule brayed. But the street was still empty. The dust rose from under the boy's scuffing feet and hung like grains of silver in the windless air.

They came to the edge of the town, and of the land. Here a small sluggish river emptied into the bay, and there were mudflats, mangroves, a warehouse and a rickety dock. Moored to the dock was a small skiff, and they climbed down into it and pushed off. The man rowed and the boy sat in the stern, pretending he was the navigator.

They cut obliquely across the bay toward a low headland that marked its northern end. At first the headland was barely visible, a mere thickening of darkness against the night beyond; but now, as they moved toward it, the night thinned and its outlines emerged clear in the dawnlight. In the skiff, the man and the boy emerged too. They were no longer merely figures, but individuals.

The boy was perhaps twelve, with a lithe small-framed body and the smooth flat features of his race. He was wearing only a loin cloth, and, though it was brown, it was lighter than the brown of his skin. His hair was black, and his eyes too, but not with the opaque blackness that was in the eyes of many of his people. As he peered ahead over the lightening water they were shining with a dark inner brightness of their own.

Then they met the man's eyes and smiled, and the man's eyes smiled back.

They were not black like the boy's, but a cool northern gray; and if there was tiredness in them there were also other things deeper than tiredness, and one of them was the smile. His face was long and flat-planed, with prominent nose and jaw, so that what you noticed in it was bone rather than flesh. It might have been an ascetic face, had it not been for the broad mustached mouth and the thatch of rumpled graying hair; and it was burned to the color and texture of reddish clay, which made the eyes appear even lighter than they really were. His hands and forearms, too, were dark and weathered, but when presently he paused in his rowing to pull off his shirt, his body appeared, in contrast, an almost startling white. Like his face, it was more bone than flesh. His shoulders, hunched over the oars, seemed all bone.

If you were a patient, my friend, he thought, glancing down at himself, I'd have you on a month's diet of yam and rice. He shuddered slightly. Luckily a doctor didn't have to take his own medicine.

The water slurred softly from the nose of the skiff. The flat disc of the bay sucked lustre from the brightening sky. The rower did not need to turn around to check his course or progress, for he knew exactly what landmark to keep dead astern and exactly how many minutes it took to reach the headland. . . . Sure, old Doc Windom, he thought. Haven't you heard? The people set their watches by him.

Except, of course, that they had no watches. They had only a clock. The vast golden eternal clock that would rise soon now, pealing, from the sea.

He rowed on quietly, as he had on so many other mornings during those past two years. On *how* many? he mused. A hundred? Two hundred? He would do it every morning, he had resolved after the first time. But being human—and often tired—he of course hadn't. He had done it when he needed to do it.

And he needed to today.

He became aware that the boy was talking.

". . . and when the plane comes this morning," he said, "you will go out and meet it?"

The man nodded.

"You will go in the jeep from the hospital?"

Another nod.

"And you will take me along? Yes, please, my doctor—" When he received no answer the boy leaned eagerly forward and the pleading came in a rush.

The man interrupted him gently.

"Don't let's talk now, Kosti."

"But—"

"Talk is for later. Look, we're almost there."

For a few moments the only sound was the creak of oars; then this too was gone, and they drifted in under the headland. Skiff and sea, earth and sky hung suspended in gray stillness.

Then flame touched the stillness. The sun rose: a yellow eye burning level across the world. The sky was a fan of light, the hills shone, and the arc of the sea blazed with blue fire. Above them the rock of the headland glittered—and below them too: a deep twilight-glitter falling away into liquid darkness.

The skiff nudged a half-sunken ledge, and the man tied the painter to a knob of coral. "Let's go," he said. "Be sure to stay inside the reef."

He dove into the water, and its soft coolness enveloped him like a silver shroud. He plunged and surfaced and lay on his back, with the sun warm on his closed eyelids; and now the tiredness behind them was gone, the tiredness in his bones was gone; heat and dust, the blat of voices, the smell of sweat and dung and formaldehyde—they were all gone; even the deep inward drone of the approaching plane was gone, forgotten and lost in the bright spell of the morning. Then he pulled himself up into a sitting position on the reef, and the boy sat beside him. They looked down at their legs, trailing long and gleaming in the water, and beyond their legs at the still depths below. And suddenly within the depths there was a quick flash, a gleam of blue and gold, and the boy was leaning far forward, pointing.

"A poutina!"

"Yes."

"Oh, if I had my spear!" The boy stared downward. "It is so beautiful—"

"—that you want to kill it?"

But the boy wasn't listening. "Even without a spear I will get it," he cried. "With my hands—watch—you will see!" And in the next instant he was gone.

The gleam receded. The boy's shadow receded. The man could see him gliding down along the rough coral walls, trying to corner the fish in a crevice of the reef. A few bubbles rose to the surface and vanished. Then gleam and shadow vanished. For a few moments the man remained peering down; then suddenly he was on his feet, for he realized what had happened, and, turning he saw the movement in the water on the far side of the reef. The fish had swum through, and, finding an opening, the boy had followed it.

"Kosti!"

The name hung in the air, unheard.

Then the man dove. He stroked down with all his strength, and though he could not swim so fast nor stay down so long as the boy, he tried to cut in from above to intercept him. The gleam was gone now, but the shadow was still there. A brown slender shadow against the white sand of the bottom, and behind it, moving slowly closer, another larger darker shadow. . . .

He reached for the boy's shoulder and missed. Reaching again, he touched his hair, grasped it, pulled. The boy's body rose swiftly, and, letting go of him, the man turned and kicked out violently with both legs. The second shadow hung suspended in twilight. There was an undulation of black fin, a yellow glint of teeth. Then the shadow receded—faded—and, stroking upward, the man raised himself onto the top of the reef.

He didn't speak to the boy, and it was a long time before the boy said anything.

Then he said, "I am sorry, my doctor."

"Maybe next time you'll remember."

"Yes, I will remember. I promise."

The man nodded and sat looking down into the water. There was no shadow any more, but only the flawless crystal of the sea.

"I am sorry," the boy repeated. "It was so beautiful. I forgot—"

They rowed back across the blue dazzle of the bay. It was no longer, however, of the sea and sunlight that they were thinking—nor even of the shadow that moved beneath them—but of the plane that, in a few hours, would land on the little airstrip beyond the village. The boy was thinking that now, certainly, he would not be allowed to go and see it. And the man was thinking that in the plane would be his wife, whom he had not seen in more than two years.

When he looked around, the blueness was gone and the water was heavy with silt. Close across it were the mudflats, the mangroves and the lopsided dock. Mooring and leaving the skiff, they walked up the street, and the dust was no longer silver but yellow. The village, which an hour before had been wrapped in darkness, lay like a parched scab on the living earth.

But it was awake now, too—and living. All around them, as they walked, were chickens, dogs, mules, oxen, and the small brown gentle people. Some of the people said, "My doctor," some only smiled or nodded gravely; but not one passed by without recognition, and in the man's heart was a warmth deeper than that of the morning sun.

Then they reached the hospital gate and turned in, going not to the main building itself but to the small bungalow on the opposite side of the compound. In his room the man brushed his teeth, combed his hair and put on a khaki shirt, shorts and a pair of sneakers. When he emerged, breakfast was already on the table on the screened porch, and, as he ate, Anna Vidal came across the compound from the hospital with a sheaf of papers in her hand.

"Good morning, my doctor," she said, coming onto the porch.

And the day began.

TWO

"THERE IS THE APPENDECTOMY," SAID ANNA VIDAL. "HE IS better. The two dysenteries are about the same. With the leg ulcer it is hard to tell, and I think you should look at him."

"Any new admissions?"

"Three men from the plantation."

"Malaria?"

"No, there was trouble yesterday."

"Again?"

"It was about a meeting that was called when they had finished work. Jan said—"

The girl cut herself off. Windom looked at her for a moment and then took another sip of his tea.

"So Jan was in it," he said.

"He was only—"

"Yes. I know. He was only lying in bed, and someone woke him up and told him about it." Windom set down his cup. "Can't you talk to your brother, Anna?" he said.

"I have tried, my doctor. Truly. But—"

"But maybe I'd better have a try at it." Windom raised his head and called: "Kosti!"

The boy appeared from inside.

"You've had your breakfast?"

"Yes, my doctor."

"Good. I want you to go to the house of Nurse Anna's mother. Tell her brother Jan I want to see him."

"At once, my doctor?"

Windom looked at his watch. "At nine," he said. "When I've finished my rounds."

Anna put in: "But the plane—"

"—won't be here until ten." Windom nodded at Kosti. The boy hesitated and his mouth opened, but no words came. Then, quick as a lizard, he turned and vanished.

Windom looked at the nurse's troubled face. "Don't be upset, Anna," he said. "I'm not angry at Jan. I simply want to talk with him."

"Jan is good, my doctor. Truly."

"I know he's good," said Windom.

He went on with his breakfast, and the nurse sat waiting. She was a young woman of perhaps twenty-five: slim of body, delicate of feature; fully three inches taller than the average woman of her race, yet by Western standards small and almost fragile. Her skin was smooth and cream-colored, her face oval, her eyes wide-spaced, large and black. And her hair was black too, straight-combed and gleaming, under the prim white starch of her cap.

Now, as the doctor ate, she bent over the case-history sheets that she had brought and presently began speaking again of the leg ulcer in the South Ward. Windom, however, listened less to her words than her voice. It was a voice that, in two years, he had never grown tired of hearing: a soft blend of her own native intonations and the King's English as spoken in the Royal Medical College of Singapore; and he would gladly have exchanged it for his own flat and textureless Wisconsinese. It is strange, he thought, how the compound can be purer than the element. And then he came back to what she was saying and nodded and finished his breakfast.

The yard, as they crossed it, was already blazing under the morning sun, and the hospital seemed in contrast almost cool. It was a rambling one-storey building of teak and stucco, dating from the late nineteenth century, and over the main doorway you could still see where the words ANGLO-CATHOLIC MISSIONARY SOCIETY had been (more or less) scraped away and PAPAAN GENERAL HOSPITAL substituted. On the right, as they went in, was the dispensary, now occupied by a student nurse and perhaps a half-dozen waiting villagers. To the left was the cubicle that served Windom as an office. Entering it, he took a white jacket from a hook and put it on over his shirt; then bent over the sheet of notes that lay on the desk.

"We'll make the rounds first," he said to Anna. "Then the dispensary. Schedule the ulcer for ten, and—"

"But at ten—"

"I mean at twelve. If any of these plantation fellows need surgery we can take them afterward."

They went on into the wards.

The hospital, at this particular time, was not crowded. Malaria was the scourge of the country, that often filled the beds and even the aisles; but now it was late in the dry season and the incidence was at its lowest. There were altogether only eight fever cases, including the dysenteries. There was the appendectomy, a goitre, three TB's (beyond the curing stage) and a woman in her seventh month of pregnancy who was threatening to miscarry. Windom spent a few minutes at each bedside; and although to the nurse he referred to the cases by the category of ailment, to his face he addressed each patient by name. In the book of his profession, this was as important as anything he did with drug or scalpel.

The ulcer was bad. There was an odor of incipient gangrene.

"Twelve o'clock," he said to Anna, as they moved on.

Then he came to the three men who had been brought in during the night. Two of them had only flesh wounds and missing teeth, but the third was badly battered, with a broken arm and probably several cracked ribs as well.

"I have given him a quarter morphine," said Anna.

Windom examined him as well as he could. But he was less than satisfied. Orthopedics without X-ray, he thought, was like navigation without a compass.

"I'll look at him later, in the O.R.," he said. Then he turned to the nearer of the other two men.

"Well, Petar?" he asked.

One of the man's eyes was swollen and closed. The other looked up at him, dark and pleading. "It was not our fault, my doctor," he said.

"No?"

"We had called a meeting, that is all. We called a meeting, and the police came."

"It was the police who beat you?"

"Yes, my doctor."

"Bilko?"

"Yes, Bilko. And his men."

"Where was this meeting held?" said Windom.

The man hesitated.

"It was on plantation property, wasn't it?"

"Yes, my doctor."

"Without permission from the management."

"Yes."

"Whose idea was that, Petar?" asked Windom. "Who organized the meeting?"

The man started to answer, then looked at Anna and stopped.

"It was Jan Vidal, wasn't it?"

Still the man said nothing.

"All right, don't tell me. Jan will be here soon, and I'll get the story from him." Windom turned to go. "You and Fidel can leave when you're ready, but be sure you keep those cuts clean. Pondar, of course, will have to stay a while."

Anna following, he left the ward and made his way to the dispensary. There were more people there now, and all of them wanted to talk to him; but there was nothing the nurses couldn't handle.

As he crossed toward his office, Kosti appeared.

"Jan will be here, my doctor," he said.

"You saw him?"

"No, he was not at home. But I saw Mamarta, his mother, and she said she would go tell him."

"Did she say where he–" He broke off. There was no use going into that. "Thanks, Kosti," he said and opened his office door.

But the boy was still beside him. "My doctor, please," he said. "Please, I know I was foolish when we swam. I was very bad; I am sorry; I am so terribly sorry. But–" The words had come out in a rush, but now they stuck. "But please," he murmured finally, looking away, "please could I come with you to the plane."

Windom held back his smile. "We'll see," he said. He glanced at his watch. "It's an hour yet."

He went into his office.

It was a small whitewashed room, containing an old desk, two chairs, a shelf of medical books, and an electric fan that didn't work. Windom sat down at the desk. He began looking through the notes that lay there, and then, realizing that he had already read them, pushed them aside. Getting up, he paced a few times back and forth across the room. It was hot and still. The only sound was the droning of insects in the shrubs beyond the window.

The sound rose and fell: like the drone of a plane. . . .

Windom looked again at his watch.

It had been—how long?—three months at least since the last plane had landed in the valley. The airfield had been built by the Americans during the war and for a brief time had been an incredible jungle depot swarming with men and machines. But with war's end that had ended too. The fliers had flown away. The jungle had crept back over the Quonset huts and rusted gasoline drums, until all that was left was a narrow strip, marked on the air charts: *suitable for emergencies.* There had, however, been no "emergencies" during the two years Windom had been in Papaan. Twice there had been the governor of the province, on his annual rounds; twice, generals on inspection tours; once, a party of engineers on a survey. And that was all. Whoever and whatever else arrived from the cities to the south, came either by truck along the jungle road or in one of the decrepit trading ships that plied the coast.

Windom took from a drawer the telegram that had arrived the day before. *Arriving plane about ten tomorrow. Lee.*

What plane? Whose plane? . . . Windom smiled as he put the telegram down. . . . Probably a maharajah's Constellation, he thought. Trust Lee.

The letter was in the drawer too: the letter that had come five days ago. He had been sitting at this same desk when Kosti brought it in, and he could still feel how his breath caught and his hands went tight when he had seen the script on the envelope and the postmark: Calcutta.

I have waited until now to write you, she had written, *because I was afraid that at the last moment I might get cold feet.*

And on the next page: *It would be fun, of course, just to drop in, but I've decided to play fair and give you a chance to get your houris (sp.?) and dancing girls out of the way.*

And on the last: *Dammit to hell, I guess I still love you.*

Windom closed the drawer. For a while he sat looking out the window at the yellow glare of the compound. Then he got up, opened a door in the rear wall of the office, and went into the small laboratory that adjoined it. On a rack on the workbench was a row of tubes in which he had been trying to isolate certain bacterial cultures. Selecting one of them, he held it to the light.

A while later he heard someone enter the office.

"Jan?" he called.

"No, it is I, my doctor."

Going to the door, he was confronted by a short pudgy man with a nervous manner and dark anxious eyes. "Oh, Lollivar," he said.

"May I speak with you, my doctor?"

"I have to meet a plane in half an hour. And I'm expecting—"

"Yes, I know whom you are expecting; but he is not coming. That is why I am here. Not on a social visit, you understand, but in my official capacity."

The mayor of Papaan sat down, took a handkerchief from the breast pocket of his white linen suit, and wiped his face. It was a round smooth face that from the front appeared wholly Oriental, but when seen in profile showed an almost angular structure, tipped by a long thin nose. Someone—probably one of the nurses, Windom thought—had once described it as "a face that couldn't make up its mind." And this was logical enough, for Dai Lollivar was a Eurasian. His mother had been a local woman, his father a French planter called L'Olivier, long since vanished, to whose name, however—with a certain allowance for the native idiom—he had tenaciously clung. Along with Anna Vidal, he was one of the few inhabitants of the valley who had lived in the outer world, and there were rumors that he had been, variously, a lawyer in Hongkong, an officer in the Siamese Navy, and a laundryman in San Francisco. In any case, he had returned to Papaan after the war and soon become both its mayor and its leading merchant.

Windom sat down at his desk.

"Well?" he asked.

"The boy Kosti," said Dai Lollivar, "goes to the house of Jan Vidal. Jan is not there, but the old woman, Mamarta, says she will get him. Then she comes to me, because that is where her son has said he will be."

"But he wasn't with you?"

"No."

"Do you know where he is?"

"Yes, I know."

"At the plantation?"

"No, not at the plantation."

"Where then?"

"With Amyan."

The mayor brought out the name dramatically, but Windom's response was merely a mild "Oh."

"You say 'oh,' my doctor," said Lollivar, "as if that is good."

"It's a lot better than his being back at the plantation."

"No, it is not better. It is worse." Lollivar slapped the table with a chubby hand. "This Amyan is a dangerous man."

"Dangerous?"

"Yes. Who do you think it is behind this thing at the plantation? Who gives Jan his orders. Who makes all the trouble."

"Amyan is old and sick."

"Yes, he is old. He is sick. But he is also—"

"He is also," said Windom warmly, "a fine decent unselfish man, and he's done more for the people of this valley than any ten other men put together."

Lollivar was taken by surprise. He pulled out his handkerchief again and mopped at his cheeks, and when he next spoke his voice was soft and conciliatory.

"Yes, my doctor, of course. I understand what you mean. He is a fine man, I am sure, and once a holy man. For many years he has been of much service. But right now, you see—like in this thing with Jan Vidal—he is making trouble."

"Not as much trouble as Schusterman, calling in the police."

"Mr. Schusterman is the plantation manager. He must protect his property."

"Or as Bilko, with those thugs of his, beating up harmless coolies."

The mayor frowned unhappily. "Yes," he conceded, "I know. Bilko is too severe, too direct. But what can I do, my doctor? He does not take his orders from me—you know that—but from the chief of police of the province."

Windom looked out the window.

"Anyhow," Lollivar continued, "it is good that you will speak to Jan Vidal. It is this Amyan, I know, who tells him what to do, but he is too old to do it himself, and if Jan no longer does it there will be an end of the trouble." He spread out his hands. "That is all that I want, my doctor. This Amyan—yes, perhaps he is a good man—but foolish. And Jan, he is good too—but young and headstrong. I do not wish anything against them, but only that they no longer have these meetings and disturbances. That there is no longer this trouble. I am a no-trouble man, you understand?"

A figure had appeared in the door, and the mayor glanced up. "Ah, good morning, my pretty one," he said.

"It is almost ten," Anna said to the doctor.

Windom got up, took off his white jacket and went to the door.

"You will speak strongly to this Jan, please?" said Lollivar, following him.

"I'll do my best," said Windom.

"He will listen to you."

"Perhaps."

They crossed the compound to where an old jeep was parked in the shade of the bungalow.

"Give you a ride?" Windom asked.

"With many thanks, my doctor."

The two men got in and Windom started the motor. But after he had driven a few yards he stopped and looked back at the small disconsolate figure standing on the bungalow steps.

"Come on, shake a leg there," he called brusquely to Kosti. "We'll need someone to help with the baggage."

THREE

THEY WEREN'T EXACTLY BUCKET SEATS BUT THEY WEREN'T divans either, and, to make it worse, there was no headroom to stand up. Lenore Windom stretched her slim legs out in front of her as far as they would go, until she realized that her knees had appeared and that Colonel Hasbrook was eyeing them.

"Creeping paralysis," she explained, tucking her feet up under her.

The colonel had looked quickly away. "It shouldn't be long now," he assured her. He exchanged a few words with the pilot in the native language. "About half an hour, he says."

"I'll last it," said Lenore.

There were only the three of them in the plane: the pilot up front and she and Hasbrook behind him, side by side. The remaining front seat and what little other space there was were occupied by baggage. It was close quarters, and the hot cabin reeked of gas and oil; but, compared to the alternative ways of making the trip, this was luxury itself, and Lenore was aware of it and grateful.

"Papaan? People do not go to Papaan," they had informed her, two days before, at the hotel in the capital. The

Visitors Bureau had suggested she hire a mule. But when she called at the American Legation things had happened even faster than she had dared hope. The name Mrs. Alexander Windom had opened all doors. The minister and his wife had had her for tea. And that same evening she had dined, by arrangement, with Colonel George Hasbrook, of the American Military Mission, who was on the point of making a flying tour of the Northern Provinces.

"I've just checked up," he had told her, "and the airstrip at Papaan is still usable."

"But you weren't planning—"

"Plans change," he said, smiling. "Sometimes very pleasantly. And besides, I've been wanting to meet your husband for a long time."

"Oh, you haven't, then?"

The colonel shook his head. "He's a regular damn hermit, you know. Best known white man in the country, but he just sticks up there in the bush. It's strange the impressions you get, though. I'd imagined him as much older."

"Older? Than what?"

Hasbrook raised his glass and smiled. "Than for this to be such a delightful dinner," he said.

He had held her hand a moment too long when they said goodnight, and she had been a little worried. But the next day he had been all right. He was young for a chicken colonel, attractive in a florid big-shouldered sort of way, and had apparently had nothing else to do but squire her around to the shops and cafés. By the time they left the city the following morning she knew that he had won a DSC at Okinawa, had a wife and two daughters in Terre Haute, Indiana, and had played left tackle on the 1935 Purdue football team.

In the plane, too, he had at first been talkative, but when her response was vague he obligingly closed his eyes and dozed. She was tired and had tried to doze too, but without success, and for most of the trip she sat looking out through the window at the green monotony of jungle below. . . . How many miles was it? Three hundred? Four? . . . "A regular damn hermit," Hasbrook had said. She smiled to herself. Well, here came the hermit's home companion.

But the smile wasn't deep. Not as deep as the coldness she felt inside her, in spite of the heat of the cabin. Not as deep as the thump of her heart, which she knew was not caused by altitude. She wanted to get up, to move around, to walk and talk and stop thinking. Most of all, she wanted a drink.

She had been very good about that, she thought. Not a single drink all the way from New York—until the two evenings with Hasbrook—and then it had not been because she wanted them but simply because it would have seemed prissy to refuse.

She wanted one now, though.

. . . *The hell you do,* she told herself angrily. It's the last thing in the world you want. And the last thing you're going to have. When you're with him: yes. When you're right and happy: yes. But like this—never. When you're alone or afraid—never. . . . Oh, Alec, Alec, she thought; this time it will be different, wait and see. This time it will be what it always should have been.

The plane droned on. She closed her eyes.

Then presently—five minutes later? fifteen?—Hasbrook was touching her arm. Beyond the window the earth was nearer and tilted, and the colonel pointed and said, "There's the field."

It was not like any airfield she had ever seen before. There was no concrete, but only grass; no planes or hangars or towers or fuel trucks, but only a dozen-odd scattered figures and, off to one side near the trees, what appeared to be a parked jeep. Then the field swung away. There were treetops, sky, trees again, and then only a blur of rushing green. The plane struck earth, bounced, struck a second time, skidded and slowed. She sat very quietly, hands folded, while it jolted over the grass, made a sharp half-turn and stopped.

But when, a moment later, she stood up, she had to rest her hand on the arm of the seat to steady herself. The heat was almost suffocating. Where the roar of the engines had been there was now a monstrous humming stillness.

Then, through the stillness, she realized that the door was open. Hasbrook and the pilot were outside, and now Hasbrook was helping her down. There were faces around her—brown faces—smooth and staring and strange; and they seemed to be pressing closer; and then there was a hand too, a hand reaching out and trying to take her shoulder bag, and she jerked away, almost in panic.

"I am sorry, my lady," a voice said, "but my doctor told me I should—"

And then a second voice: "All right, Kosti."

She looked up and there he was. As brown as the others; tall, gray-eyed, thin. . . . Too thin, she thought; much too thin. . . . Then the others were gone. Everything else was gone. She felt his cheek against her cheek and his hands against her shoulders, and she was no longer in a strange place among strangers but in the place where she belonged.

This is home, she thought, almost fiercely. This is home.

Then she was in her home: crossing the screened porch and small sitting room beyond; standing in the doorway of his—and now her—bedroom.

"The Papaan-Plaza," said Windom.

"Nicer," she said. "Plazas have clanking radiators."

"I know a room of your own would be better, but—"

"No, this is better."

There were two camp beds set close together, with a mosquito bar looped above them. There were two chests of drawers, a clothes cupboard, straw rugs, and, beyond a connecting door, a tin-walled bathroom.

"The plumbing works," Windom told her, "if you don't take it by surprise."

On the two chests were bowls of freshly cut tropical flowers.

"How lovely!" said Lenore.

"Anna picked them for you."

"Anna?"

"My head nurse."

"Oh." She bent her face to the fragrant blooms. "They're beautiful."

Kosti glided in and out with the baggage. A minute green lizard appeared from behind the cupboard, eyed them briefly and vanished. Then the sound of footsteps and voices became audible outside.

"I think it's the staff," said Windom.

"The staff?"

"From the hospital. To welcome you."

"Oh dear." Lenore looked apprehensive. "I don't have to—"

"All you have to do is smile. If some of them stare, smile harder."

She had taken a hibiscus blossom from one of the bowls and was fastening it in her hair.

"All right?" she asked, turning.

He smiled. "Daché couldn't do better."

She went toward him, raised her face and kissed him.

"All right, too?"

He put his arm out and drew her closer and held her tight. He kissed her nose and then her cheek and then her lips, and then they stood quietly in each others arms and she saw the little bristles on his throat under the jawline, where he always forgot to shave.

"Alec," she murmured.

"Yes, Lee?"

"I'm here, Alec."

He held her another moment. Then she found a piece of Kleenex, wiped the lipstick from his face, and they went outside.

Later they sat with Colonel Hasbrook on the screened porch, and Kosti brought cool drinks.

"It's a pleasure to meet you at last, doctor," said the colonel. "You're quite a legend down-country, you know."

Windom smiled. "Now you can put them straight."

"The minister asked to be remembered. And all the rest too. They wish you'd come down for a visit."

"Perhaps I shall, one of these days." Windom's smile broadened. "I might even come tomorrow, if I could pick up an X-ray machine."

"An X-ray, eh? That's what you need?"

"It's one of the things. Don't get me started on the list."

Hasbrook rubbed the broad wedge of his jaw; then he leaned forward a little. "On the contrary, doctor," he said, "I'd like you to give me that list." Windom started to speak, but he waved off the interruption. "As a matter of fact, we were talking about you just a few days ago down at the legation. About the work you're doing up here."

"It doesn't amount to—"

"It amounts to plenty. Do you know what the minister said? He said, 'That Doc Windom's the best ambassador the U.S. has in this part of the world.' And I agree with him."

"That's fine for the ego, of course. But—"

"I'm not buttering you up. I'm giving the facts." Hasbrook took a pull on his drink and set it down carefully. "Look, doc—you don't get out of the woods much and maybe you don't see the larger picture. But things aren't too good in this damn country. No better than in the rest of southeast Asia. The U.S. is doing what it can; it's trying to carry the ball. But it's not easy, I'm telling you, and we're no more popular than the English or French or any of the rest of them. The government's a corrupt mess. Up north are the Reds. And in between—" Hasbrook paused and shrugged. "In between, there's you. The only American who's really living out with the gooks. The only one they've got some respect for and might listen to."

"I'm not a politician, colonel," said Windom. "I'm a doctor. And as for what you call the gooks—"

"You're out here doing a job for them; and they know it. And that's why we in turn want to do a job for you. That X-ray machine—whatever else you need—put it down for me and we'll get it for you."

He went on talking. Windom nodded and occasionally spoke. His attention, however, was only half with the colonel. In ordinary circumstances such a visit, and such an offer, would have held him engrossed, but it so happened that he was sitting in the same room as his wife for the first time in two years.

Lenore sat in a rattan chair in the corner, quietly listening. . . . Two years, he thought. Did they show? No, scarcely at all. . . . When he had first seen her at the airstrip she had seemed taller and thinner than before, but now he realized that that had been only because of the smallness of the people around her. She had not changed. She was the same. The long lovely legs, the slim waist, the flower-blue eyes and carefully careless yellow hair: they were all the same, bright and light and glowing in the hot drabness of the little bungalow. That, he thought, had always been the primal quality beneath all her other, often conflicting qualities. Lightness. Of step, of gesture, of smile, of voice. Even during the worst of their troubles she had never lost it, and she had not lost it now: the lightness of a girl in the heart and body of a woman.

". . . and when I found what charming company I would have," the colonel was announcing gallantly, "a flight up to Papaan took top priority."

He raised his glass, found it was empty and set it down. Then Anna Vidal appeared in the door and said, "I am sorry to bother you, my doctor, but it is now almost twelve."

Toward late afternoon they got into the jeep and drove through the village. Along the streets and in the bazaar the people watched them with shy friendly eyes.

"Oh, they're adorable, Alec," said Lenore. "And the women's clothes—those tube skirts and voile jackets. I can't wait till I get some for myself."

"You're a mem sahib now," Hasbrook reminded her, grinning. "Mustn't forget your dignity."

"Dignity hell," said Lenore. "Shopping spree tomorrow."

They came to the end of the village, and Windom stopped by the rickety wharf. For a few minutes they looked out toward the headland across the glittering bay.

"As good as Antibes?" asked Windom.

"Better than Antibes," Lenore answered. And her hand touched his on the seat of the car.

Then they drove inland: through the village again and out into the country beyond. The dust rose in red veils behind the wheels of the jeep, and the river, which bisected the broad valley, was little more than a chain of stagnant pools between dry mudflats.

"Used to be a million mosquito eggs to the square inch,"

said Windom, pointing. "That's one thing we've had pretty good success with."

At intervals they passed native houses: a few of stone or timber, most of bamboo with thatch roofs. Along the road were creaking ox-carts and brown naked children, and here and there a woman with tucked-up skirts was doing her washing in the shallows of the river. There were some vegetable patches and strips of grazing land and, beyond these, the airfield, with the small plane gleaming and incongruous under the trees at the far side. Then the trees closed in, and the road cut deep and shaded between them.

"Where are the rice paddies?" asked Hasbrook. "I never saw a valley in this country without paddies."

"You've seen one now," said Windom. "There aren't any."

"Climate wrong?"

"No, it could be all right, with irrigation for the dry season." Windom paused briefly. "That's the big problem here," he added.

"Irrigation?"

"Not the irrigation itself. It could be done, and the people want it. But the plantation owners don't. All the land from the village on back is theirs, and all they want is rubber."

"So they bring in the rice?"

"Yes, they bring it by truck and boat. But there's not as much that way, and it costs more. Some of the people have been getting pretty insistent about having their own crop."

"Insistent—how? What have they been doing?"

"Well, they've had a few protest meetings. And there's some talk of a strike."

"What a country," said Hasbrook. "If it's not droughts it's floods. If it's not malaria it's strikes."

They drove on, and on either side of them now the long ranks of rubber trees stretched into shadowy distance. The air was still and almost cool. Now and then they could see a figure moving along the aisles with knife and cup, but it was no more than a flicker of movement in the immense geometry of the groves.

"It's beautiful," Lenore murmured. "As quiet and dim as a church."

"And wouldn't our friends up north like to take over the mortgage?" said Hasbrook. "I'll bet there're enough tires in it to roll every truck in the Red Army."

They continued for perhaps five miles; then Windom slowed down and said, "All the rest's the same."

He started to turn, and, while he was backing up, a truck appeared, coming along the road in the opposite direction. There were two men in it—a native driver at the wheel and a white man beside him—and as they drew abreast they stopped and the latter got out.

"Good afternoon, doctor," he said, approaching the jeep.

Windom nodded pleasantly. Then he introduced Lenore and Hasbrook. "This is Mr. Schusterman," he said. "The plantation manager."

Schusterman was a smallish wiry man with a bold nose and keen deep-set eyes. He was dressed, like Windom, in khaki shirt and shorts, but with the addition of a revolver in a holster at his waist. Offering his hand and smiling, he said, "It is an honor to have such distinguished visitors."

"Only one distinguished visitor." Lenore smiled back. "I'm an immigrant."

"Yes, of course, an immigrant. That is good. Very good." Schusterman spoke English with an indeterminate European inflection. "And now madame is inspecting her new homeland?"

"Just a quick once-over," said Windom. "Colonel Hasbrook's leaving tomorrow, and I wanted him to have a look at the plantation."

"Well, at least it is quiet today."

"Nothing more's happened?"

"No, not here." Schusterman's small eyes regarded Windom curiously. "I was wondering, doctor, if anything had happened with you."

"With me?"

"I had heard that you called in Jan Vidal."

"Yes, I wanted to talk with him. But he didn't come."

"I see. And do you know, perhaps, doctor, why he did not come?"

Windom hesitated.

"It was because he was too busy talking with this Amyan." Schusterman turned to Lenore and Hasbrook. "I am sorry to bore you with these local matters," he apologized, "but we have had some trouble here."

"About the rice?" said Hasbrook.

"Yes, about rice." The manager turned back to Windom. "It is quiet today—but only because they are talking. Wait and see. When they are finished talking there will be worse trouble."

"Who are these men?" asked Hasbrook. "Agitators?"

"Amyan is an old man," said Windom. "A former Buddhist monk. Jan Vidal is one of the foremen at the plantation."

"He *was* a foreman," Schusterman amended.

Windom's lips tightened. "You've discharged him?"

"Yes, of course I have discharged him. He is lucky he has not been put in jail."

"By your friend Bilko?"

Schusterman looked at him a moment before answering. "No, not by my friend Bilko," he answered quietly. "By the Sergeant of Police Bilko, who is charged with maintaining law and order."

"Three men came into my hospital last night," said Windom. "Badly beaten, and one of them seriously injured. I didn't notice Bilko or any of his police coming in."

"That, I assure you, is only because effective measures were taken."

"Yes, most effective, I'd say. And most–"

"Most necessary," Schusterman interrupted. "I should think you had been in the East long enough, doctor, to understand how such matters must be handled. Bilko is an official and responsible to higher authorities. I am manager of this plantation and responsible to its owners. We are in troubled times, in a troubled part of the world, and this sort of thing cannot be tolerated."

He stopped, and there was a silence. Then he said: "I am sorry. I have no wish to argue. But you are a physician–a man of science, not of practical affairs–and perhaps there are certain things you do not understand."

"Yes," said Windom. "Perhaps there are."

He seemed about to go on. Then he changed his mind, waved, and drove off down the road.

FOUR

THE INSECT CHORUS ROSE. THEN THE MOON ROSE. FROM THE screened porch of the bungalow Lenore Windom watched it climb swiftly through the banyan trees beyond the compound.

It was about ten o'clock. An hour before, Colonel Hasbrook had yawned discreetly, excused himself and gone off to the room that had been prepared for him in the hospital annex; and shortly after, Windom had been called over to one of the wards. She had been a doctor's wife for many years, and being left alone did not upset her. Or at least she was resolved that it would never upset her again. While she waited she rearranged her clothes in the cupboard and drawers in the bedroom and changed from her traveling clothes into a nightdress and light robe. Then she walked slowly through the little house: from the bedroom to the living room (that was also the dining room); from there to the porch; from the porch back through the living room to the kitchen. The kitchen was dark, and the cook and the boy Kosti were gone for the night. Snapping on the light-switch (thank the Lord for that, she thought; she had not dared hope for electricity), she looked at the stove, the sink and the small refrigerator. They were clean, she noted. Well—reasonably clean. Then she opened a cupboard, a huge cockroach scrambled out, and she jumped.

"Steady, girl," she told herself.

Back in the living room she continued with her mental notes: curtains, a proper table, at least two new chairs, something for the walls. Against one wall was a bookcase, and she examined its contents; but there were only medical books, a few journals and stacks of ancient magazines. From New York she had sent along cartons of reading matter—along with canned foods, household gadgets and gifts—but they were coming by ship, and it would be a month or more before they arrived.

You were always *going* to read a medical book, she thought. Now, damn it, you really are.

On a sideboard were decanters of gin and whisky. She found a glass; then changed her mind, set it down and went out on the porch. Sitting on one of the rattan chairs, she watched the moon rise.

How quiet it is, she thought. . . . And in the next instant realized it was not quiet at all. The shrilling of the insects was as loud as—she smiled—as the racket of the buses down on Madison Avenue.

Then she was no longer smiling. Dear God, she thought: this time—please—let me make him happy.

A little while later there were footsteps outside, and she thought it was he. But instead of his entering the door, there was a soft knock.

"Yes?" she asked.

There was no answer, and she crossed to the door. "Who is it?" she asked.

A voice answered in words she could not understand, and through the screening she could see a small shawled figure. After a moment's hesitation she opened the door.

"The doctor isn't—" she began; then drew back, startled,

as the figure thrust out a hand at her. "No, I'm sorry—I haven't any—"

Suddenly she realized that the hand was not begging, but was holding something out to her. It was the hand of an old woman, and under the shawl she could now see a dark shriveled face and toothless mouth.

"Da, da," the woman seemed to be saying, her brown claw pressing against Lenore's body.

"Please, I don't—" She felt panic again, as at the moment when she had stepped from the plane. Then, in the next instant, relief, for she saw her husband approaching across the compound.

Windom spoke to the woman in her own language: at first severely, then more gently, finally with a smile and a pat on the shoulder. Then he took whatever it was she held in her hand, and she turned and moved quickly away.

"What was it?" Lenore asked, as they went in through the door. "What did she give you?"

Windom opened his hand and showed a copper coin.

Lenore looked at it blankly.

"My fee," he said, smiling.

"Fee?"

"She was treated in the dispensary today and forgot to pay when she left. Poor old thing—she has yaws."

Lenore was staring at him. "You mean—you mean you take *money* from these people?"

"When they can afford it, yes. It's usually only a little, like this, but a few hundred coppers a week at least helps pay for their medicines." Windom put the coin in his pocket. "Also, strangely enough, they rather like to pay. It makes them feel they're really getting something. And it's good for their pride."

"But—"

Windom chuckled. "But what would my old patients

have done if I'd sent them one-cent bills? Probably just what they did with the fifty-dollar ones: put them on the bottom of the pile." He came close to her, smiled and put his hands on her shoulders. "You're going to find a lot of queer things here, Lee," he said, "and you're going to get used to them, just as I did. They're wonderful people—wait and see. They're wonderful, and you'll like them."

She was no longer conscious of his words. Only of his hands, light and warm on her shoulders. Then he dropped them and said, "The appointment book says time for a drink."

"I—I don't—"

"Together, Lee. It's always been good—together."

"Well—"

"What'll it be?"

"Do you have the makings for a stinger?"

He smiled. "The secret formula?"

"Yes, the secret formula."

He went inside, and she was again alone on the porch. Only this time not really alone, for his voice was still there. The gray eyes, the slow smile, the arms reaching out to her: they were all still there, before her, inside of her. No, not alone, she thought. Not alone any more—ever.

The rising moon had cleared the tops of the banyan trees, and the dust of the compound glistened like phosphorus. Off in the distance there was the faint sound of laughter. A dog barked. Then Windom returned with two glasses.

"Try it for size," he said, handing her one.

"Custom-made."

They stood facing each other, sipping the cool drinks; and once, as they raised them, their eyes met, and then Windom turned and sat down.

"I've only had the refrigerator a few months," he said. "It

really belongs over in the hospital, of course; but the flesh was weak."

"Oh."

"Three of the shelves are for the serums and vaccines. One's for stingers."

"Fair enough," she smiled.

Then there was a silence, and, through it, the drone of the insects. Lenore sat down beside him.

"Alec—" she said.

"Yes."

"I'm sorry I got upset before. About the old woman."

"It was natural. She startled you."

"But I didn't mean to be rude. Or unkind." She paused. "I want so much to be just as you want me to be. For it to be *right* this time."

"It's going to be right," said Windom. "It's right already."

"Then you're not angry?"

"About the old woman? Of course not."

"Or about—" She hesitated. "About my coming?"

"What do you think?"

"I'm not sure what I think. I'd like you to tell me."

It was a moment before Windom answered. Then he said: "I think that what you've done is about as wonderful a thing as a woman could do."

"Oh, Alec." Her hand reached out and touched his. "I've wanted to come. So much. For so long. These last two years—you can't imagine what they've been for me. It's been like living without eyes, or a heart."

She turned his hand over and put her own within it.

"You've been happy here, haven't you?" she said.

"In most ways, I suppose."

"You've been doing what you want to do."

"Yes."

"And that's what you're going to go on doing. What you

want to do. What you must do." Her hand tightened on his. "I know what you've been thinking: that I've come here to bring you back. But that isn't true, Alec. Believe me, it's not true. For ten years I tried to change your life into my life, but it isn't that way any longer. Now I want to live yours."

In the dim light it seemed to her that he was shaking his head. "No?" she asked. "You don't believe it? You don't think I can?"

"There's only one way you and I can live together, Lee," said Windom gently. "Not if it's your life. Not if it's mine. Only if it's ours."

Instead of answering, she raised his hand and put it to her cheek. "I love you, Alec," she said. . . . But when he started to speak she stopped him quickly. "No, don't say it because I say it. Don't say it until you're ready."

"Lee, I–"

"The crazy thing," she went on, "is that I've loved you more since you left me. *Because* you left me. Or maybe it's the natural thing. I don't know."

They were silent again, and she rested her head against his shoulder.

"I'll tell you another natural crazy thing," he said. "I was jealous this morning."

"How nice. Why?"

"Seeing you come out of that plane with another man."

"Oh, the colonel. Haven't I told you? The colonel and I are going to get married."

"When he graduates from high school?"

"Please be civil about my fiancé. He's been very pleasant –and very helpful."

"Uh."

"You don't like him, do you?" Lenore raised her head. "Really, I mean."

"What makes you think that?"

"You haven't changed that much. I can still tell when you don't like someone."

Windom said nothing.

"And this time I think you're being unfair. Maybe he's not the most brilliant man in the world, but he's perfectly nice. Certainly he's being nice to you, promising you all that hospital equipment."

"For the gooks."

"Oh."

"I don't like the word nigger. I don't like the word kike. I don't like the word gook."

"He didn't mean anything by it, I'm sure."

"No," said Windom, "they never do."

There was a pause.

"Anyhow," she said, "why bother about it? He'll be gone tomorrow."

She returned her head to his shoulder.

"Alec," she said.

"Yes?"

"*I* won't be gone."

Then for a while there was no more talk, but only the moonlight and the drone of the insects. Only her cheek against his khaki shirt, and her hand in his, and his other hand gently stroking the back of her head under the hair.

"Hello, stranger," she said.

"Hello."

And still later:

"Stranger—"

"Yes?"

"Let's go in."

"All right."

"The old way."

"All right, the old way."

He rose and picked her up in his arms and carried her in through the living room to the bedroom, where he set her down on the floor. "If I dropped you on one of those cots," he told her, "I'd break every bone in your body."

There was a moment, then, when they stood facing each other, and the light was on; and in the light, for just that moment, it was different and constrained, and the man before her almost *was* a stranger. Then he said, "Odds or evens who gets the bathroom first," and they matched fingers and she won, just as she always had, and the two years disappeared.

When she came out of the bathroom and he had gone in, she sat on the edge of one of the cots, but she did not comb out her hair as she usually did, because the feel of his fingers was still there underneath it. She took off her robe and mules and lay down, and the cot was hard all right, but its hardness was cool, and when she snapped off the lamp the moonlight was cool and silver.

Then Windom came out of the bathroom. He was wearing only a pair of shorts, and she saw how white his body was, against the darkness of his face and arms; and how thin. Standing between the cots, he let down the mosquito bar, so that it enclosed both of them like a translucent tent. For an instant—longer?—he remained standing there, as if undecided; then sat down on the edge of her cot.

"Welcome home, Lee," he said.

"Welcome home, Alec."

She put out her arms and drew him to her, and for a while neither of them spoke, until, smiling in the half-darkness, she said, "Lie on the other side, darling. You're always happier on the other side."

Then there was stillness again. Stillness and coolness. Coolness and warmness. There was the cool-warm cot and the silver netting, and that was all there was—*he* was all there was—and welcome home, she thought, welcome home, oh my dearest. And yes, she was home again, he was home again, back where he belonged again . . . except . . . not yet, not quite, no; and suddenly where warmth had been was cool emptiness, and what should have happened didn't happen.

He lay still in her arms.

"Lee, I'm—"

She kissed his mouth quiet.

"I'm sorry, Lee. I suppose I—need time—"

"There's plenty of time."

"Don't be—"

"Don't you be. It will be all right." She kissed him again. "We'll be all right.

He held her tight, pressing his face against her shoulder.

"Lie still," she whispered. "Lie still."

FIVE

He lay still. The minutes passed, or maybe the hours . . .

Lee, he said. Lee.

But he didn't say it aloud.

He was lying on his back, with his eyes closed, and then he turned on his side and opened them and lay watching her, asleep on the cot beside him. He had turned and opened his eyes many times, and each time he half-expected that she would not be there; that there would be only the cot, the netting, himself, as there had always been.

But she was there.

She had come back to him.

Back, he thought. That was hardly the right word. It was he, not she, who had done the going away; and there was certainly no *back* for her about a bungalow in a village in a jungle valley in southeast Asia. She had come almost exactly one half of the circumference of the earth, and while that wasn't so far as it had once been, it was still a pretty fair distance, with no *back* about it. At first he had been simply surprised; and then touched and grateful. Perhaps that had been part of the trouble, he thought. He had been too touched, too introspectively involved in meanings and emotions, to respond to the simple fact of her presence.

The psychos would have a word for it, he thought wryly. A less distasteful word than impotence.

In the darkness he could hear the soft rhythm of her breathing. It was very different from the way she had breathed on those nights in New York, when she lay drugged with alcohol or nembutal while he walked the floor, struggling to think straight, to feel straight, praying that the phone would ring with an emergency call. It would not be like that again: he knew it. And she knew it, or she could not have come. But if not like that, like what? Like the beginning?

My God, it had been wonderful at the beginning! Light and tender and golden. Of the few women he had known before her, half had been tramps, who worried about money, half nurses, who worried about babies. But Lee had worried about nothing. She had laughed. She had taken and given. And in her arms he had learned more of what a woman is—or can be—than in all the beds and wards and operating rooms he had ever been in.

They had met in a small town in northern Wisconsin, where he was resident at the hospital and she was on a skiing party with friends from Chicago. She had hurt her leg in a fall, was brought into the accident room, and five days later sat up in bed and said to him calmly: "I should have had my head examined, not my knee. Do you know what, Alec? I want to marry a doctor."

At first, of course, he had not known how rich she was, and when he learned he tried not to think about it. But there was no not-thinking about it when, early that spring, he visited her in New York and found himself in a world that theretofore had existed for him only in the pages of an occasional book. Not that there was anything phony or meretricious about Lenore Scofield or her family. Her father was senior partner of an investment-banking house, her mother a Somebody who was related to even bigger Otherbodies. It was simply that their home was on upper Fifth Avenue and not in upper Wisconsin; that they lived on eighty thousand a year and not three.

"You couldn't give it up, Lee," he told her. "It's not being spoiled. Only human."

"I can do it."

"For a year, yes. Maybe a few years. But afterward—"

She argued, but not successfully. Then, before he knew what was happening, she had reversed the field.

"All right, Mr. Mohammed," she said. "So you come to the mountain."

"To New York, you mean?"

"Yes."

"What could I do in New York? What would I use for patients?"

A month later, when she came west again, she had the answer to all that. Item One: her father was president of the Board of Trustees of the Episcopal Hospital. Item Two: Dr. Gordon Ashburn, the eminent gynecologist (and incidentally an old family friend), was looking for a young and capable assistant. "And the best part," Lee pointed out, "is that soon you'll have his whole practice. He's so old now he can hardly pick up a fee, let alone an instrument."

"But I'm a G.P.," he protested. "Not a GYN-man."

"All doctors are G.P.'s to begin with, aren't they? You have to specialize sometime."

"No, I don't. Medicine is too damn full of specialists already, and—"

And the argument went on.

On the surface it appeared light and casual—as did everything in which Lee was involved. But that was only surface; for to Dr. Alexander Windom, aged twenty-eight, it was the major decision of his life. He knew that, in general, there were two directions which a medical career could follow: the high road (which meant specialization, selectivity, the best associations, the best milieu); and the low road (which meant general practice and service in a small community). He was convinced that, by background, training and temperament, it was the second for which he was suited. And one night, the summer after their first meeting, he spent the better part of a week's salary on a phone call to New York and soberly told Lee of his decision.

"All right, darling. Goodbye," she had murmured. And that was all. . . . Except that the next day she flew out to him, two days later they were married, and the following autumn he began work as assistant to Dr. Gordon Ashburn in an office on Park Avenue near Seventy-second Street.

Dr. Alexander Windom, aged forty-six, lay in the darkness and listened to his wife's breathing. There had been times when it seemed to him that it had been bad from the start. But it hadn't been. When he was honest with himself he knew that during those first years he had been very happy. He knew it now, lying on his cot, with the familiar figure asleep beside him.

At first Lee had been all any man could have asked of a wife. Not only gay, not only light and lovely and laughing, but tender and understanding, and with deep pride in him, as she guided him through the labyrinth of a strange new world. He was accepted almost immediately, both by her circle of friends and by Dr. Ashburn's glittering galaxy of patients. He went from office to house-call to hospital to library and lecture hall (for he continued studying while he practiced), and still found time, when evening came, to be unreluctant escort and lover to his wife. In fact there was time for everything—except enough sleep—and, at thirty, sleep did not greatly matter.

After a few years, as Lee had predicted, Ashburn retired;

and, although a few patients went elsewhere, he found himself with a practice that most men twice his age would have envied. Soon he took on his own assistant, but, even so, the pressure increased. Talk of "that brilliant young man from the Middle West" had begun to trickle along the Manhattan grapevine; and after certain of his experimental hormone treatments were conspicuously successful, it seemed to him that half the mink coats in the city were draped on the chairs in his outer office.

He was human enough to feel satisfaction in his progress, but there was doubt and self-questioning as well. There was the knowledge that, well as he was doing, he and Lee lived on a scale of almost twice what he earned. And there was the day in the hospital library when he overheard two of the internes talking. "Practice?" said one. "How in hell can you get a practice in this man's town?" "Only one way," said the other. "Marry it." "You mean Windom's way." "Yeah, Windom's way . . ."

He drove himself relentlessly, trying to keep up with his studying, his papers for the medical journals, his work in the wards and clinics. But it was harder at thirty-three than at thirty, harder at thirty-five than at thirty-three. "Easy, darling, easy," Lee told him. "After all, we have enough money without your killing yourself." But, as many a successful man had discovered before him, it wasn't as simple as that.

At her insistence they took vacation trips: to the West Indies, Mexico, Europe. In Europe, he had resolved, he was going to attend a series of lectures in Paris, another in Vienna, but somehow it worked out to only one of each, and the remainder of the time they spent at Biarritz and Cap d'Antibes. "A real two-month rest for you," Lee called it—and, in a fashion, it was. Except that the resting came exclusively between 4 A.M. and noon.

They had left France a few weeks before war broke, and

for the next two years in New York things continued much as before. In daily living, at least. But not in the daily newspapers. And not within himself. The excitement of quick success had worn off. It was stale and meaningless now. The routine of office, house-call, hospital; his ladies with menopause and faulty metabolism, his ladies who wanted to be pregnant and his ladies who didn't want to be pregnant; even Lee (who didn't want to and never was), with her lightness and laughter, her parties and "fun people": they had all become stale and meaningless and not a little ridiculous, on their tight bright little island of security in a world fighting for its life.

Twice, without telling her, he wrote to the War Department, offering his services in the now quickly expanding army. But both times he left the letters unmailed and went on with his usual round. It could not be said that he was out-and-out unhappy—he was still far too much in love with Lee to be that—but the old zest and satisfaction were gone. He went through the motions. He marked time.

Then came Pearl Harbor, defeat, the chaos of awakening and girding . . . and a few months later, the night when he told her of the field unit that was being organized by the hospital. To his surprise, she had not protested or become emotional, but sat quietly listening, as if to something she had known all along; and when he had finished she had simply asked: "You're sure in your mind, Alec?"

"I'm sure," he had said.

"Because you feel it's your duty?"

"Yes."

"And because you *want* to go?"

"Yes."

And that had been that.

The unit had been sent first to a camp in Mississippi and then across the Pacific to what was left of southeast Asia. Organized as a field hospital, it was not a front-line outfit, but functioned in the rear area behind the fighting troops; and, except at rare intervals, its work was less concerned with combat surgery than with sanitation, tropical fevers and native girls impregnated by G.I.'s or Tommies. No heroes they. Nor even, properly speaking, soldiers. As one of the doctors put it after a year in the bush, the danger was not in being shelled or bombed, but simply bored, to death.

At least it had been that way for most of them. But not for him. Almost alone among his colleagues, he liked the tropics. He liked the native people. And although, as a gynecologist, he drew practically all the pregnancy cases, there was other work which he found as absorbing and rewarding as any he had ever done. When the unit first came to Papaan malaria hung like a blight over the valley. Six months later it was all but gone. Dysentery, dengue, yaws, leishmaniasis, intestinal parasites—the whole catalogue of fevers and infections that afflicted the region—were, if not eliminated, at least brought under reasonable control. "When I get back," he wrote to Lee, "I may be a bit rusty on my hormones, but I'll be the top latrine man for all Park Avenue."

Indeed, half his job in those days had been not medicine at all, but sanitation, and in carrying it out he worked partly with his army corpsmen and partly (which he preferred) with the natives themselves. Before the war there had been an Anglo-Catholic mission in the valley, and, as a result, most of the people were Christian, many spoke English, and a few were literate. Among the last were the old man Amyan, who had relinquished the robes of a Buddhist monk to become the town's counselor and elder statesman, and the Vidal family, which had then consisted of father, mother, son Jan and daughter Anna. And all had helped as much as they could—particularly the girl Anna, who had attached herself to him and his work with almost fanatical devotion. No labor was too much for her, too tiring or too dirty. "To help my people is what I have always wanted to do more than anything," she told Windom, her soft oval face glowing. "How I would wish to be a doctor, like you, or at least a true nurse—"

But he was to have an even closer tie than this to the Vidals. And with it his one brush with real war. Late in 1944 the long-static front, to the north of the valley, burst suddenly into activity; patrols of both sides ranged back and forth through jungle and rubber groves; and the hospital was ordered to withdraw several miles to the south. At the time, however, Windom had been in one of the hill villages and knew nothing of what had happened, and on returning to Papaan he would have driven straight into a Jap command post, had not old Vidal intercepted him on the road and hidden him in a shed near the forest's edge. The next day he had managed to work his way southward. But when, a few weeks later, he returned with his unit, it was to find that the Japs had discovered what Vidal had done and shot him out of hand.

Soon after, the tide of war turned completely. They moved far to the north, and that was the last of Papaan. But not altogether of the Vidals; for at war's end, while waiting in Singapore for transportation, he had managed to arrange for Anna to be admitted into the again-functioning nursing school of the Royal Medical College. He had hoped to see her once before leaving, but it did not work out that way. A few days after he had a letter from her, saying that she would be coming on the next boat, his unit received its movement orders and sailed for home.

That had been—when? The fall of '45. Almost six years ago . . . It did not seem that long. . . . Six years seemed like nothing, and a night seemed forever. He glanced at the clock on the night table, and the illuminated dial showed 2:15. The moon had climbed high now—he judged it was almost directly overhead—and the room was darker.

Sleep, he told himself. Sleep. But there was no sleep. He was about to move over and try the other cot, when Lee stirred slightly and her hand touched his shoulder. Then she murmured something that sounded like, "Jeff—Jeff—"

Suddenly he remembered. It *was* "Jeff." Jeff was the Sealyham terrier she had bought after he had gone off to war. "To keep the bed warm," she had explained ruefully on his return. And he had smiled. He was smiling now.

But neither smile lasted . . .

For it was after his homecoming that their real trouble had begun. Its origins, of course, lay far back, before the war, in their so different backgrounds, temperaments and attitudes; but then it had been only an undercurrent, and what drew them together was far stronger than what might have pried them apart. Now all their differences were on the surface—bare, naked—clarified and magnified by three years of separation. Lee's father had died during his absence, and she had more money than ever, in her own right. She was used to living as she pleased, keeping her own hours, choosing her own friends. Outwardly she still seemed as young as before—a girl rather than a woman—but inside there was a hardness, a lacquered, almost metallic quality, that had not been there before. Her movements were quicker, her laughter more brittle.

And she drank more. Much more.

Strangely, perhaps, their sexual attraction to each other was as strong as ever; and he knew, as well as if he had never left her, that she had not been unfaithful. But paradoxically, it was this very attraction, their compulsive mutual need, that intensified the friction between them and made it impossible for them to accept half-measure and compromise.

In his practice he had been the confidant of many unhappy wives and had advised them sanely, tolerantly and, he hoped, successfully. But here in his own life, involved in his own emotions, he felt himself as weak and feckless as a schoolboy. Increasingly, during the two years that followed, there were scenes, silences, pacing of floors, slamming of doors—all the tawdry banal stage-trappings of the traditional breaking marriage.

11 P.M. The phone ringing . . .

"It's Bob and Helen. They've just left the theatre and want us to meet them at Twenty-One." "It's too late, Lee. I have to be at the hospital at eight." "Just this once—please. It's been so long since—" "I'm sorry, Lee." "Oh, all right." Pause. "But damn it, *I'm* going." Slammed door.

1 A.M. The phone . . .

"It's Mrs. Lewis. I'll have to go up and—" "Again? Can't she wait until morning?" "I'd better take a look." "Always time for all those cows, but never for me." "I'll only be an hour. Go back to sleep." "What is there to do but sleep?" But when he came back she was sitting in the dining room, with the scotch and a glass on the table.

There was more to it, though, than just he and Lee. He was unhappy in his work. He had thought that his former dissatisfaction was simply a by-product of war, but now that the war was over he was more dissatisfied than ever. Veteranitis, he thought. It would pass. But it didn't pass. Month by month it grew worse—his sensation of imprisonment intensified—until he knew that, whatever the price, he must break out of the tight little world of thyroid and menopause, wealth and neurosis, in which he felt himself trapped.

"You should get away for a while," said Lee. "Let's go back to Europe."

But Europe wasn't the answer. Biarritz and Antibes weren't the answer. For brief intervals—at a ship's rail, on a sunlit beach, in the darkness of a hotel bedroom—they succeeded in recapturing some of the magic of their early days; but after the ship's rail there was the ship's bar, after the beach the casino, after the night the morning. And one morning he said to her, "We'd better go back, Lee. It's no use running away."

"Running away?"

"From our problems."

"I thought I was your problem."

"No, it's not you. Not us—really. It's our whole—well—way of living. And my work . . ."

"Oh," she said. "Your work."

And after that things were even worse between them; for she couldn't stand being secondary—even as a problem.

Which had come first: his own half-formulated thoughts or the letter from Anna Vidal? Not that it mattered. They both came. Anna told of her life in Singapore, her graduation from nursing school, her gratitude, her pride. And that now she was back in her own country, in the valley of Papaan. *The old mission,* she wrote, *has not returned; but the buildings are still here, and we have been permitted to use them as a sort of hospital and dispensary. Since you Americans left there is again much malaria and other fevers, and the nearest doctor is many miles away. Still we have made a start and are, I think, doing some good. . . .*

A month later he in turn wrote a letter—to the International Medical Foundation. An answer came back: they were interested. When, soon after, he met the directors of the foundation, they were even more interested. But then he waited. Over and over he decided the time had come—and still waited.

Then the time came—without decision.

Among his patients was Lee's younger sister, Diane—a spoilt high-strung girl, recently married, who had, against her wish, become pregnant and was terrified of childbirth. At first she had begged him to send her to an abortionist, but he had of course refused, and after he had talked with her long and patiently, she appeared, for a while, calmer and more reasonable. As her time drew near, however, she again became panicky, declared that she couldn't face the ordeal, and demanded that, instead of a normal delivery, he perform a Caesarian section. Almost hysterically resentful when he again refused, she had stormed from his office and apparently gone straight to Lee; for when he got home that night Lee was as indignant as she.

"You have to do it," she told him.

"No I don't. And I won't."

"Why not?"

"Because it would be malpractice," he said. "Because she doesn't need it."

"Of course she needs it. She's scared to death. She's sick."

"She's no sicker than I am. She's just a damn neurotic."

"Oh, I see—a neurotic. Just like me, I suppose? You and your holier-than-thou judgments. You and your tank-town ethics . . ." And so on, one thing leading to another (including drinks), until she jumped up from the dinner table and announced, "All right, this is it. I've put up with all I'm going to, and I'm through—do you understand? I'm leaving."

Then he looked up at her a moment and said at last, quietly: "It isn't necessary, Lee. I am."

He moved for a few weeks to a hotel. Unregretfully he closed the office that, after all the years, had never seemed his, but still Dr. Gordon Ashburn's. Before he left for the East there was some talk of divorce, but Lee had done nothing about it, and when, at erratic intervals, she wrote him, her stationery still carried the name *Mrs. Alexander Win-*

dom. One letter—the first—had been overwrought and emotional. The rest were mere notes about money or common possessions. In the past year there had been only two of them—until the one from Calcutta.

And now . . . he was again listening to Lee's breathing . . . now the pendulum had swung again. Or rather hung poised, waiting to swing. He tried to force his mind into the future, but it would not go. It was held in the *now* as closely as the two cots were held in the tall sheath of the mosquito bar.

Now she was here. That was all.

It could not be as it had been at the beginning: he knew that. No more than it could be as it had been at the end. . . . Did he want her? . . . . Yes. From the moment he received the last letter he had known that he wanted her. From the moment he saw her step from the plane he had wanted her more than he had ever wanted, or ever could want, any woman in the world. And yet, as he lay there with her at last in the bright darkness, something in him—his body? his mind?—had *not* wanted her. . . .

He turned on the hard cot. Go to sleep, he thought. Lie still.

He lay still.

SIX

TOWARD MORNING IT RAINED. FOR PERHAPS TEN MINUTES A torrent beat down on the valley, and then abruptly it stopped. When, a while later, it began to grow light, mist rose in slow billows from the fields and riverbanks and, up on the higher ground, twined through the long aisles of the rubber groves. Through the mist, along the river and road, men, mules and bullock carts moved on to the work of the day ahead.

But up in the rubber groves nothing moved at all.

In her frame-and-thatch house on the outskirts of the village the old woman called Mamarta Vidal was preparing breakfast. Reckoned by years, and Western standards, she was not old at all; for she was not yet fifty. But fifty, in a jungle village in southeast Asia, is a very different matter from fifty in New York or Paris, or even Bombay or Singapore. She was hunched and twisted in body, and wrinkles seamed her brown face. Her lips and what few teeth remained to her were stained purple from the juices of betel nut. Her hands, moving among the pots on the stone oven, were like the claws of an ancient bird.

After a few minutes her daughter Anna came in from the

other room. It had been her weekly night at home; but now she was again dressed in her nurse's uniform, and its starched primness contrasted startlingly with the brown dinginess of the old peasant house.

Her mother glanced at her with eyes that managed at the same time to be watery and sharp. "You should have slept longer," she said. "You do not have to be at the hospital until eight."

"I want to be there early this morning," said Anna. "There were many things that did not get done yesterday, with all the excitement."

"Excitement? . . . Oh, you mean the mem-doctor."

"Yes. And the plane and everything."

"What is she like, the mem-doctor?"

"She is very lovely. Tall and light and cool. But now at first, of course, she is also unsure."

"Unsure? Of what?"

"Of being in a strange place, I suppose."

"Strange?" Mamarta grunted. "What is there strange about Papaan? It is where she comes from that is strange, not here." She poured the contents of one of the pots into an earthen bowl. "Do you know what I have heard the other day about America? I have heard that in their houses they have shrines that are wooden boxes, and when they pray in front of the boxes there is light and music and the saints move around inside."

She and Anna sat down to their breakfast of baked eggs, millet cakes and tea. Outside, the sun rose. Then the front door opened and a young man came in.

Both women stared at him.

"You are not at the plantation?" said Mamarta.

"You can see I am not," said Jan Vidal.

"Why? What are you doing here?" The old woman looked at him closely. "Where have you spent the night?"

"At Father Amyan's."

"Amyan's? . . . But the sun is already up. By now you should be back at the plantation."

"I have been discharged from the plantation."

Anna half-rose from her seat. "Oh, Jan—"

"I have been discharged," he went on, "and so I am not going there. But I am not the only one. Nobody is going there today."

"Nobody?"

"We have called a strike."

Jan Vidal crossed the room slowly and stood looking out the window. Like his sister, he was tall for his race; but, where she was slight and small-boned, he was broad, solid and powerful. He was dressed nondescriptly in denim work-trousers, sandals and a white singlet, and his straight black hair needed a combing. His face was smooth and boyish, even for a man still in his twenties, but now, in the early sunlight, its lines were tense with his inner excitement.

Mamarta rose, went to the oven and filled another bowl. "Eat your breakfast," she told him.

"I am not hungry," said Jan.

"Eat your breakfast."

He started to speak again, thought better of it and sat down at the table.

"You should have talked to Doctor Windom," Anna said to him.

"The doctor?"

"Before you did anything. He wanted to see you yesterday."

"I couldn't go yesterday," Jan said. "I was busy."

"With Amyan?"

"Yes, with Father Amyan."

"I think that maybe you see too much of this Amyan," said the old woman. "There are those who say he is—"

"I will tell you exactly what he is," her son interrupted her. "He is a saint."

"A saint? Mother of God, he is not even—"

"—a Christian, no. Nor even a Buddhist any more." Jan leaned across the table and his dark eyes glowed. "Do you know what his religion is?" he said. "It is human beings. Human rights."

"Eat your breakfast, boy," Mamarta told him.

He took a few gulps in silence.

"We all know that Amyan is a good man," said Anna quietly, "but he is an old man, and sick, and perhaps no longer very practical."

"Not practical? I suppose it is the others who are practical? Who suffer injustice for years and do nothing about it. Who wait for an old sick man to tell them they must strike for their rights."

"This strike—it begins this morning?"

"Yes."

"Where are the men?"

"In their homes. Around the village."

"And what will they do now?"

"We have called a meeting for eleven o'clock in the north pasture across the river. There we will elect a committee to call on Schusterman and his assistants."

"To ask for what?" said Anna.

"To ask for what we have asked for all along. Either the right to buy our own land from the plantation; or, if they won't do that, at least the right to grow our own rice on rented land."

"And if they won't give you either?"

"We will go on striking."

"With violence—"

"No, not with violence. That is what you do not understand about Father Amyan. He is a saint, I tell you. Like

Gandhi. He will have nothing to do with violence." In his excitement Jan rose to his feet. "That is the great thing that will happen here," he said. "A strike without violence. Resistance without bloodshed. That is what Father Amyan has taught us can be done. And what will be done. . . . Wait and see, Anna—mother. We will do it. And we will win!"

There was another pause; then he put a hand on Mamarta's shoulder. "Do not be angry, mother," he said.

"I am not angry," she answered.

"Or upset."

"I am not upset."

"What don't you like then?"

"There is only one thing I do not like." The old woman fixed him with her keen watery eyes. "That no one is going to knock in the head of that policeman Bilko."

Jan grinned and said, "Maybe we can cheat a little on Bilko, when Father Amyan is not looking." Then he turned to the door.

"Jan—" said Anna.

"Yes?"

"I think you are right, too. There must be the strike. There must be the fight for what is decent and just. But before you go to the meeting—now, this morning—please talk to Dr. Windom."

Her brother hesitated.

"He is on your side—our side. You know that. He will not try to stop you, but only give you good advice. He is so wise, Jan. So kind. And—"

Jan was watching her with a curious expression. "And perhaps his head nurse is in love with him?" he asked.

Anna flushed. Her dark eyes blazed out at him, and then abruptly she turned away.

"All right, all right," said her brother. "I did not mean it. . . . And I shall see him."

He started out again, but this time it was Mamarta who stopped him.

"There is another thing, son," she said.

He turned resignedly. "Yes, mother?"

"Before appearing in public will you go and comb your hair."

In the center of the village, near the bazaar sheds, was the office where Dai Lollivar functioned both as merchant and mayor. During the course of a day half the tradesmen and officials of Papaan made their appearance in it, and Lollivar was used to dealing with them casually and summarily. But there was nothing either casual or summary in his manner this morning, as he offered a chair to his unexpected visitor.

"If I had known you wanted to see me, Mr. Schusterman," he explained, "I would have been happy to come up to the plantation."

"Yes, I know," said Schusterman. "And I would have spent the day waiting for you."

Lollivar lighted a cigarette and puffed on it nervously.

"As you can probably guess," said Schusterman, "what I have come here about is this strike."

"Ah yes, of course."

"It must be stopped."

"Of course."

"And this meeting must be stopped."

"Meeting? I have not heard of any—"

"You are hearing about it now. It has been called for eleven o'clock this morning, across the river from the village."

"This morning?" Lollivar's moon-face showed acute unhappiness. "That is not good, is it?"

"No, it is not good. That is why you will have it stopped."

"I? But what can I—"

"If the meeting were on plantation property," said the manager, "I could handle it myself. But this field across the river is not plantation property. It is village land, and under your jurisdiction."

"Yes, I see—yes: my jurisdiction. But—" Lollivar spread his hands. "But what would you have me do? They will not listen to me."

"It is not a question of listening—or talking. It is a question of action."

"You mean the police?"

"Obviously." Schusterman glanced at his watch. "In fact, so obviously that I have asked Sergeant Bilko to meet us here to discuss our plans."

The mayor had already extinguished one cigarette and lighted another. Now he put out the second. He rose, walked across the room and back to his desk again. Then he pulled out a handkerchief and patted his cheeks.

"I—I see your point, of course, Mr. Schusterman," he said at last. "The plantation must be kept going. Law and order must be preserved. But it would be my—er—suggestion—with the utmost respect, of course—that—"

The manager's small eyes regarded him coldly. "That what?" he asked.

"That we do not, at least right away, call in Bilko."

"Why not?"

"Because—well—because, you see, Bilko is not a—how shall I say it?—a popular man. In the year he has been here he has not been liked by the people, and now there is much bad feeling about what happened the other day."

"You mean at the plantation?"

"Yes, at the plantation. When the three men were hurt."

"What did you expect me to do?" said Schusterman. "Let them start a riot."

"No, no," Lolliver assured him. "Do not think for a moment that I criticize you. Law and order must be preserved. It is only that under the circumstances—with the feeling of the people, you know—perhaps it would be wiser to—"

He broke off, for now suddenly it was Schusterman who had risen. The manager spread his hands on the desk and leaned forward.

"What would be wise, Mr. Mayor," he said quietly, "is for you to listen to me. Rubber is what this country lives on. The plantation is what this valley lives on. There has been trouble at the plantation; now there is a strike. Thousands of trees stand waiting to be tapped, and no one taps them. Instead, they call a meeting, where agitators will incite them to more trouble." He raised a hand and slapped it sharply down on the desk. "This cannot be, do you understand me? It cannot be permitted. Either you will use your authority to stop this meeting, or I shall wire the provincial authorities that you are incapable of handling the situation."

Lollivar fumbled with a third cigarette. Then he looked up, as a figure appeared in the door.

"Come in, Bilko," said Schusterman.

The sergeant of police approached the desk. He was a short thick-set man in a khaki uniform, with a fleshy face and square close-cropped head.

"We have been discussing the situation," the manager said. "Do you think you can handle it?"

"Yes, it can be handled," said Bilko.

"But there will be hundreds at the meeting," Lollivar put in. "And once it has started—"

"It will not start."

"Good," said Schusterman. "That is the whole strategy: it must not start. If they are kept apart—in their homes—they cannot do anything. Then in a few days they will be discouraged and go back to work." He looked at Bilko anxiously.

"But are you sure you can do this," he asked, "with only fifteen men?"

"We can do it for a few hours," said Bilko.

"And then?"

"By then I will have had a small talk with the leaders."

"This Amyan—"

"Yes, Amyan. And Vidal."

"A talk?" Lollivar put in. "You mean you will—"

"I will point out to them that they are making a mistake," said Bilko blandly. "And I believe that I can convince them. When they are convinced—poof—" He snapped his fingers. "The others are nothing. They will hop like crickets back to their rubber trees."

"Good," the manager said again. "It is the right way. It will work."

Bilko went to the door. "I shall be going then. My men are waiting." He clicked his heels and bowed slightly. "With your permission, sir?"

Schusterman nodded.

The sergeant's flat eyes moved to Lollivar. "And yours, too, Mr. Mayor?"

Lollivar took out his handkerchief. "Yes—er—I suppose it is the only way," he murmured. Bilko went out, and he looked at Schusterman. "There must be no trouble, of course. There must be law and order—"

Breakfast over, Windom drove Colonel Hasbrook to the landing field. The pilot had arrived only a few moments before them, and while he warmed up the plane's engine the two men waited in the jeep in the shade of the trees.

"It shouldn't take more than an hour to Jagila," said Windom.

"The quicker the better," the colonel said. "I'm afraid the rest of my tour's going to be a bit of a letdown."

"It was damn good of you to bring my wife up."

"I could do with a few more assignments as tough as that. I hope you won't mind, doctor, if I say that Mrs. W.'s a very attractive woman."

Windom smiled. "I don't take it as an offense."

"You're a lucky man. My old girl wouldn't come any nearer this part of the world than Santa Monica Boulevard. Or, I don't know—" Hasbrook winked. "Maybe *I'm* lucky."

"Where do you go after Jagila?"

"Ramdang, Thetka, Kailipon. All garrison towns, up near where the Reds are operating. Then back to the capital about the end of the week. . . . Anything I can do for you there?"

"I don't think so, thanks."

"Outside of the X-ray, I mean. Don't worry, I'm going to go right to bat for you on that."

"I can't tell you how—"

The colonel raised a big hand. "A pleasure, doctor. Of course, it may take a little while—you know how things move through those good old channels—but we'll see you get it, don't worry. Hell, it's like I was saying to you yesterday. The sort of work you're doing here is better propaganda than all the loans and V.I.P. delegations and radio programs put together."

"I'd never exactly thought of my work as—"

"You may not have thought of it, but that's just what it is." Hasbrook lowered his voice. "Look, doc," he said, "let's face it: what's the U.S. doing out here anyhow? Not having any love affair, I can tell you that. These inspection trips I take, for instance. Seeing what they need. Getting them guns and trucks. Half of them would just as lief use the guns on us as on anyone else. They've got no use for us—never have had, never will—and the only use we've got for them is that they hold the line against the Reds. As long as we've got to do that, we need them—whether we like it or not. And because we need them"—the colonel tapped with his finger on Windom's knee—"we've got to make them need us.

"That's where you come in," he said, "because that's exactly what you've been doing. And when I put in for that X-ray for you I'm going to tell the big brass all about it. You're doing as important a job keeping the gooks healthy and making them like it as any of the rest of us are teaching them to fly or shoot."

The plane gave a final warm-up roar, and the pilot gestured from the window.

"Well, doc, it's been a real pleasure," said Hasbrook.

He got out of the jeep, shook hands and walked over and climbed into the plane. Within two minutes it had taxied off, turned, made its takeoff run and disappeared over the trees to the west.

Windom drove back toward the hospital. There were the usual plodding ox-carts and staring children along the road and the usual women doing their washing in the shallows of the river; but as soon as he came to the village he realized that something out of the ordinary was going on. The main street was all but empty. Most of the house and shop doors were closed. Here and there he saw small groups of men gathered in yards and alleys, but they were deep in talk and showed no awareness of him as he passed. A block from the hospital another car swerved around a corner and raced past him, and he saw that there were two policemen in it—with two rifles.

Entering the hospital compound, he parked the jeep and was going toward his bungalow, when Anna Vidal appeared on the steps of the main building and came quickly across to him.

"My doctor," she said, "I am so glad you have come."

He looked at her sharply. "What is it, Anna?"

"Jan is here."

"In the hospital?"

"Yes."

"What's happened to him?"

"Nothing has happened. That is, he has not been hurt. But he is in trouble. There is trouble everywhere. I have put him in your office and told him he should wait for you."

Windom followed her across the compound and into the hospital. The dispensary, on the right of the entrance, was empty, but when he opened the door on the left Jan Vidal rose to meet him.

"I must speak to you, my doctor," he said tensely.

Windom looked him up and down and saw no sign of injury. Then he went around behind his desk and sat down.

"You weren't so anxious to speak to me yesterday," he said. "When I was looking for you."

"I am sorry, my doctor. I was—busy."

"So I gather." Windom paused, his eyes on the young man's face. "Well, let's have it."

"Father Amyan has been arrested," said Jan.

"Oh?"

"About an hour ago. I was on my way to his house, when some men stopped me and said the police had just come and taken him away. They said they were also looking for me. But I went through the back streets and came here."

"It's about the strike?" asked Windom.

"Yes, about the strike. And the meeting."

"What meeting?"

"One that we had called for this morning."

Jan's eyes kept moving restlessly to the window. Anna, who had come in with the doctor, stood silently in a corner.

"Sit down, Jan," said Windom.

"But any minute now they may—"

"Sit down. They won't bother you here."

Jan sat down, and for a moment Windom looked at him without speaking. Then he asked quietly: "What do you expect me to do?"

"I am sorry to bother you with this, my doctor," said Jan. "Truly I am. But I have come to ask your advice, because I do not know where else to go."

"Have you talked to Lollivar?"

"Lollivar?" Jan blew out air between his lips. "And what would be the good of that?"

"He's the mayor, after all."

"Yes, the mayor. And also something besides. Also a merchant whose biggest customer is the plantation, and he would sooner stand up against the prime minister of the country than against this Schusterman, who buys from him." Jan paused, then continued earnestly. "No, my doctor," he said. "There is only you I can come to. You are a wise man—that I know. And a kind man who has always been good to my people."

"No better," said Windom, "than your people have been to me."

"It is not that I am afraid of being arrested; you must believe me, my doctor. With Father Amyan in jail, that is where I would want to be—with him. But in jail I could be of no use. Soon it would all be over, finished, hopeless."

"And if you're not in jail?"

Jan's eyes flashed. "Then we can win," he said. "If we are all together—working together—we can win. The meeting this morning: no, that is no longer possible. Schusterman and Bilko have seen to that. But that is not important; there can be other meetings, in other places. The important thing is that the men are not forced back to work. That the strike goes on."

He leaned forward, his brown hands gripping the edge of Windom's desk. "You know how it has been in Papaan, my doctor. With the poverty. With no land and no rice of our own. Such things cannot go on forever, and the only way they will not is if we take action—if we strike. I know what it is that you fear: that there will be violence and bloodshed. But there will not be, I promise you. Not from us. What happened at the plantation the other day, when the three men were beaten—that was not our fault. We were promised that we could have a meeting, and when we met the police came with their clubs. Father Amyan is a man who will have nothing to do with violence. He is a man of peace and humanity. And the rest of us, we are not criminals, not bandits, but only poor men trying to find a decent life. That is the truth, my doctor. You know it is the truth."

Again, for a few moments, Windom studied the young man before him. In his rough work-pants and soiled singlet he looked no different from any other simple plantation laborer. He was not educated as his sister Anna was educated, and his speech had none of the refinement which she had acquired during her two years in the outer world. But it was not a lout or a hooligan at whom Windom was looking. It was a man thinking deeply and feeling deeply. It was a man with a light in his eyes, and the light was strong and pure.

"Yes, Jan," he said. "I know it's the truth."

"What can we do, then?"

"Go on with the strike."

Jan said nothing, but his eyes were fixed on the doctor's face, and his grip on the desk tightened until the knuckles showed white.

Windom stood up.

"The meeting is off," he said, "and there probably won't be any more trouble today. Spread the word around that the men should stay in their homes. Meanwhile I'll get hold of Lollivar and Schusterman and see if we can't talk this thing out."

He started for the door.

"As for yourself, I think you'd better stay here in the hospital for the time being. Suppose we say"—he smiled—"for observation."

Jan seemed about to speak, but no words came. Anna, however, who, while the two men talked, had remained silently in the corner, now came quickly forward. And before Windom could stop her she had seized his hand and kissed it.

SEVEN

THERE WAS A NEW AND SEVERE CASE OF AMOEBIC DYSENTERY; one of the malaria patients was running a high fever; and a ten-year-old girl had been brought in from one of the up-valley villages almost blind from trachoma. It was close to noon before he returned to the office to find Dai Lollivar sitting there.

"I have been waiting an hour to speak to you," said the mayor. "It has been a most difficult morning."

"What's happening now?"

"Everything is happening. Amyan is in jail. The people threaten to riot. The police threaten to shoot."

Windom had remained by the door. "I'm going out to the plantation," he said.

"The plantation?"

"To see Schusterman."

"That is not necessary. Schusterman is in the village with Bilko, and they are coming here."

"To the hospital?"

"They have heard that Jan Vidal is here."

Windom crossed the room and sat down at his desk. Lollivar sat opposite him and dabbed at his face with his handkerchief.

"That is why I am here," he said. "To speak with you before they come. For I would not want you, my doctor, to misunderstand my position."

He paused uncomfortably, and Windom waited.

"I am a man of peace," the mayor went on. "Of law and order, you understand? All that I wish is that there be no trouble. I am the mayor of the village—yes—but I am also a man of business, and when there is trouble of this sort it is terrible for business." He raised a hand quickly. "Not that it is myself I think of, of course. It is the people, the rubber crop, the welfare of the valley."

"There seems to be some difference of opinion about its welfare."

"Yes, exactly. There is difference of opinion. There are anger and threats. You and I, my doctor"—Lollivar leaned forward confidentially—"we are men of the world. We understand that there are two sides to a question and wish only that there be no trouble. That is what I say to Schusterman. That is what I say to the plantation workers. It is a bad thing, this strike. It is a bad thing about the rice and the land rentals. Why must we have always these bad things? I ask them. Why must there be such arguments and unpleasantness, instead of that everyone is reasonable—you understand—and then there will be no trouble and—"

"About their arresting Amyan—" Windom interrupted. "What's your position on that?"

"Position?"

"What did you say to the plantation workers?"

"I say to them that it is most unfortunate. That we shall see what can be done."

"And to Schusterman?"

Lollivar spread his hands. "With Mr. Schusterman it is of course difficult. He is a most determined man, you understand. Most—ah—inflexible, and one must proceed with tact."

"Meaning you didn't say anything to him."

"But of course I say something to him. I say that it is a difficult situation. That Amyan is perhaps a dangerous man, but popular with the people. That it is unfortunate and—"

He looked up in relief as a knock sounded on the door.

"Come in," said Windom.

And the boy Kosti appeared.

"The lady, she asks I say to you that lunch is ready, my doctor."

"Tell her I'll be right over," said Windom.

"And also, my doctor, Mamarta Vidal is outside. She says that she must see you about—"

But before the boy could get any further, another figure, no taller than he, appeared in the doorway beside him. "My son—" demanded the old woman. "He is here? He is all right?"

"Yes," said Windom, "he's all right."

"He is not hurt?"

"No, not hurt."

"Praise be to the Virgin—" The old woman stopped, noticing Lollivar for the first time. Then her watery eyes flashed and she came farther into the room. "Ha, I thought it was a man who sits there," she said. "But it is not. It is only the stuffed pig who calls himself the mayor."

Lollivar made as if to rise, but Mamarta had planted herself directly in front of him. "The fat coward pig," she went on, "who is against his own people. Who allows an innocent man to go to jail. Who thinks of nothing but his stomach and pockets, while—"

The mayor was still trying unsuccessfully to get out of his chair. Windom had half-risen. Then Anna Vidal came hurrying in.

"Mother!" she said sharply.

"Be quiet," the old woman told her. "I am busy."

Anna took her arm. "It is the doctor who is busy. You must not disturb him like this."

"It is not the doctor I disturb. It is this fat-guts here. This cow-faced Iscariot."

She turned on Lollivar again, but Anna held her back. "It is the doctor's office, mother," she said, "and he has much to do. Come, we will see Jan. He is all right. We will talk to him."

She led Mamarta toward the door. But before they reached it another figure appeared.

"I am not intruding, I hope," said Schusterman.

Before Windom could answer the old woman had redirected her barrage. "No, you are not intruding. You are expected. Where Judas is, there is the devil too."

"Come, mother," said Anna.

"You have come for my son, hey?" Mamarta demanded. "Well, you will not get him. The doctor will not let you. The whole village will not let you."

Anna pulled her gently toward the door. Schusterman stepped aside, ignoring her, and behind him was revealed the squat figure of Bilko.

"Ah," said the old woman.

But this time that was all she said. Puckering her seamed cheeks, she spat a glob of betel juice on the floor at the policeman's feet. Then, shaking off her daughter's hand, she marched from the room.

Anna and Kosti followed her out and closed the door. Lollivar had retreated to the window and was again busy with his handkerchief. Schusterman crossed to the chair he had vacated and sat down opposite Windom, while Bilko moved up behind him.

"You appear to be having a busy morning, doctor," said the plantation manager.

"So does the whole village," Windom said.

"Sergeant Bilko and I will not keep you long, however. We have merely come for Jan Vidal."

Windom said nothing.

"He is here, is he not?"

"Yes, he's here."

"Will you please call him in."

"I'm not sure yet." Windom rubbed his jaw meditatively. "First there are a few things that I think we should discuss."

"Yes? What things, doctor?"

"You are here to arrest Vidal, is that right?"

"That is right."

"Why?"

"Why? Good God, man, you know why. You know what has been going on."

"What law has he broken?"

"Let us not quibble, doctor. This is a question of keeping the peace. Of preventing riots and bloodshed."

"I haven't noticed the strikers doing any rioting or bloodshedding. The only injured people who have been brought in here were—"

"I repeat," said Schusterman "—let us not quibble. There has been a breach of the peace. There has been stoppage of work and threats of violence. And the police must take such steps as they deem necessary."

"Or as *you* deem necessary?"

"I—the police—it is the same thing."

"Oh, I see. They take their orders from you?"

"I did not say—"

Windom looked at Bilko. "Whom do you take your orders from?" he asked.

The sergeant didn't answer.

"From the mayor, isn't that right?"

"From the mayor, yes—in local matters. And for more important things, from my superiors in—"

"You haven't had any orders from your superiors about this, have you?"

Again Bilko didn't answer.

"Have you?"

"No," said Bilko.

"Or from the mayor?" Windom turned to Lollivar. "What orders have you given?" he asked.

Lollivar swallowed. He looked from Windom to Schusterman and back again to Windom. He reached for his handkerchief, changed his mind, and brought out a cigarette instead. "I have explained to you, my doctor," he said at last, "that the situation is—er—most difficult. We do not want trouble. No, all of us are civilized men—men of good will—and all we wish is that—"

Schusterman got to his feet. "It is nonsense that we waste time like this," he interrupted. "Mr. Mayor—sergeant: you will be so good as to wait outside. With your permission, doctor, I think perhaps we can settle this matter in a few minutes."

Lollivar and Bilko left the room—the former with obvious relief, the latter impassively. Then Schusterman sat down again.

"The mayor is a fool," he said. "The other is only a stupid policeman. We can speak better alone." He paused briefly, then leaned forward and fixed Windom with his small sharp eyes. "You will tell me, please, what is on your mind, doctor?"

"What's on my mind," said Windom, "is the way you're handling this strike."

"I see. And how would you recommend I handle it?"

"Let the men meet and talk it over. Then hear their grievances."

"I already know their grievances."

"What have you done about them?"

Schusterman bit his lip. Then he said patiently: "May I point out to you, doctor, that I am not the owner, but only the manager, of this plantation? The decisions and policies of its operation are not made here in Papaan, nor even in the capital of this country, but across the world in the great cities of the West. They are not, I assure you, made even by the nominal owners. They are made by governments, as part of their international policy.

"The people here are peasants—coolies. They think about land, and they think about rice. But has it occurred to you what would happen if they had their own land and rice? They would be independent of the plantation. They would be able to set their own wages. Or not work at all. The importance of this country is its rubber, and rubber must come out of it. Nothing can be allowed to interfere with that, and as long as I am in charge here nothing will. The coolies have been told many times that they cannot have their own land and rice crop, and I am not going to allow them to be stirred up again by agitators and Communists."

"What Communists?" asked Windom. "Amyan? Jan Vidal?"

"Yes, I know, they are—what is the phrase?—'agrarian reformers.' " Schusterman smiled thinly. "But we have had our experience in China with agrarian reformers, have we not, Dr. Windom?"

"I've been here two years now, and—"

"And by now you should know this country better than apparently you do. Let me tell you something that perhaps you do not realize. It would take only the smallest shift in balance, the least relaxation of vigilance, for this whole area to be lost to us. Two hundred miles to the north is Red China. In the hills between is the bandit Than-kar and his men, in the pay of the Reds. Do you think that word does not go back and forth between here and there? That they are not waiting for any opening, any sign of weakness?" The manager paused, and when he spoke again his voice was quieter. "You and I are the only white men in this valley, doctor. Let us work together—as white men. If we have the leaders of this strike in custody, the others will be back at work in two days, and the trouble will be over. Otherwise—" He stood up. "But there can be no otherwise. Come, let us get this Jan Vidal and have an end to it."

Windom didn't move.

"You will not do it?"

Instead of answering, Windom rose, crossed to the window, and stood looking out across the yellow dust of the compound. Then he turned back to Schusterman and said, "No, I won't do it. I can't do it."

The manager started to speak, but Windom went on quietly: "As you say, we're the only two white men in this valley. We should be able to agree, to work together. I know the importance of rubber in this country. I know the importance of the plantation. But I don't care how important they are: you can't run the show any more as if these were the old colonial days. You've got these people wrong, Schusterman. Amyan and Vidal and all the rest of them. They're not Reds or agitators or bandits or anything of the sort—I promise you that. But they're not dumb animals either. Most of them have had some education. A few, like Amyan and Anna Vidal, have had a lot of education. They've been through a great war; they know something about the world they live in; and they're not going to let anyone set the clock back to the time when they were hopeless illiterate coolies."

Windom paused and smiled slightly. "Now we've each made our little speech," he said. "Perhaps we can go on from here."

Schusterman stood watching him for a moment. There was anger in his eyes, but his voice, when he spoke again, was cool and controlled. "The only thing it is necessary to go on to, doctor," he said, "is to put an end to this strike."

"Fair enough. The strike certainly isn't doing anyone any good."

"But you will not—"

"I will not help end it by force—no."

"What would you suggest: prayer?"

"I suggest what I said before. A meeting."

"It is out of the question. The police have already—"

"All right, not a mass meeting. A conference. Between you and the leaders."

"You expect me to sit down with these—"

"I expect you to be reasonable," said Windom. "And I shall expect them to be reasonable. If you want, I'll be glad to act as mediator."

Schusterman started to speak, stopped, and drew a slow breath. His lips were a thin colorless line under the bold beak of his nose. "I am afraid you still do not understand the situation," he said, slowly and quietly. "The agitator Amyan is in jail. The agitator Vidal will soon be in jail. One does not *mediate,* doctor, with criminals under arrest." Abruptly his manner changed. "In any case," he added, shrugging, "it is obvious we are getting nowhere." He turned and called:

"Bilko!"

The door opened and the policeman came in, followed hesitantly by Lollivar.

"You will order your men," said Schusterman, "to search the hospital for Jan Vidal."

Windom shook his head. "No," he said, "I am afraid that will not be possible."

Bilko looked from one to the other.

"I am sorry, doctor," said the manager. "I do not wish to

cause any more trouble than necessary. But the police have the right to—"

"The police have no right whatever to remove a patient from a hospital."

"A patient?"

"Exactly. If you'd care to look at our records you'll see that Jan Vidal was admitted this morning."

"Admitted—for what?"

"For observation," said Windom.

There was a silence. Schusterman seemed about to speak; then stopped and bit his lip.

"Very well, doctor," he said at last. "I don't know what you hope to gain by all this, but for the moment you win. I am not going to cause a disturbance in your hospital, nor am I going to stand around any longer arguing. In any case, we have the most important man already in custody. That, I think, may prove enough for the present, and later—"

"Later," said Windom, "I shall be glad to see you. Whenever you're ready to call a meeting."

Schusterman turned and left the room, and Bilko followed him out. Lollivar started after them; then stopped in the doorway and looked back at Windom. "My doctor, I know—" He cleared his throat. "I mean it is most difficult, you understand, and—" He glanced nervously after the others. "And I will of course do everything in my power—"

Then he too was gone.

Presently Anna Vidal looked in the door.

"They have gone?" she asked.

"Yes," Windom said. "They've gone."

Anna came in, and her mother came after her. "You have sent them away," the old woman said. "You have not let them harm my boy." She all but ran to the doctor; but this time he saw what was coming and put his hand on her shoulder before she could seize and kiss it. "You are our protector," she murmured. "May the Virgin bless and keep you."

Then suddenly, she was no longer looking at Windom, but past him, at a spot on the floor near the door. "Oh, my doctor," she cried. "I am so sorry! So ashamed!"

She crossed the room quickly, knelt down, and with the hem of her skirt wiped the blob of betel juice from the planking. "Truly, my doctor, it was not the floor I meant to spit on, but Bilko's feet. Please forgive me that I did this. The next time I will aim better—in his ugly face."

Windom went over and raised her to her feet. "What I'm worrying about, Mamarta," he told her, smiling, "is that some day you might get angry at *me*."

"Come now, mother," said Anna. "The doctor is busy." She looked at Windom. "Do you wish me to get Jan?"

"Please," he said.

Anna and her mother went out, the old woman again muttering blessings. Windom sat down at his desk and after perhaps a minute Jan Vidal came in.

"I cannot tell you, my doctor—" he began.

"Don't tell me anything," said Windom. "Sit down and listen to me."

He described briefly what had just taken place. Then he added: "I want you to promise me that you won't leave the hospital."

"For how long?" asked Jan.

"Until Schusterman agrees to the meeting I've suggested."

"And if he does not agree?"

"I think he will. I think he'll have to. Anyhow, it's worth waiting a few days to see."

"But meanwhile Father Amyan—"

"I'm going to do everything I can for Amyan," said Windom. "There's nothing you could do right now, except get yourself into the same fix he's in."

"It is terrible that he should be there in jail, while I am hiding like a coward."

"Everyone knows you're no coward. But there's no need to be a fool either. If you go rushing out of here now, one of two things will happen. Either they'll arrest you straight off, and that will be that; or you'll collect a mob and there'll be violence. You want the other side to be reasonable. All right, *you* must be reasonable. Stay out of sight for a while. Send out word to the others for them to stay in their homes. In a few days I'll talk to Schusterman again, and, unless I'm very wrong, he'll be ready to listen."

Windom paused. "Will you do as I ask?" he said.

The young man hesitated briefly. Then he answered, "Yes, my doctor, I will do as you ask."

He rose, as if to go, but Windom gestured him back into his seat. "There's one other thing, Jan—"

"Yes, my doctor?"

Windom sat for a few moments without speaking, his gray eyes steady on Jan's face. "I've known you and your family for quite a while now," he said. "I know a good deal about you. But I don't know everything about you. And I'm going to ask you one question."

Jan waited.

"This strike is purely a local thing, isn't it?"

"Local?"

"It was decided on by the people here in the valley? By you and Amyan?" Windom leaned forward a little. "You are not following orders from anyone outside?"

"From outside?" Jan's face showed bewilderment. "I do not know what you mean."

"I mean from Than-kar. From the Communists."

The young man stared at him. "My doctor, surely you do not believe that? You do not think—"

"We're not discussing what I think, Jan. I'm asking you

a question. Has this strike—have you and Amyan—any connection with Than-kar?"

"No—of course not." Jan was terribly agitated. "So that is what they are thinking and telling you. . . . But you know it is not so, my doctor. You have been in Papaan for two years. You know how it has been—what sort of people we are—and that we are not—"

The rush of words was interrupted by a knock on the door.

"Yes?" said Windom.

And the boy Kosti came in again.

"The mem-doctor," he said, "she asks I tell you that it is already—"

Windom stood up.

"Coming, Kosti."

Jan Vidal had risen too and was standing close beside him. "My doctor, please—" he began again. "You must understand—you must believe me—"

"I believe you," said Windom.

He put out his hand, and Jan took it.

"But now—"

"Now I have to go," Windom crossed to the door. "Find your sister Anna and she'll fix you some lunch."

EIGHT

It had been not quite light when Windom and Colonel Hasbrook drove off to the airfield. Left alone, Lenore sat at the breakfast table on the bungalow porch, looking across the dusty compound at the hospital building beyond. The hospital was not at all what she had expected it to be, although what that had been it was hard to say. A bamboo shack, perhaps. Around it, a jungle clearing, with shrines, pagodas, dancing girls and a sacred white elephant. She smiled inwardly. Twentieth Century-Fox proudly presents *Lenore and the King of Siam.*

She glanced with distaste at her still half-full teacup. Then she rose and started to get one of the tins of instant coffee she had brought along with her. Almost at the same moment, however, she changed her mind. You like tea, she told herself. You *adore* tea. Returning to the table, she drank what was left in the cup.

It was growing hotter. The compound was a yellow glare. A few indistinguishable figures moved in and out of the entrance of the hospital—and then something moved on the shaded porch. It was purplish black, perhaps six inches across, and all legs, or at least it seemed to be all legs until it stopped, and then two things that might have been eyes were staring at her.

She pushed sharply back in her chair, and a cup and saucer fell to the floor. Then the boy Kosti appeared from inside, and the legs scuttled away.

Kosti made no move to go after it. "It is only a *moki* spider," he said cheerfully.

Lenore said nothing.

"The *moki* he is nice. He eats the ant eggs." The boy stooped to pick up the broken china. "It is good to keep always a *moki* in the sleeping room," he went on. "Then there are no ants in the bed."

"Yes, of course," Lenore murmured. She managed a smile. "You'll have to be patient with me, Kosti."

"Patient, my lady?"

"There are a lot of things you'll have to teach me."

Kosti's brown face lit up. "Yes, my lady," he agreed, "there are many things I will teach you. About the *moki*—that is only one. There is also the blue spider and the scorpion and the green mamba. There are the leopards and pythons in the forest across the river and the bats who sleep under the roof when it is bright and hot. . . ."

He went on with mounting enthusiasm, as he put the breakfast things on a tray. Then at last he disappeared toward the kitchen. For a while Lenore stood by the table, her eyes moving slowly across the flooring of the porch. But the thing with legs did not reappear, and presently she too went inside.

Going first to the bedroom, she selected a box of candy and a bottle of toilet water from the gifts she had brought with her, and, moving on to the kitchen, gave one to Kosti and the other to the cook. There was abundant gratitude, much excited sampling and sniffing; but when Lenore subsequently tried to get around to the business of the household it was with a signal lack of success. The cook, a plump blank-faced woman named Lahana, spoke practically no English and Kosti, whom Lenore tried to enlist as interpreter, was still absorbed in the subject of Papaan's fauna. By the time the interview ended she had no idea whether lunch would consist of rice or roast cobra.

When she returned to the porch Windom was just driving into the compound in his jeep. She watched him park it, get out and start toward the bungalow; but, as she was about to open the screen door, the nurse whom she had met the day before came quickly across the compound and intercepted him. After a moment's conversation he turned and went with her toward the hospital. Lenore was about to call out to him, then changed her mind and closed the door.

Again, as on the previous evening, she walked slowly through the rooms of the bungalow. She opened cupboards and drawers, examined tableware and linens. On a bench in the living room there was a small radio, and she turned it on; but, finding only a drone of unintelligible voices, she quickly silenced it. For a while she stood in front of the bookcase, then took out a volume called *Manson's Tropical Diseases,* carried it to the porch and read a chapter titled "Mycetoma and Blastomycosis."

Nine o'clock had become ten. Ten became eleven. Three men, one of whom she recognized as the plantation manager, crossed the compound toward the hospital entrance, and the dust rose behind them like grains of sulphur in the sunlight. On the porch no shred of air stirred. Even in the thin cotton dress she was wearing, her waist and thighs were damp with sweat, and a strand of hair kept coming loose and dangling limply over her forehead. Going inside, she doused her face and arms with water, pulled her hair up tightly onto the top of her head, and changed from the dress into a sleeveless shirt and shorts. Then she went into the kitchen and made herself a long drink of tonic water, lime juice and ice. Only one more thing needed to make it right, she thought. But she resolutely ignored the gin bottle as she passed through the living room toward the porch.

She was halfway through Manson on beriberi when she realized there was someone at the door. Looking up, she saw a white uniform, a soft oval face, and shy dark eyes.

"Oh. Come in," she said smiling. "Miss–" She hesitated. "It's Miss Vidal, isn't it?"

Anna smiled back at her. "I would be happy if you would call me Anna, my lady."

"Come in, Anna." Lenore had risen and held the door open. "Sit down, won't you? I've been wanting to thank you for the flowers in my room. They're lovely."

"It was nothing, my lady. I wanted only to–" Anna was blushing. Her face was like a rose petal under the starched primness of her cap.

Lenore smiled again. "And you're lovely too," she said. "You'll have to give me lessons in how to keep so fresh and cool."

The nurse's blush deepened. There was a moment's pause.

"The doctor isn't here," said Lenore. "I thought he was at the–"

"Yes, he is at the hospital."

"He must be busy this morning."

"There was an operation. It was a little difficult. And now there are–" Anna hesitated–"some people he must see." She looked out across the empty compound, then back at Lenore. "I have come to ask if there are some ways in which I can help you, my lady."

First they went into the kitchen, and this time there was an intelligible colloquy with Lahana the cook. "In a few days," said Anna, "you will know all the words that are needed for the meals and the house." Then they went through the other rooms, and she made suggestions about clothes, cleaning, ventilation and insects. "Kosti is right," she explained. "The *moki* is an ugly thing, but useful. Especially in the rainy season when the ants and moths are everywhere."

"Aren't there insecticides?" asked Lenore.

"Yes, in the hospital we use them, of course. But the doctor, he does not like the smell, and here in his own house he will not—" Anna stopped abruptly. Her eyes broke away from Lenore's in embarrassment. "I—I am sorry, my lady," she murmured. "I did not mean—"

"It's all right, Anna."

"He has been here alone so long. I am used to . . . Please, you understand?"

"Don't worry about it," said Lenore. Then she smiled. "I see I'll have to get myself up to date on my husband's taste in smells."

Back on the porch she offered Anna a drink and then a cigarette. But the girl was still ill at ease. "I must get back to the hospital, my lady," she explained. "There is only the doctor and I, you see, and—" Once again she broke off, embarrassed. "I shall come tomorrow—yes. And if there is anything at all I can do—" Before she had finished she was at the door and out.

Now there was stillness again. Lenore read Manson's chapter on leishmaniasis. At noon Kosti appeared to announce that lunch was ready, and she sent him across to the hospital to tell Windom. "The doctor says he will come at once," the boy reported on his return.

She read the chapter on leprosy and yaws.

"Excuse, my lady," said Kosti, reappearing, "but Lahana say it is now a half-hour and the lunch it is—"

She sent him to the hospital again.

"The doctor says he will come at once," he said.

"Alec—"

"Yes?"

"What is it? Tell me."

He had sat through lunch almost without speaking, and now that it was over he stood at the window, staring abstractedly out at the glare of the compound.

"Was it a hard morning?" she asked.

"Hard?" Windom turned back to her. "Well, sort of, I suppose. There are a couple of dysenteries that I can't seem to get over the hump."

"But that's not it—is it?"

"It?"

"You never brought the hospital home with you. And I don't think two years have changed you that much." She rose and went up close to him. "Tell me, Alec," she said. "I saw that—what's his name?—the plantation man was here this morning. It has something to do with him, doesn't it?"

"There's been some trouble at the plantation. A strike."

"Oh. But how does that concern you?"

"It doesn't, really. Anyhow, don't worry about it. It's not important."

"No, I can see you think it *is* important." Windom didn't answer, and she looked up at him earnestly. "Tell me about it, Alec. Please. It's not a question of worrying; just of knowing. Don't you see? I have to know what you're doing. It's the only way we can be close again. The only way it will be any good."

She paused and put her hand on his arm. "Please, Alec," she said. "I'm right, and you know it."

"Yes, you're right," he said.

And he told her what had happened during the past two days. She listened quietly and seriously, asking a question here, making a comment there. But when he had finished, she smiled and kissed his cheek. "Poor Dr. Windom," she said. "The man who was going to get away from it all."

He smiled back. "At least their hormones are in good shape."

"And they pay a cent a visit."

"Sometimes two."

"And you like that fine."

"Yes, I like it fine."

They were silent a moment, and she stood watching him, and when she spoke again she was no longer smiling. "Then I'm going to like it too," she said.

He went back to the hospital, and she read Manson on intestinal parasites. Or, more accurately, she read two pages on intestinal parasites, then dropped the book to her lap and closed her eyes. And when she opened them again he was standing over her.

"All right, let's go," he said.

"Go? Where?"

"On a mission."

She was confused and not yet fully awake. "A mission? You mean—it's something important?"

"Yes," he said. "Something important."

Leaving the bungalow, they got into the jeep, and Windom drove out of the compound and through the almost deserted streets of the village. At the end of the street they got out and, circling a warehouse, walked along the dock beyond. And then suddenly Lenore realized where they were going, and as Windom helped her down into the skiff she pressed his hand tightly in her own.

He rowed, and she sat in the stern, facing him, and for a long time the only sound was the soft creak of oars. They moved out from the brown river water into the blue of the bay, and soon blue was all there was, blueness of sea, blueness of sky, with only the headland between them, pointing a dark green finger into the empty miles. The sun was still a good two hours from the horizon, but the fierce heat of midday had passed. Closing her eyes, Lenore felt the light lying warm and gentle on the lids. Then, opening them, she looked at her husband and smiled.

The headland moved closer. Soon it was directly above them, and on the other side of the skiff were the plunging purple shadows of the reef. This time, however, Windom did not stop at the reef, but rowed on around the headland, and on its far side were a small horseshoe cove and a curve of beach. Nosing the skiff in, he pulled it up on the sand. Then they lay in the soft sand, side by side.

"Alec—" she said.

"Yes?"

"Thanks, Alec."

Her hand moved a little and found his and held it.

And now it was Windom who closed his eyes. . . .

When you open them, he thought, you will be lying on Paradise Beach, Hog Island, Nassau, Bahamas, and the girl you married last Wednesday will bend over you and laugh and kiss you on the lips. You will be lying on the beach at Antibes, Biarritz, Montego, Acapulco, and the wife you have been married to for two years, five years, seven years, ten years, will bend over you and laugh and kiss you on the nose. Those had always been their best times: on beaches. On the warm sand, in the cool water, under the sun. It was when they left the beach that the trouble started; when it was time for dinner, for the drinks, for the party—or for no party. When it was time for the office, the hospital, the lab, the night call.

When it was time for reality, he thought.

No . . . He felt the sand soft beneath him and the sun soft above. . . . The one was as real as the other: the beaches, the laughter, the magic, no less than the bickering, the arguing, the estrangements. Here—now—a nameless beach on a nameless headland on a jungle coast—were real. The hand in his hand was real.

And then he opened his eyes, and she was no longer lying beside him, but sitting up, watching him, and as their eyes met, she bent her head and kissed him.

But this time she did not laugh.

"This is the best beach of all," she said.

"It is now." He smiled.

"No, it's always been the best. And it always will be."

"For the first few months I was here," he said, "I didn't know there was a beach within a hundred miles. Then one day I went out in the skiff with Kosti, and we came around the headland, and here it was."

"And you've come often since?"

"Now and then."

"With Kosti?"

"Sometimes with Kosti."

"And sometimes with—"

"Sometimes alone."

There was a pause, and he could hear the soft lapping of water at their feet. Then she asked:

"Has it been all right, Alec—alone?"

"You asked that last night."

"I'm asking again."

"I've been busy," he said. "I think I've been doing some good."

"You've become very close to these people, haven't you?"

"In a way, I suppose. Not in exactly the same way you can be close to your own people. But—"

"But you care for them. Really, I mean."

"Yes."

"And they care for you. I've seen it already, Alec—in just

two days. Kosti and Lahana. The old woman who came last night. And your nurse—what's her name?—Anna."

"Anna's pretty wonderful. I hate to think what the hospital would be without her."

"She's very charming."

"Then there's her brother, Jan. You haven't met him yet. He's quite a person too."

"He's the one who's in trouble—with the strike?"

"Yes."

"And you're helping him?"

"I'm trying to."

Lenore hesitated before speaking again. "Are you sure it's the wise thing, Alec?" she asked. "Mightn't it mean trouble for you too?"

"What do you expect me to do?"

"You're a doctor—not a politician."

"I'm a doctor, yes. But I'm also a man living among other men. These people don't want trouble any more than I do. But what they want is fair and right, and they should have it."

"And that's the only reason—you're certain?"

"Reason?"

"Why you're involved in this strike. It isn't just because—" again Lenore hesitated—"because you've become so close to some of them?" Windom was about to answer, but she cut him off, and now suddenly her words came in a rush. "No. No, Alec—I'm sorry. I'm foolish. That's not why I'm here: to question or argue with you. I'm here to *be* with you. Believe me, please. It's all so new, of course, and there are lots of things I'm sure I still don't understand. But that's all I want, truly it is. To understand. To help you—"

Her hand touched his. Her eyes were raised to his face. "Do you know what I was thinking this morning?" she said. "That, if you'd let me, I'd like to work in the hospital."

"But–"

"Oh, I'm no nurse–I know that. But there are things I could do, aren't there? Helping with the records, maybe. Or feeding and bathing patients. And meanwhile I could be learning the rest. . . . Please, Alec. Please. . . . It can't be the way it was before. You living one life, me another. It has to be *we*–in everything. We together . . ."

Windom didn't answer. But his eyes, deep and gray, were looking steadily back at her.

"What is it, Alec?" she said. "What are you thinking?"

"I'm thinking of something I said last night," he told her.

"Last night?"

"In the bungalow, before we went to bed. I said that your coming here was a pretty wonderful thing." There was a pause, and the eyes smiled.

"I was right," he said.

And now again they sat together for a while without speaking. There was the light touch of their hands on the warm sand. There was the sun, larger now and redder, sloping down toward the wooded crest of the headland, and beyond the headland the gleaming plain of the sea.

"It's waiting," said Lenore.

With a quick effortless movement she was on her feet and stripping off her clothes. Her body, lithe and white, seemed to catch and hold the sunlight, as for a moment she stood motionless before him. Then, turning, she ran lightly across the sand and into the water.

Then she was swimming. And Windom, rising and undressing, followed her. Here in the sheltered bay there was no surf, and the sea closed in about him silk-soft and smooth. Lenore was a strong swimmer, and out ahead he could see the flash of her head and arms as she moved steadily forward; but, striking out after her, he thrust forward as hard as he could, and when after a minute or two he raised his eyes, he was almost abreast of her.

"Still the champ," he grinned.

"Especially when I'm treading water," she agreed.

Then they swam on, more slowly, side by side, their arms moving in rhythm, their bodies suspended without effort in the salt silken bay. Around them was the glitter of sunlight, beneath them green depths of cool shadow, and he could feel the pure coolness on his flesh, in his eyes, in his blood, as the dust of the years, like the dust of the valley, drained out and away from him into the purity of the sea. And now they came to the reef, and he found the smooth level place which he knew, and they pulled themselves up onto it and sat with their feet dangling in the water and their thighs and shoulders touching, and Lenore's hair shone like wet gold above her laughing eyes.

Suddenly she was bending over and pointing.

"Oh, Alec—look!"

And glancing down, he too saw the quick rainbow glint in the shadow below.

"What is it?" she asked.

"It's what they call a poutina. They're a sort of angel fish."

"It's so beautiful—" She leaned far out over the still water. "And so quick . . . See, there it is now. . . . There . . . There . . . Now it's gone." She peered down along the steep coral walls. "I think it swam through to the other side of the reef."

Turning, she looked out into the water beyond. And Windom looked too. But there was no glint. No shadow. Only the deep blue of the ocean spreading to the bare blue of the sky.

They swam leisurely back to the beach and came up out of the water hand in hand. The glare of the day was now altogether gone. The sand gleamed coral pink. And Lenore's body was pink too—firm and fresh and glittering from the sea—and Windom pressed her hand and swung her gently toward him. He took her body in his arms. He felt it, firm and cool against his own. And then no longer firm but soft, no longer cool but warm, and her arms were around him too, her face was raised, her eyes were shining. There was the softness of flesh, the softness of the sand, the faint lapping of the sea upon the sand. And that was all there was: the sea, the sand, the two bodies upon the sand—with the years gone, the constraint and strangeness gone—and what had not happened the previous night happened now, and they were man and woman again, husband and wife again. . . .

"You see," Lenore whispered. "It's all right. We're all right."

Then again there was only the sound of the sea, as they lay together on the nameless jungle beach that had suddenly, magically become home.

The sun was almost down when they rose, dressed and pushed off in the skiff. And as they rowed back across the bay the sky turned quickly from blue to sunset red and from red to sombre purple. The dock and warehouse glided up out of obscurity, and then Lenore pointed, and, turning, Windom saw a small gesticulating figure on the dock.

"It's Kosti," he said.

The skiff drew closer and nudged the pilings, and as the boy scrambled down to them they saw that his eyes were wide with excitement.

"I have been looking for you everywhere, my doctor," he panted. "Father Amyan has been killed."

NINE

AN HOUR EARLIER THE RUMOR HAD BEGUN TO SPREAD. A SHOP-keeper whose place was next door to the jailhouse reported that he had heard a shot. The gate to the jail's outer compound, usually open, was shut and barred. When a policeman appeared outside and some villagers asked him what had happened, he had refused to answer; and when they persisted he had threatened them with his revolver.

That had been at about five. By five-thirty more than a hundred people were gathered in the street outside the jail. Perhaps half of them were striking plantation workers, the rest a heterogeneous group of neighborhood dwellers and passers-by. For a while they had simply stood in silence, as if waiting for the police to open the gate. Finally some of the men, bolder than the rest, approached the gate and beat on it. But there was no answer from inside.

Another ten or fifteen minutes went by.

Then the gate swung suddenly open, and behind it were four policemen with rifles. One of them, a corporal, ordered the crowd to disperse.

"We want to see Father Amyan," they insisted.

"You cannot see him."

"Yes, we can. We will."

"The prisoner Amyan is dead," said the corporal. "He was shot while trying to escape."

And the gate swung shut.

Leaderless, the crowd melted away. The village lay quiet in the evening light. But through the quietness the news went swiftly from street to street, from house to house. It was carried by two plantation workers to a room in the hospital, and when presently they left again, Jan Vidal was with them.

"Where did he go?" Windom demanded of Anna, as she stood before him, tense and distraught, in the cubicle of his office.

"I do not know, my doctor," she said.

"You didn't see him go?"

"No. I was in the North Ward, and the first I knew, one of the student nurses came and told me Jan had gone off with two men."

"Who were they? Did she know?"

Anna shook her head. "She did not see them close enough to tell."

Giving her a few brief instructions, Windom crossed the compound to the bungalow. Lenore was waiting for him anxiously on the porch.

"Don't leave the hospital grounds," he told her. "When Kosti and Lahana leave you can go to the main building and stay with Anna. But don't leave the grounds."

"But you—" she began.

"I may be gone a while."

"No, Alec—please. You can't tell what might—"

"Don't worry about me. The people all know me. I'll be all right."

And before she could speak again he was out the door and clambering into the jeep.

Night had now fallen. But the village was still quiet, the

streets almost deserted, as he drove the few hundred yards to the Vidals' house. Light showed in its windows, but when he knocked and entered he found old Mamarta alone. She was standing at the table, and lying upon it was an enormous curve-bladed native sword, which she was apparently in the process of cleaning and polishing.

"You remember it, hey, my doctor?" she asked. "It was my husband's, who used it for Japs. Before that it was his father's and his father's father's. Now it is Jan's, and he will use it better than any of them." She tried to hold up the blade, but it was so heavy she could scarcely lift it. "It is the only sword in Papaan big enough to go through the fat guts of Bilko." She cackled happily.

"Has Jan been here?" asked Windom.

"Yes, he has been here."

"Where has he gone?"

"About his business." Mamarta rubbed energetically at the sword with a shred of cloth. "There is much business, my doctor, to be done in Papaan tonight."

As he was about to go, a figure appeared in the door. It was another old woman, almost as small as Mamarta, and even more excited. "Quick, Mamarta. Quick, my doctor," she cried. "Come—look—you must see!"

They followed her out, and she pointed, and there, beyond the village, was a red glow in the black western sky.

"They have set fire to the plantation," said the second old woman.

"They are roasting that Schusterman like a cock on a spit," Mamarta added with enthusiasm. "Then they will come back for the sword and attend to Bilko."

Windom got back into the jeep and drove off. He drove faster than he had ever driven in the valley before, and soon the village was behind him, the riverbank and open fields were behind him, and he was careening along through the twisting roads of the rubber groves. At intervals his headlights picked up figures along the way: some alone, some in groups, some on foot and others on mules or bicycles. Occasionally a voice called out to him. But he did not stop. And presently the red glow was no longer only in the sky, but directly ahead of him, a bright screen of flame crackling and billowing behind the black boles of the trees. Then the road bent sharply, and he came out into an open space, and all around him were running figures and shouting voices. Braking to an abrupt stop, he leapt from the jeep.

As far as he could see in the dim confusion, most of the flames were coming from various of the outbuildings that surrounded the plantation house, and some of them had already burned almost to the ground. But the main building was now afire too, and a red glow showed in the windows of its nearer wing. A man ran close beside Windom, carrying a lighted torch, and he seized him and knocked it from his hand.

"Where is Jan Vidal?" he demanded.

The man looked at him apprehensively. "I do not know, my doctor."

"Where is Mr. Schusterman?"

"I do not know, my doctor."

The man turned and ran off, and Windom went quickly on to the plantation house. Circling the burning wing, he found a side door, opened it, and groped from one dark room to another. "Schusterman!" he called. "Schusterman!" and then "Jan!" "Jan!" But the only sounds were shouting voices outside and the loudening crackle of flames.

Coming out another door, he found himself in the center of a confused mob. Several men were throwing burning faggots into a window. Close by, two others were holding a figure pinioned to the ground, while a third kicked it. Windom recognised the victim as a Chinese clerk who worked in the plantation office. The man who was kicking him was an ordinarily mild and timid coolie named Ikar, a father of ten, whom he had been treating for two years for tuberculosis of the kidneys.

"Stop it" Windom ordered him.

But the kicking continued.

Then Windom hit him. It was not anger at the man that he felt. It was anger at anger. At violence. And even as he struck, he thought: and now you too. Returning violence for violence, anger for anger.

Ikar staggered back and looked at him dumbly, but did not strike back. The other two men released the Chinese, and he scrambled to his feet and disappeared.

"Where is Schusterman?" Windom asked.

The men shook their heads. "We have not seen him," one said. "He is not here."

"Where is Jan?"

"He is not here either."

"Where is he?"

"He has gone back to the village."

"To the jail."

"To settle our account with Bilko."

There was a pause. The firelight flickered on the circle of sullen brown faces, and, turning, Windom saw that the whole main section of the plantation house was now in flames. There was no way of saving it.

"You had better get back to the village too," he said quietly.

He went back to the jeep, got in and drove off. Although the road was now more crowded than before, he managed almost as fast a pace as on the way out, and in less than fifteen minutes he was again in the village streets. There were no flames here, no hoarse shouts or darting shadows, and he knew that, whatever the story would prove to be, it was already an accomplished fact. Then he turned a corner into the street where the jail and police station were located, and the fact was before his eyes.

The street was filled with people—men, women and children—moving about in the aimless tides of a crowd. But among them were others who were not moving: figures hunched and sprawled on the ground, wounded and dying. The jail gate was now open, splintered by many blows and hanging crazily on one hinge, and in the courtyard beyond were more wounded, more dead. Most were plantation workers. Windom saw three policemen. He saw two women and a boy who could not have been more than ten. Among them moved their families and companions, searching out their own. Somewhere a voice shrieked with high insane monotony. Beside a still figure, a shawled woman was kneeling and beating her head against the ground.

Windom entered the jail building, thrusting his way through the crowd at the door. Beyond the door was a vestibule, beyond that a small office; and in the office were two more bodies. One, lying on a table, was an old man with a seamed sunken face and a fringe of white hair, his body straight and his hands folded, as if already laid out on a bier. The other, sprawled on the floor near his feet with his face in a pool of blood, was the police sergeant Bilko.

Four plantation workers stood by the table, one at each corner—a guard of honor for their dead leader—and a fifth man sat in a chair on the far side of the room, his face bent into his hands. As Windom came in he looked up at him silently.

"All right, Jan," Windom said. "Let's start clearing up the mess."

There were eight killed outright and thirty wounded. Or, rather, thirty wounded badly enough that they had to be taken to the hospital. How many more went home to be treated with herbs, spittle and incantations, no one would ever know.

Among the dead were three policemen, including Bilko. Among the wounded, four. Of the rest, about half had thrown down their arms and joined the strikers, and the other half had managed to escape. Apparently Schusterman, too, had escaped. No one seemed actually to have seen him since the rioting began, but a group of peasants from upvalley reported that earlier in the evening one of the plantation trucks had roared through their village, heading south.

There was no ambulance in Papaan. But the hospital was well stocked with stretchers, left over from the war days, and within half an hour these had been brought and the wounded carried away. Their families followed in straggling procession, some in dazed silence, some wailing their grief, and soon the hospital compound was as crowded as the jail-yard had been a while past.

In the wards there were not enough beds to go around, and soon the aisles between them were lined with the stretchers. Windom moved quickly from one to the next. For the moment there was little that could be done except first aid: tourniquet and dressings for the hemorrhage cases, the hypodermic for pain. Anna and the student nurses followed him, bearing the necessary instruments and equipment, carrying out his quick instructions when he moved on. Then he came to a stretcher over which a woman was already bending, trying to staunch the bleeding of a man who had been shot in the throat. "Here, let me have the dressing," he said. And it was not until the woman turned to give it to him that he realized it was Lenore.

Her hand was trembling. Her face was as white as the nurse's uniform she was wearing and the towel that was wrapped around her head.

"You shouldn't be here, Lee," he told her.

"No?" she murmured. "Where should I be? Playing solitaire?" She bent again over the man on the stretcher. "Go on," she said.

But at that moment the wounded man gave a shuddering gasp. Bubbles welled up in the red hole of his throat, and suddenly a great gush of blood streamed up over her hands. Then, with a quiet sob, she raised her hands, blood and all, to her face and would have fallen if Windom had not held her.

"Anna!" he called.

And she and the student nurses came quickly. The two other girls raised Lenore to her feet and led her from the ward. Anna knelt beside Windom and helped him do what he could for the dying man.

There were three more deaths altogether. There were two long hours in the stifling ill-lit operating room for surgery that could not wait for daylight. There were the stenches, the retchings, the groans, the babblings of delirium. All that was missing, thought Windom, were the Japs. But even worse than the Japs were the huddled figures in the compound outside—kneeling, praying, waiting.

With Anna, he went out and spoke to them, reassuring some, telling others what he had to tell them. He urged them all to go home and return in the morning, and a few left. But not many.

Then he re-entered the hospital; and, as he passed the door of his office, it was opened cautiously from inside, and someone spoke his name. Going in, he found the mayor, Dai Lollivar.

"What are you doing here?" he asked.

"I have been waiting for you, my doctor."

"Are you hurt?"

"Hurt? No, my doctor, the Lord has spared me. Or at

least my body. But in my spirit I am wounded—I am sick. More than by bullets or knives."

"How long have you been here?"

"An hour. Perhaps two. It does not matter. I have not minded waiting."

"You weren't at the jail?"

"The jail, my doctor?"

"Or at the plantation?"

Lollivar didn't answer.

"You've been hiding here the whole time?"

"Hiding?" The mayor's moon-face was pained. "Who speaks of hiding? Here in this room, my doctor, we have spoken of trouble, and how we must avoid it. So the trouble begins, and that is what I do. I do not go to the trouble, but away from it. I try to set an example. If no one goes to the trouble, there is no trouble."

Windom almost smiled. But Lollivar was looking up at him anxiously. "It has been bad, has it not?" the mayor asked. "There are many wounded, many killed."

"Yes," said Windom.

"Bilko has been killed."

"Yes."

"That is bad—bad. Also it is good, of course, for this Bilko was an evil man. But mostly it is bad." Lollivar produced his handkerchief and wiped his face. "And Mr. Schusterman," he said. "He is dead too?"

"No."

"He has escaped?"

"They think so."

"That is good. Very good . . . But it is also bad. . . . He escapes. He goes to the capital, to the authorities, and tells what has happened. And then they think I am responsible. I am the mayor, they say, and it is my fault." Lollivar looked at Windom earnestly. "You will explain to them, will you not, my doctor? That I have done nothing wrong. That I have wanted only peace and no trouble. . . ."

Anna appeared in the doorway.

"I have been with Tok Danil," she said to Windom. "He is the one with the fractured pelvis, and I am afraid he is weaker."

The mayor went on talking, but now it was to himself.

The clock on Windom's desk showed two-thirty. And now it was Jan Vidal who stood, stooped with tiredness, at the office door.

"Well," said Windom, "are you satisfied?"

Jan didn't answer.

"Come in. Sit down."

Jan crossed the room and took the chair across the desk from him. Windom offered him a cigarette, but he shook his head.

"How many are dead?" Jan asked.

"Eleven."

"How many are ours?"

"Eight."

"There will be more?"

"It's hard to tell."

There was a pause.

"What next, Jan?" asked Windom.

"First we must take care of the wounded."

"That's my job."

"Yes."

"And yours?"

"In the morning we will have a meeting. Then we will begin to clear paddies for the rice."

"You'll plant your rice at last, eh?"

"Yes, we will plant our rice."

There was another silence. Windom looked out through

the window at the darkness of the compound, and Jan, raising his eyes, looked at him.

"What will you do, my doctor?" he asked at last.

"Do?"

"What will you report to the authorities?"

"How many dead there have been. How many wounded."

"That is all?"

"I'm a doctor, Jan; not an official. Besides, I imagine Mr. Schusterman's report will keep the authorities well occupied."

"He will report only his side."

"Of course."

"And he will lie."

"Possibly."

"But then they must hear the truth." Jan leaned forward in his chair. "They must hear our side. And not only from us."

Windom didn't answer.

"You are no longer on our side, my doctor? You believe now that we are wrong."

"I believe that violence and killing are wrong."

"Violence and killing—yes, of course. But was it we who started it? We who are responsible?" Jan's big hands gripped the edge of the desk. "My doctor, you did not see what I saw when we broke into the jail. They had beaten Father Amyan. They had whipped and burned him. The marks were plain on his body. And when still he would not tell them what they wanted—when he would not betray his own people—then they killed him. They said he was trying to escape; but that is a lie, and you know it. Father Amyan was old. He was sick. He was the gentlest of men. . . . And they murdered him."

Jan's voice broke. His eyes filled with tears. Then in the next instant they had turned hard and dark, and he rose to his feet. "So we have killed back," he said. "We have done at last for that pig of a Bilko. Yes, in doing it some of us have died too. Good men, good friends, women, a child. It was a terrible thing—but a necessary thing. We would do it again. We will fight on if we must. We will make a life for ourselves and our children and our children's children, and the soul of Father Amyan will look down and be proud of us."

He looked at Windom, almost as if in defiance. Then again, abruptly, his manner changed. "You have been our friend, my doctor," he said quietly. "Our friend and our helper. Do not, please, leave us because of what has happened. Do not now be against us."

Windom looked at him for a long moment in silence. Then he too got up.

"I'm not against you, Jan," he said.

"And you will—"

"Suppose we leave it at that for tonight." He glanced at the clock. "It's almost three. Get some rest."

He was standing alone by the windows when Anna came again to call him back to the wards.

There was a band of gray in the eastern sky as he came up onto the porch of the bungalow.

"Alec?" said Lenore's voice.

"Haven't you been to bed?" he asked.

"Come on," she said, appearing from inside. "I've some coffee and sandwiches ready."

"I'm not hungry, thanks."

"You've had nothing since yesterday lunch. Come on."

In the kitchen, where the light was on, he saw that she was still wearing the nurse's uniform with a towel around her hair. She brought the coffee from the stove and the sandwiches from the refrigerator and sat beside him at the table while he ate and drank. When his cup was empty she poured him more coffee.

Then after a few moments she seemed to be listening to something, and, getting up, she left the kitchen. Following her, when he had finished eating, he crossed the living room, came to the bedroom door—and stopped. Lenore was bending over the nearer of the two cots, and on it, lying crosswise in a row, were four small motionless figures.

"One of them woke up," she said, "but he's asleep again now."

Approaching the cot, he saw that they were the four children who had been in the hospital: the up-valley girl with trachoma, a second, younger girl whose left foot had been amputated, and two five-year-old boys crippled by rickets.

"It seemed so horrible for them over there," Lenore said. "And Anna and the student nurses were almost crazy with work."

"When did you bring them here?"

"Early last night. When they were carrying in the others."

Windom peered down at each child in turn. Then he took Lenore's arm and they went into the living room.

"Good going, Lee," he said.

"Kosti helped me with them. It was nothing."

"No, it wasn't nothing."

Lenore didn't look at him. "I was so ashamed," she murmured. "There in the ward, when that poor man was dying —and I couldn't—"

Windom put his hands on her shoulders and pulled her gently toward him. "Lee, stop it," he said. "You're not a doctor. You're not a nurse."

"No, I'm not a nurse. I can't do what Anna Vidal can do. What any little brown coolie girl can do—" He was holding her close to him and now at last she looked up into his face. "I came here to help you, Alec—"

Her own face was pale and tired; her blue eyes almost dark in the gray dawnlight. Suddenly she bent her head against his shoulder. "I want to so much," she whispered. "So terribly much."

TEN

TWELVE DAYS LATER TWO MEN WERE TALKING IN A GOVERNMENT office in the capital. One, named Tanit Belhedron, was vice-commissioner for the Northern Provinces. The other was Carl Schusterman.

More accurately, Schusterman was talking—at length and with emotion. The commissioner listened. He was a slight man with a smooth face, smooth lacquer-black hair and small flat-lidded eyes. His white linen suit was tailored and immaculate. In his lapel he wore a sprig of jacaranda blossom; on his left hand a ruby ring.

Now and then, as the other talked, he made a notation on a pad that lay on his desk. At intervals he asked a question. "Believe me, Mr. Schusterman," he said, when his visitor paused, "I understand your vehemence and your concern. But you must be patient."

"But I have been here for a week."

"Exactly. For *only* a week. And it is less than two since the events of which you speak. In such a matter as this you must expect certain delays."

"My company," said Schusterman, "demands the protection to which it is entitled."

Belhedron nodded. "And it shall have it. My government,

I assure you, is going to preserve law and order. And we are as aware as your company of the importance of its rubber production."

"By now the trees have probably been slashed, and the crop ruined."

"No, our reports indicate that that has not happened. And if it has—" the commissioner shrugged—"what's done is done."

"Why have not the provincial police taken control?"

"The provincial police, if I may say so, could scarcely take control of a bazaar pickpocket. The one capable man up there was this Bilko—and now he is gone. The rest are worse than nothing. As likely as not, half of them up there have already joined the criminals."

Belhedron looked meditatively at his ruby ring; then rubbed it gently against his lapel. "You are upset, Mr. Schusterman," he went on. "You are outraged and impatient, and that is understandable. But you must not let your impatience delude you into thinking that nothing is being done. It is precisely because so much is being done that it must take some little time."

"I am afraid I do not follow you."

"This—shall we say?—disturbance at your plantation was not, as you of course know, an isolated incident. There has been trouble at many other plantations throughout the northern rubber district. Not as drastic as at yours, perhaps—but of the same nature. And with the same cause. As you have seen, the situation has gone far beyond the point where it can be handled by the police. It has gone beyond the powers of my own department. It may interest you to know that it has been exhaustively discussed during the past week on the very highest levels of our government. It has even been the subject of discussion between our government and certain other much larger and more powerful governments."

Schusterman made as if to speak, but the commissioner continued. "You know—we all know," he said, "that these disturbances are not local matters. Who were the so-called leaders in this trouble at Papaan?" He glanced at his notes. "One Amyan, an ex-Buddhist monk. One Jan Vidal, a plantation foreman. Do you think these peasants are the real leaders? You know as well as I whom they take their orders from."

"From Than-kar."

"Precisely. Behind them is the Red bandit Than-kar; and behind him his masters in Peiping and Moscow. Far from being a local matter, it is not even simply a national one. It is international. And that is exactly the level on which we plan to deal with it."

"You mean—"

"I mean that we shall send troops. Not the garrison companies that we have scattered around the provinces; they're no better than the police. But real troops, from here in the capital. American trained—with American arms. It may be a little while, Mr. Schusterman, before your company gets back its plantation. But you will get it, never fear. And we shall teach these Reds a lesson they shan't forget."

The commissioner picked up the telephone on his desk. "Is Colonel Hasbrook here yet?" he asked. "Good. Ask him to come in." Then, turning back to Schusterman: "You have met Colonel Hasbrook, I believe. He is handling the military equipment of which I just spoke. That, of course, is the concern of the army, not of this department; but it has occurred to me that—" The door opened, and he broke off and got to his feet. "Do come in, colonel. Good morning."

Hasbrook shook hands with the two men. Then he grinned at Schusterman. "All in a piece, I see."

"Most luckily, yes."

"Sounds like a tough crowd up there."

"Oh yes." Schusterman smiled back thinly. "But not quite tough enough, I am afraid."

"It was good of you to come, colonel," said the commissioner. "Mr. Schusterman and I have been discussing the Papaan affair, and there is one particular aspect on which I would very much like to have your opinion."

"Captain Lutz tells me the troops are coming on fine," said Hasbrook. "Having some trouble getting on to the new equipment, of course, but nothing that a week or two won't fix."

"Excellent. I am delighted. Though military matters, of course, are not directly my province." Belhedron cleared his throat. "What I was wondering, colonel, is if you could give us some information about your compatriot up there."

"My compatriot?"

"About Dr. Windom."

"Oh." Hasbrook leaned forward in his seat. "Has anything happened to him?"

"We do not know."

"Is he still in Papaan?"

"As far as we can ascertain—yes. As you are aware, the telephone and telegraph lines have been cut, and the sort of word-of-mouth information we have had is often not too reliable."

"Good God, you don't think he's been killed?"

"No, we think that unlikely. Mr. Schusterman here considers it *extremely* unlikely. That is what we want to ask you about, colonel."

"Ask me about?"

Belhedron made a triangle with thumbs and forefingers and regarded it meditatively. "On your recent tour of duty," he said, "you spent a day and night at Papaan."

"Yes."

"You stayed with Dr. Windom."

"Yes."

"What, may I ask, was your impression of him?"

"That he's a remarkable man."

"Remarkable?"

"A man giving everything to his job. Unselfish. Devoted."

"You mean devoted to the people there?"

"To the people. To his work. He's made a great thing of that hospital, I'm telling you. He's trained nurses, taught the natives to keep clean—"

"We have a rather complete dossier," said the commissioner, "on Dr. Windom's professional record. Now we are wondering about his other activities."

"What do you mean—other activities?"

The commissioner changed his tack slightly. "The morning that you left Papaan," he said, "was the day the trouble started."

"I believe so. Yes," said Hasbrook.

"It had not actually started before you left?"

"No."

"But you must have known that it was threatening."

"I knew there was talk of a strike at the plantation. That something was in the air. But as an American army officer, I didn't feel it was my place to get involved in it."

"You were quite right, colonel. But to get back to Dr. Windom. To what extent was *he* involved in it?"

"Windom? To my knowledge, not at all."

"Mr. Schusterman here says that he was greatly involved."

Hasbrook looked from Belhedron to Schusterman.

"—that, if he was not actually one of the instigators of the strike," the commissioner went on, "he was doing everything in his power to help it."

There was a short pause.

Then Schusterman said: "You will perhaps recall, colonel, the afternoon we met, when the doctor was driving you through the plantation. Then perhaps you will also recall the conversation we had. About the trouble there had already been. About the foreman Vidal, whom I had discharged."

Hasbrook nodded.

"Was it not clear to you what Windom was about?"

There was another pause—longer than before. Then Hasbrook shook his head.

"No, gentlemen," he said. "You're barking up the wrong tree."

"I beg your pardon?" asked the commissioner.

"You're letting your imaginations run away with you. Windom may be close to the natives—yes. That's part of his job, and only natural, living with them all this time. But to claim that he's mixed up in what's happened—in rioting and killing—is going too far. You can't make me believe it."

"We are not trying to make you believe anything, colonel," said Belhedron blandly. "We are simply trying to acquire some information."

"I've already told you what I know. And what I think."

"I am not now referring to his life here in this country. I am thinking of his previous history. In fact we have already asked your diplomatic people to check back on it."

"To find what?"

"To find, for one thing, if he has a record of political activity. To find if he has had any previous Communist associations."

"Communist?" Hasbrook stared at him. "That's fantastic!"

"It may appear fantastic to you, colonel. However, if you consider the last few years of world history, I think you would agree that the fantastic has become more common than the commonplace."

"But Windom was one of the top doctors in New York.

An army major. His wife comes from an old banking family, and—"

"Colonel, colonel," Belhedron interrupted gently. "There is no cause to take this personally. Or as a reflection on your country. Quite the contrary, I assure you. The United States is as concerned as we are in defeating communism. You yourself would not be here now, if it were not. Very well. We have information that one of your countrymen has given aid and comfort to Communist-inspired agitators. It is information that must be investigated, and, if it is true, drastic action must be taken. In the interests of your country as well as of mine."

Hasbrook got up and walked slowly across the room. For a few moments he stood looking out of the window, and his broad, usually placid face was clouded. Then he turned back to the others.

"Captain Lutz," he said, "tells me that the troops will be ready by the end of next week."

"So I understand," said Belhedron.

"And that it will take another week to move them up to Papaan."

"Approximately."

"In three weeks, then, we should have some of the answers." Hasbrook picked up his cap, which he had placed on the commissioner's table. "But I'm willing to bet," he added, "that the answers on Windom aren't going to be what you think."

"I hope you are right," said Belhedron.

ELEVEN

BANDOR, G. 28. ADM. 4/9/51. SHOT IN ABD., LEFT UPPER quadrant, rupturing spleen. Op., splenectomy 4/9. Medication . . . Prognosis . . .

Laurang, M. 37. Adm. 4/9/51. Knife wounds in throat and rt cheek. Op., débridement 4/10; sutures removed 4/15. Med. . . . Prog. . . .

Dastil, H. 19. Adm. 4/9/51. Fract. left occiput skull; mult. contusions. Irrational three days; gradual improvement. Med. . . . Prog. . . .

Ahmol, R. 32. Adm. 4/9/51. Bullet wound rt. lumbar area. Probed 4/10 (unsuccessful); probed again 4/13, bullet removed. Infection of wound noted 4/13, septicemia (?) 4/15. . . .

Pohander, A. 44. Adm. 4/9/51. . . .

During the first week there were thirty-five cards in the "current file" on the office desk, thirty-five men, women and children on the cots and pallets in the wards. During the second week nineteen were discharged, but, of those who remained, all were on the "serious" list and four were "critical." Meanwhile, by malevolent coincidence, a wave of enteric fever swept the eastern section of the village, and no sooner was a bed vacated by one patient than it was occupied by another.

For twelve hours a day Windom moved back and forth from the wards to the operating room. For another four, on an average, he jeeped about the village from home to home, visiting the wounded who had been moved from the hospital to make room for the fever cases and the fever cases who could not be admitted at all. When she could, Anna took over for him. But in most instances he was needed himself. The families of the sick and injured crowded the compound, waiting for him, and even stopped his jeep as he drove through the dusty streets.

In a strictly medical sense the fever was not too difficult to deal with. It was of a type that flared and receded quickly, and he was equipped with proper means for its treatment. With the badly wounded, however, it was a different story. He needed an X-ray machine. He needed far larger quantities of penicillin and streptomycin. In spite of every precaution, two men developed septicemia; two more required amputations; another had a bullet lodged close to the spine, and it was not until the second exploratory operation that he was able to find and remove it. For days it seemed certain that at least some, if not all of them, would die.

But in the end he pulled them all through. He worked with an almost fierce concentration and fixity of purpose—improvising, substituting, experimenting; and strangely, though his body grew numb with tiredness, his mind seemed clearer, calmer, more at peace than it had been for a long time past. He was a man absorbed in the job at hand; in the exercise of his skills. Here the tissue that must be débrided. Here the artery that must be clamped. The hemostat, please. The scalpel. The drain, the suture. The syringe.

Anna stood beside him: tired, too, but unresting until he rested.

"Go get some sleep," he would tell her.

"Later, my doctor," she answered.

And when now and then she left his side, it was only to return a few minutes later bringing him a lime drink or a cup of tea.

Even the bungalow was now little more than an annex of the hospital; for Lenore had insisted on keeping the four sick children there, at least until such time as the main building should be less crowded. There were of course still no cots available, but she had bedded them down on the living room couches. And with Lahana's and Kosti's help, she herself took charge of their feeding, bathing and routine medication.

"It's not much," she said, "but at least it makes a few less for Anna."

For two weeks Windom was in the bungalow for little more than a quick meal, a change of clothes, sleep. And their talk was limited to the developments of the day and the problems of the next. Only once, when they were alone together for a few minutes at supper, did they range farther afield; and that began with Windom's mentioning that one of the wounded policemen was almost ready to be discharged.

"But *can* you discharge him?" Lenore asked.

"I think so," he said.

"He won't make trouble?"

"No."

"When will the other trouble start?"

"The other—?"

"About the police who were killed. About the plantation."

Windom shrugged. "It depends on how long it took Schusterman to get to the capital. And on what they decide to do."

"They'll send people, won't they? More police or something."

"I suppose so."

"There'll be arrests and trials." She paused, but Windom said nothing. "It may be awful, mayn't it? As bad as what's happened already."

"It will depend on whom they send."

"What will you do, Alec?"

"Do?"

"Will you be on the side of the people here? Will you try to help them?"

"Of course."

"Yes—of course. But—" Lenore hesitated. Her eyes were troubled. "But some of them will have to be arrested, won't they? The ones who really rioted. Who did the burning and killing. . . . They'll ask you about it, Alec. And you'll have to tell them."

"What I'll tell them," said Windom, "is the truth."

"But the truth is—"

"The truth is that these people were driven to what they did. That any self-respecting lot would have done the same thing."

"But burning the plantation—killing the police—"

"All right, they went too far. Because they were goaded too far. But if the government tries to treat them like criminals or bandits, they're going to hear plenty from me."

"That's what I'm afraid of, Alec."

"Afraid?"

"That they'll hear too much from you. That they'll think you're involved."

"I *am* involved."

"You know what I mean. That you're somehow responsible. That plantation manager—he probably thinks so already. You didn't get along, I could see that; and I'm sure he'd like nothing better than to make trouble for you."

Windom smiled and got to his feet. "A prescription from

your physician," he told her "—stop worrying about me."

"What else should I worry about?"

"Well, as a starter, I could suggest ten surgical cases, eighteen dysenteries and one fallopian pregnancy. Or even the rice crop would do."

She smiled back, but in the next instant reached out and took his hand. "You'll be sensible, won't you, Alec?" she pleaded. "Sensible and careful—"

"I'll make Lollivar look like a daredevil," he promised her.

And he went back to the hospital.

Once too, during those days, they went out again to the headland. This time, however, it was not during the afternoon, but in the middle of the night.

For an hour he had lain on his cot, tired but sleepless, and then the moon rose, and, getting up, he went to the window and watched it climb the black sky behind the banyan trees. Suddenly he realized that Lenore was standing beside him, watching too.

"Come on," she said.

"Where?"

But he knew where.

They drove through the empty streets, crossed the dock and climbed down into the moored skiff. Then they rowed out across the bay, and the headland swam up at them, green and silver in the darkness. There was the soft coolness of the sand; the soft warmness of the water; the quick gleam of phosphorus as their arms rose and fell, and, beyond the reef, the broad gleam of moon and ocean. There was the beach again. There was the cool warmness of flesh. And that was all there was. . . .

Lenore smiled up at him.

"Husband," she said.

"Wife."

"Not doctor."

"No."

"Not nurse."

"No."

"Not hospital, not sick, not hurt, not tired, not worried."

"No."

"Not war, not peace, not things, not people."

"No."

"Not anything but us."

"No."

There was the sea; the moonlight. There was her smile. And then she was no longer smiling but lying quietly beside him: hand in his, eyes closed.

"It wasn't a mistake, was it?" she murmured.

"No," he said, "it wasn't a mistake."

The dead were buried. The fever passed. Two weeks after the "trouble," there was enough room in the hospital to move the sick children back from the bungalow, and by the end of the third week only a handful of the wounded were still left in the wards. In the village, the streets and bazaars were no different (except for the absence of policemen) from what they had been before. The bullocks plodded. The children scampered. The women gossiped. The merchants haggled. The trouble had come, the trouble had gone, and neither the Holy Virgin nor the Dapsang Buddha, nor even Dr. Alexander Windom, could undo what had been done or bring back the dead.

The business of life was living.

And raising a rice crop.

The work of preparing the crop had been begun on the first day after the riot. Seed had been brought in from neighboring valleys and sown in hundreds of small beds in the outskirts of the village; and now, out along the river, acres were being cleared, ditches dug, embankments raised, fields plowed into paddies. In a few weeks the shoots would be ready for transplanting and flooding, and at the same time, by happy coincidence, the heavy rains were due to begin. Already there had been occasional light falls, and day by day the monsoon clouds were piling up more heavily on the horizon to the south.

Sitting in the hospital office, where Windom had summoned him, Jan Vidal could scarcely suppress his excitement.

"Even this first season," he said, "we shall have a crop big enough for the whole village. And for the whole year it will cost us less than buying rice from outside for three months."

"You've done a good job," Windom told him.

"To work is easy, my doctor, when the heart is in it. Already the biggest part is over, and soon we can turn to other things."

"Such as the plantation."

"The plantation?"

"That's why I asked you to come here, Jan. To talk about it."

"What is there to talk about? The plantation is dead. Finished."

Windom shook his head. "No," he said. "It must be kept going. It must be cared for. I want you to get the men together and explain that. They are to go back and tend the trees. They are to rebuild the houses they burned down."

Jan stared at him without speaking.

"They must," said Windom.

"No, they will not do it. They will refuse."

"They won't refuse when you explain to them why they must do it."

"Why? There is no reason why. For years we have been like slaves to this plantation, and now at last we are free of it. Do you expect us to go back and be slaves again?"

"I expect you to think like an intelligent man, Jan. Not like a child." An edge of annoyance showed in Windom's voice. "You people have showed your strength. Maybe not in the way you should have; but you've done it. You're going to have your rice crop—which is what you wanted. But you know perfectly well this valley can't live on rice alone. There has to be employment. There have to be wages. And the only place they can come from is the plantation."

Jan listened sullenly.

"If you let the rubber trees go to ruin, you'll be playing right into the hands of the people you're fighting. They'll call you saboteurs—they'll call you bandits—and they'll be right. And more than that, you'll be fools. You're as dependent on the plantation as it is on you, and if it's decently run it can make Papaan a happy prosperous place. All right, that's your job now. To see that it's decently run. To care for it; not to ruin it."

"We are not going to go back to the old days," said Jan. "We have fought for our rights and won them. And we are going to keep them."

"If you're reasonable, I think you'll have a good chance to. But not if you're fools. You don't think Schusterman or the plantation owners—or the government itself—are going to let things stand the way they are? They'll be back here soon, and you know it. And they'll take over the plantation again."

"Not if we—"

"Don't talk nonsense. If you *what?* Fight? Get yourselves all killed or jailed? In the eyes of the law you've committed serious offenses, and no government in the world would let you get away with them." Windom paused, leaned forward a little and spoke with quiet earnestness. "Look, Jan—the government people will be coming here. They'll come in force, take the plantation, hold an investigation. So far they know only one side of the story, but now they'll hear the rest.

You'll tell them. I'll tell them. And I think they'll believe us and be reasonable. I think they'll let you have your rice crop."

"But—"

"But only if you are reasonable too," said Windom. "Only if you meet them halfway. And the first thing in doing that is to get back to work at the plantation. To take care of the trees. To rebuild what you've destroyed."

There was a silence.

"Well?" asked Windom.

"You have always been our friend, my doctor," said Jan.

Windom said nothing.

"When we have been sick you have healed us. When we have been in trouble you have helped us."

Windom still said nothing.

"You are a white man, but you have not come among us as the other white men. You have come not to take but to give. When you have spoken it is always to say the thing that is best for us."

After another moment Jan got to his feet.

"I shall call the men together," he said.

"Good," said Windom.

The clouds marched up from the horizon, and raindrops spattered in the dusty streets. Then the drops turned into streams and the dust into mud. All one night the rain fell, and the next day the entire village, except the very old and the very young, went out to the rice paddies. By evening, half the rice crop had been transplanted. By the next evening, all of it.

"Tomorrow you can get back to the plantation," said Windom to Jan Vidal.

"No—the day after tomorrow, my doctor," he answered. "Tomorrow is for celebration."

Flags and streamers had appeared magically along the village streets. Crowds thronged the bazaar. A juggler, a snake-charmer and a dozen drink-vendors materialized from nowhere, and a band, composed of a flute, a saxophone, a drum and a set of temple gongs, paraded endlessly around the central square. The mayor, Dai Lollivar, made a long speech, and Jan Vidal a short one.

"In our new freedom," he said, "let us remember the great man who has made it possible. Let us remember Father Amyan."

For a few minutes, then, the crowd was silent. But soon the band was dinning again, the children racing about, the hawkers shouting their wares. Today was carnival day, and nothing was going to stop it for long. Old Amyan was in the earth. But so was the rice crop.

In the afternoon Windom and Lenore drove out to a pasture near the riverbank, where half the village seemed to be gathered.

"Good Lord," she said, "it looks like a baseball field."

"It is," he told her.

There were whitewash lines, a rickety backstop, and two teams called (as near as an outlander could make out) the Gaspos and the Sokeraties. There was a variety of ancient balls, bats and gloves, stamped with the fading legend, *Quartermaster Corps, U.S. Army*. And presently there was an umpire named Windom. Two hours, and an indeterminate number of innings, later the game ended, with both sides claiming victory and a crowd surging about the center of the diamond.

"We won!" shouted the Gaspos.

"No, we won!" howled the Sokeraties.

"Quiet! Quiet!" commanded Jan Vidal, louder than all the rest. "There is only one among us who may say who has won, and that is our honored umpire."

The shouts died away. A great circle of eyes fastened on Windom.

"The Gaspos won the batting," he announced. "The Sokeraties won the fielding."

And the crowd dispersed happily.

But when dark came they were all back again in the central square. The dim street lights had been augmented by hundreds of torches and flares. The band was playing. In the center of the square a low platform had been erected, and when Windom and Lenore arrived, they were led forward and ceremoniously seated on a bench that had been placed before it. Besides them were Lollivar, Jan Vidal and the more important elders of Papaan. Around and behind them stood the rest of the villagers, packed close together in solid ranks, their faces bright and expectant in the flickering light of the torches.

Watching them, Lenore, too, felt an expectancy that was almost excitement. Here at last was something of what she had expected the East to be. Not dust and rain, hospital and patients, rubber crop and rice crop; but an intimation of another world, dark and teeming, ancient and secret. A heavy scent filled the air: of a thousand bodies, of the burning torches, of incense. Overhead, the moon and stars were brilliant, but to the south the monsoon clouds piled high against their silver light.

Suddenly the band stopped playing. The crowd fell silent. Then a single voice split the stillness with a high ululating note. . . . A command? A lament? An incantation? . . . Then there was music again, but this time not as before. Now there were only the drum and the gongs, beating in soft monotonous rhythm. A hushed wave of anticipation passed through the crowd. And the dancers appeared.

They came up from the shadows beyond the platform in slow measured procession, their tall headdresses swaying, their bright costumes gleaming as if they themselves were moving torches. They danced only with their arms and legs, in patterns that were at once rigid and fluid, angular and soft. Their bodies were held stiff and straight as trees, and their faces were like immobile lacquered masks. Some were men and some were women, and first the men held the center of the platform, thumping their bare feet to the measure of drum and gong, swinging their arms as if they held great invisible swords. Then they withdrew to the rear, and the women moved forward. The rhythm grew softer and more gentle. Hands danced. Shoulders and thighs danced. Motionless, the brown slender bodies danced, under the tight shining sheaths that covered them.

Lenore watched in fascination. Without understanding the details, she knew that the pattern evolving before her was a thing of a hundred meanings and suggestions: intricate, stylized, incredibly ancient. It told of war and feats of war, of life ending and life beginning, of planting and harvest, of the fertility of earth and of man. It told of hope and fear, of lament and thanksgiving. It told of a world, strange and dark, soft and sunlit, that had existed long before the first invader had come and would endure long after the last had gone. *As it was in the beginning,* Lenore thought . . . *is now, and ever shall be* . . .

The women, in turn, withdrew. The men moved forward again. Then for the first time men and women danced together, but at opposite sides of the platform, in long swaying files. The beat of bare feet grew swifter. The beat of drum and gong grew louder. And then suddenly stopped. The two files froze into converging lines, with their apex at the far end of the platform, and from that apex a single figure emerged.

It was a woman, Lenore saw. But whether she was one of those who had already been dancing, or a new performer, she could not tell. As quickly as it had arisen, the sound of drum and gong subsided, until they were only a deep half-heard rhythm. The dancer's feet made no sound. They moved in the slow intricate patterns of old ritual. In the gleam of the torches her body swayed, sinuous and proud.

In her hands, raised before her, she held a small box of jade and ivory. She is not a dancer, Lenore thought, but a priestess. Now the battles have been fought, the victories won, the earth sown with seed; and the priestess comes to the altar carrying the offering of thanks.

She is beautiful, she thought. . . .

The moving figure was closer now. The torchlight shone on her silver vestments and the tall cone of her headdress. It touched the rose softness of her bare arms and throat, the rich black of her hair, the mask of her face. . . . Then, in the next instant, the mask seemed to dissolve. The figure was no longer silver, but white. The headdress was white. . . . The dance seemed to have stopped. The figure stood motionless before her. Or, rather, *almost* before her. Before Windom. And now Anna Vidal bent low and held out to him the offering of the jade and ivory box.

"With our gratitude, my doctor," she murmured.

And her eyes were shining.

TWELVE

THE RAIN BEAT DOWN. EACH DAY, TOWARD NOON, THE CLOUDS parted and the sun beat down, but the tender rice shoots were deep and safe under the brown water in the paddies. Up on the higher ground, men with knives and pails moved again on their long rounds through the rubber groves. And in the center of the groves more men were at work: clearing the charred ruins, hauling timber, measuring, sawing, hammering.

"Before, we work too hard for too little," they grumbled. "Now we work even harder, and for nothing at all."

"No, it is not for nothing," Jan Vidal told them. "It is for the future, when the owners return. So that things will be better."

Any time now they expected a platoon of police to appear. Or a plane-load of officials. Neither came, however; and, with the telegraph wires still down, no news came either. Some three weeks after the "trouble" the rumor spread that a detachment of troops had moved up from the capital into the lower part of the province. But it was obvious, all agreed, that this could have nothing to do with Papaan.

"They are going to the northwest," the men said, "for the fighting against Than-kar. Perhaps that is why no one has come here. They are all too busy with Than-kar and his Reds."

Then a plane came.

It flew in from the south, quick and silver in the noonday brightness; and first it flew in a circle over the village, but did not land. Then it banked out toward the plantation. The men working on the new buildings saw it coming in low over the treetops, and before they even heard the sound of the machine guns the bullets were thudding among them. Five men fell. And before their companions could reach their side the plane was a speck in the distance.

Lansang, the sub-foreman, looked at Jan Vidal with hard flat eyes. "Yes, of course," he said. "When the owners return, then things will be better."

One man had been killed instantly. A second died a few hours later on the operating table. Again Windom spent the night with probe and scalpel, swab and syringe. Toward morning he snatched two hours' sleep in the bungalow, and at seven he was back at the hospital.

"Where's Jan?" he asked Anna.

But she didn't know.

And he didn't appear.

Within an hour, however, Dai Lollivar was there, sitting breathless and distraught in the cubicle of Windom's office.

"They are coming, my doctor," he said.

Windom nodded. "I'm afraid so."

"What shall we do? Mother of God and the Living Buddha—what shall we do?" But the mayor did not wait for an answer. "I shall tell you," he said. "All this night I have been thinking about it—without sleep, without rest—and there is only one thing to do. . . . Look. Listen . . ." He leaned forward, his plump hands spread on the desk. "The troops come—yes? They think we are bandits; in revolt, lawless. So we show them we are not lawless. We have no police, no; but we have a law and a jail. And in the jail, when they come, will be the leaders of the trouble. Jan Vidal, Lansang, Petar, a few others. That will be enough. They will see the trouble is over and the law is being enforced."

"Enforced?" asked Windom. "By whom?"

"By me. The mayor."

"I see. And just how do you propose to get these men into jail?"

"That is why I have come to you, my doctor. For me, I know they will not go. But for you, yes—they will. You will speak to Jan Vidal and tell him he and his friends must go to jail. That way they will help the whole village; perhaps save us all. The troops come. They look. They see that all is quiet and the mayor is in charge. They go away." Lollivar's eyes fixed on Windom in hopeful appeal. "You will do it, yes?" he asked. "You will call Jan here and explain to him, and when he has agreed I will make the arrest. . . ."

Whatever Windom's answer might have been, it was forestalled by a peculiar noise from outside. And a moment later the boy Kosti backed past the open doorway, firing an invisible gun at invisible foes.

Windom called him in. "What's going on, Kosti?" he asked.

"Everything is going on, my doctor!" The boy's eyes were bright with excitement. "The enemy is coming. We fight them. Bang, bang—so. It is a great battle, a great victory. Like—like—" He paused, searching for a worthy simile. "Like in Hopalongo Kassidi—"

Windom smiled. Then he stopped smiling. Clutched in the boy's hand, he saw, were a dozen or more rifle cartridges.

"Where did you get those?" he asked sharply.

"At the warehouse, my doctor."

"What were you doing there?"

"The same as everyone was doing. Getting guns—bullets. I would have got a gun myself, only—"

Windom was on his feet. "What do you mean, everyone?" he interrupted. "Who? How many?"

"Jan, Lansang, Petar, almost all the men."

"And they were taking the guns?"

"Yes."

"Are they still there?"

"No, now they have gone."

"Where?"

"To the jail."

"The jail?" Windom repeated.

"Yes, my doctor. They say that is the strongest place in the village. They will hide there behind the gates and walls and when the enemy comes they go bang, bang, bang."

Lollivar had risen too. "Mother of God!" he moaned.

Then Anna hurried in.

"Have you heard, my doctor—" she began.

"We're hearing now," said Windom.

"You must go to Jan."

"Yes."

"Now. At once. In the jeep we can be there in five minutes."

"You'd better stay—"

"No—please, my doctor. The patients are all right. The student nurses are with them." Anna's voice was low and pleading. "I too am worried for Jan. And perhaps I can help."

For an instant Windom hesitated. Then he nodded. "Well, they're where you want them," he said to Lollivar as he crossed to the door.

It took them only three minutes to the jail.

As on the last occasion he had been there, the yard was

crowded, but this time not with mourners. Men were moving about in all directions, carrying rifles, crates and bales. On the steps a group was knotted together in some sort of wrangle, and inside were even more people—fetching, carrying, arguing, shouting. Ordinarily Windom could not move a block through the village without being stopped and greeted by half its inhabitants, but now no one so much as noticed him.

Followed by Anna, he made his way to the small office where, three weeks before, he had found Jan sitting with the bodies of Amyan and Bilko. Jan was there again, but this time not in silence and grief. Men were running in and out, asking questions, taking orders. Two were receiving guns and crates from the others and stacking them against the wall. In a corner, Mamarta Vidal squatted like a brown gnome, sorting out foodstuffs and ammunition which she was taking from a pile of sacks.

"Mother, go home," Anna told her sharply. "This is no place for you."

"The place for me," said the old woman, "is where there is trouble for my family." She looked at Windom. "Excuse me that I do not rise, my doctor," she apologized. "But my skirts are full of yams and bullets."

"Mother, please—" Anna said.

But Mamarta ignored her and went on sorting.

Windom stood looking at Jan Vidal, and Jan looked back at him. The flow of men in and out suddenly stopped, and the two who had been stacking crates and rifles moved quietly to the door.

"Commander Vidal's headquarters, I presume?" said Windom.

"This is headquarters, yes," Jan answered.

"Headquarters for what?"

"For the defense of Papaan."

Windom's gray eyes were steady on his face. "Have you lost your mind, Jan?" he asked quietly.

Jan said nothing.

"You expect to defend the village against a battalion of troops?"

"Not the village—no. We cannot defend that. But here in the jail, yes. We can hold out for days."

"Call it weeks. And what then?" Jan didn't answer. "And what about the rest of the village *while* you're holding out. The women, the children, the old ones. What's going to happen to them?"

Again no answer. Windom put a hand on Jan's arm. "You can't do it," he said, "and you know it. Get your men together and call off this crazy thing."

Jan looked at him sullenly. "What do you expect us to do? Have a celebration because troops are coming? Meet them with cakes and wine?"

"The first thing I expect is for you to show a glimmer of reason."

"Reason?" Jan's sullenness swelled into anger. "I seem to remember your talking about reason before, my doctor. We must be reasonable and rebuild the plantation—yes? We must be reasonable and wait quietly to be machine-gunned. Now I suppose we are to be reasonable while they stand us all up against a wall?"

"They aren't going to—"

"No, of course—they aren't going to. You know just what they will do, and you tell us what we should do. Just as you told us before, and we did what you said, and look what has happened—"

"Jan—you can't talk like that to the doctor!"

Anna took a step forward, but her brother turned on her savagely. "How do you want me to talk?" he demanded. "What I say is true. He tells us that if we do this and that, then everything will be all right. They will meet us halfway. So we do it, and what happens? They meet us with bullets."

"That is only because they think—"

"—that we are bandits. Enemies." Jan looked at them defiantly. All right. If that is what they make us, that is what we are. All our lives we have been—what? Coolies, slaves, pack animals. Now we are something else, and perhaps it will be better."

"Yes, better," Mamarta Vidal put in from her corner. She cackled happily. "We will show them whose slaves we are—hey, my son? Just like we did the Japs."

"These aren't Japs that are coming," said Windom. "They are your own people."

"No," Jan said. "They are not our people. Once, perhaps, they were. But no more. They are the owners' people, the rulers' people, the white men's people. They have sold themselves to the white men. For money. For power. And they are no longer our people, but our enemies."

Anna's eyes blazed. "How dare you speak so! Is not the doctor a white man? And who has ever been better to us, or helped us more? You are my brother, but I am ashamed of you. And you should be ashamed of yourself. You will tell him that you are sorry, do you hear me? You will tell him now, you fool!"

Overwrought though he was, Jan recoiled before her anger. "I did not mean it against the doctor," he said. "He has been good to us, yes. He has helped us. But he is still a white man, and there are some things in which he cannot help us. Which he cannot even understand." He turned back to Windom. "We are not bandits, you know that. We are honest men; humble men. But even a humble man—even a mule or a bullock—can be driven only so far. They have killed Father Amyan. They have killed our brothers and friends. Now they are coming to kill the rest of us, but they will not find it so easy. For we are going to fight them. Not only for our rice crop. Not only for our lives. But for our freedom, our self-respect . . ."

There was no longer anger in his voice, but something deeper and quieter than anger. His dark eyes, fixed on Windom, held not only challenge but pleading. "Yes, you have helped us, my doctor," he said. "You have healed our bodies when we have been sick. But now it is more than bodies and sickness; it is men and the lives of men. And with our lives we must do what we have to do."

There was a pause. Jan's eyes went to the men who were watching at the door, and he beckoned them in.

"No, Jan," said Windom.

Jan turned and looked at him.

"You can't go on with this. You mustn't."

"You still think it is wrong?"

"Not what you say. But what you want to do."

"All right, you think it is wrong."

"Not only wrong, but stupid."

A half-dozen of the men had come into the room. They stood in a silent group, waiting.

"You cannot stop us," said Jan.

"No," Windom answered. "I can't stop you. But there's one thing I can and will do."

"Yes?"

"I will leave Papaan."

There was another silence, longer than before. Then Mamarta Vidal got quickly to her feet, yams and bullets spilling around her onto the floor. "No, no, my doctor," she croaked.

Anna said nothing; but her body went rigid and her lips white.

"If you go on with this," said Windom quietly, "I will go

back to the hospital now. I will pack my things and get into the jeep and drive away this morning."

Jan stared at him. "Leaving the wounded?"

"Leaving the wounded."

"Leaving us all?"

"Leaving you all."

Mamarta seized one of his hands. "No, no," she wailed. "You cannot! You will not!"

"My doctor—" Anna murmured. But no more words came.

Jan started to speak, stopped, looked at the group of men. The men looked at one another, their eyes puzzled and troubled.

"What would you have us do, my doctor?" asked one. "Wait here to be killed?"

"To be made prisoners?" said another.

"To be slaves again?"

Windom shook his head.

"What then?" Jan demanded.

"My suggestion—if you've got around to listening to it—is that you leave the village."

"Leave it? For where?"

"For the hills. The forest." All the men seemed about to speak at once, but Windom went on. "I don't mean everyone," he said. "Only the plantation men; the ones involved in the trouble. And I don't mean for long. A few days, perhaps, at most, a few weeks."

"And then?"

"Then the troops will come. With them, the officials, the authorities. And I shall speak with them."

"What do you mean, speak with them?"

"I shall tell them what has happened here. Not the rumors and lies they have heard, but the truth. I shall tell them about the rice crop and the strike; about Amyan and Bilko;

about what you were driven to and what you have done. And I think they will listen to me and believe me."

Again the men exchanged glances.

Jan shook his head. "We cannot do it. We must stay here and—"

"Stay here and what? Shoot down a dozen soldiers before you're shot down yourself? Watch your wives and children being shot—your homes being burned?"

"It is running away. We cannot go."

Windom shrugged. "All right. Then I'll go."

He turned toward the door, but two figures quickly blocked his way. One was Mamarta, clutching again at his hand. And the other, beside her, was Anna.

"Please, my doctor—please," she murmured. Then once again she turned on her brother. "He is right," she said, her voice taut and strained. "He is right and you know it, and it is only because you are a stubborn fool that you will not admit it."

"For you, we all know," said Jan, "the doctor is *always* right."

"Yes, he is always right. He is wise. He is good. And if you knew him as I do—"

"—I would worship him like a god, hey? I would burn incense for him because I cannot go to bed with him."

There was a sharp sound, as a hand slapped his face. But it was not Anna's hand. It was Mamarta's. "Hold your mouth, lout!" She glared up at him. "You will not speak so to your sister."

A nervous snicker ran through the watching men. Anna turned abruptly away. Windom looked at Jan for a long moment before speaking.

"Sometimes I think your sister is right," he said quietly. "That you are a fool."

"I—I am sorry, my doctor—"

"Never mind being sorry. Never mind me—or what you think of me. You've got something more important to think about, and that's your village and your people. You want to be their leader. All right, lead them. But don't destroy them. You're a man now, not a boy, and being a little tin hero isn't enough."

"You cannot say to me that I am—"

"All I say to you, Jan, is stop and think. If you want to go ahead with this craziness, I can't prevent you. All I can do, and what I will do, is leave. But I beg you—with all my heart I beg you—don't do it. Don't throw away the little you've won. Don't sacrifice everything you care for to your own stupid pride."

He paused and put a hand lightly on Jan's shoulder. "Think it over," he said.

Then he turned and left the room.

Rumor traveled fast in Papaan. When, a half-hour later, he came up onto the porch of his bungalow, Lenore was waiting for him, tense and anxious.

"Will we be leaving, Alec?" she asked.

"No," he told her. "No, we won't be leaving."

THIRTEEN

"Of the plantation men," said Jan Vidal, "sixty-eight will go. That is all of us, except six who are still sick or weak and nine who have refused."

"What are they going to do?" asked Windom.

"Stay here. But it does not matter. They are the no-goods." Jan consulted a slip of paper. "Also," he added, "there are twenty-two not from the plantation who wish to come. There are thirty women and children. Which makes a total of one hundred and twenty."

"Why the women and children?"

"Some of the men will not go without their families. And some of the women will not stay without their men."

"Won't they make it more difficult?"

"A little, perhaps. But it is better that way than the other."

Jan was quiet, unemotional, businesslike. According to Anna, he and his lieutenants had conferred for about an hour after Windom left the jail. Then they had called all the men together in the jail-yard. And now he had come to the hospital.

"You have enough food?" Windom asked him.

"Yes. Each man will bring staples for three weeks, and our

meat we will get by hunting." He paused and looked up. "For this we will need the guns, my doctor."

"That's all right," said Windom. "When will you be ready to go?"

"Tomorrow morning."

"Good."

"We will go up to the head of the valley," Jan continued, "and then follow the trail toward the northwest."

"To Blue Mountain?"

"Yes, to Blue Mountain and then beyond. It is wild country there, well hidden, good for game; yet high enough so it is not true jungle."

"How will we find you?"

"We have talked of that too, and it should not be difficult. Near the ridge of Blue Mountain there is an open space which gives a long view of the trail below. We will leave a few men there as outpost, and when you send for us they will lead the messengers on to our camp." Jan paused and regarded Windom steadily. "*—If* they are your messengers, my doctor," he added. "If they are not—if they are the others—we will do other things."

"They'll be my messengers," Windom assured him. "Or, better yet, I'll come myself."

"You are certain you can do this thing?"

"Let's say confident, Jan."

"We will keep our rice paddies?"

"Yes."

"The crop will be ours?"

"Yes."

"And there will be no reprisals for what has happened?"

"No."

Doubt and hope struggled in Jan's face. "If you can do this—" he said haltingly. "If you can do this, my doctor, it will be—"

"—At least better than being dead or in prison," supplied Windom. He smiled a little, stood up and extended his hand. "Good luck to us, Jan."

Jan took it and held it tightly. "Thank you, my doctor. And I—I am sorry that I—"

"Forget it," said Windom.

The village seethed with preparations and excitement. Crowds filled the streets, the bazaars, the warehouse, and spilled over into the compound and hallways of the hospital.

"How I wish I could go with the men," lamented Lollivar. "It is my place, really—at their head—leading them, counseling them." He dabbed at his face with his handkerchief. "But this is my place even more," he pointed out. "Where the danger is even greater. Where firm hands are needed for control and wise judgment for negotiation . . ."

"Please, my doctor—please let me go," begged Kosti. "I am big enough. I am strong. I can carry a load and a gun the same as a man."

Windom shook his head gently.

"Other boys are going."

"Only those whose—" Windom cut himself short. Only those whose parents were going, he had been about to say. And Kosti's father and mother had been killed by the Japs.

"Only those who are not important here," he said.

"Yes, of course I am going," declared Mamarta Vidal to Windom and Anna. "And neither you nor that son of mine is going to stop me."

"But Mamarta—" said Windom.

"But mother—" said Anna.

"But nothing," said the old woman. "I am not staying here to welcome any army of Bilkos. And besides—if I stay here—who will cook Jan's food and keep his clothes mended?"

"And you, Anna," said Windom. "If you'd feel better—happier—"

"I will stay here, my doctor," she answered.

"I could manage—"

She shook her head. "My place is here."

In the thin gray rain of the next morning she stood beside him at the hospital gate, as the procession moved out toward the valley road. There were men with guns and men with sacks and bales; men waving and shouting and men plodding glumly with their eyes on the ground. There were a half-dozen boys racing ahead excitedly, and Kosti watching them from the bungalow steps. There was a bullock cart piled high with foodstuffs and supplies, and on the top of the pile, Mamarta Vidal, with a great curved sword lying across her knees.

Windom waved. Anna waved. Lollivar, appearing breathlessly from down the street, waved too and called out: "When you return, my brave people, it will be as heroes in triumph. . . ."

Mamarta Vidal spat out a gob of betel juice. One of the bullocks passed wind. Then Jan was standing beside Windom.

"We are leaving our village to you, my doctor," he said.

Windom nodded.

"Our fields, our homes, our families, our future." Jan paused, his eyes dark and steady on Windom's face. "You know this, do you not?" he added quietly. "We would leave them to no one in the world except to you."

Then he was gone: a part of the procession; one figure

among a hundred figures moving off along the street in the rain.

All day the rain fell. And most of the next. On the third day it stopped, and there were intervals when the sun appeared, but it was only a pale remote gleaming beyond veils of mist. No breath of wind stirred. The valley lay sodden and torpid under a pall of heat.

The village waited. . . . In the streets and the bazaar life moved in a sluggish half-current, flowing through a dubious no-man's-land between yesterday and tomorrow, between anticipation and fear. The women still gathered with their washing at the riverbank. The men tended the rice paddies. Carts jolted along the muddy roads. But no one went along the road as far as the higher ground of the plantation. The rubber groves were as deserted as the wild forest beyond them, and the half-finished buildings at their center stood ghostly under the mist and rain.

Out of the rain, on the fourth morning, came the drone of an engine, and presently a plane appeared out of a rift in the clouds. But it merely circled low over the empty plantation and then vanished into the south.

And no troops appeared.

"They are held up by the rains," the villagers said.

"They will not come for weeks."

"Or not at all."

"They are going to the north to fight Than-kar."

"And our men can return to us."

Of those who had gone there had been one early report: the announcement by an up-valley farmer who came down to the market that they had camped for a night in his fields and moved on the next morning up the trail toward Blue Mountain. But since then there had been no word at all.

"You will send me after them, yes—please?" begged Kosti.

"I will follow them and find them and bring back messages." And when Windom turned down the suggestion: "Then you will send me to the south, and I will look for the troops. I will be a spy—a patrol."

Some, like Kosti, waited impatiently. Some waited lethargically. A few, such as Lollivar, waited purposefully. Over the entrance of his office was a large sign that read: WELCOME TO OUR VISITORS FROM THE MUNICIPALITY OF PAPAAN. And outside his shop in the bazaar: RARE GIFTS FROM THE NORTHERN PROVINCES TO TAKE HOME TO YOUR LOVED ONES.

In the hospital the air hung heavy and stagnant in the corridors and wards. The patients lay strengthless on their damp cots. At the operating table, while he performed a colostomy on one of the men who had been machine-gunned, Windom had to call in an extra student nurse to stand beside him and wipe the sweat from his eyes.

"Now that you've finished with the wounded," Lenore pleaded with him, "you should rest a little."

"Yes, I may, for a few days," agreed Windom.

But the next afternoon word arrived that several cases of cholera had broken out in a village down the coast. And that night he told her he would have to go.

"Go? Now?" Lenore asked.

"In the morning."

"For the day, you mean?"

"I'm afraid it will be longer than that. Cholera is bad business."

"Longer?" she looked at him miserably. "Oh no, Alec! Not now. Just when you're out from under for the first time and we could be together a little." She paused, close to tears. "It's unfair. It's like—"

Windom smiled thinly. "Like being married to a doctor," he said.

"You *have* to go, Alec?"

"You know I do."

"Let me come too, then."

He shook his head. "No, Lee."

"Please."

"Not with cholera. It's impossible."

"Is Anna going?"

Something in her voice made him look at her a moment before he answered. "No," he said, "Anna's not going either. One of us has to stay at the hospital."

"Couldn't you stay and she go?" A begging, almost desperate note was creeping into her words. Then, abruptly, she checked herself. "I'm sorry, Alec," she murmured. "I didn't mean it. If you have to go, you have to: I know that. It's only—only that I was hoping so—that maybe we could—"

Her voice trailed away, and Windom put his arms around her. "When I come back," he said.

"Yes, when you come back. Only by then probably the troops—" She clutched at another thought. "Mayn't they come while you're gone?" she asked. "Wouldn't that be very bad—if they came while you're gone?"

"I've thought of that," he said. "But I can't let a whole village be wiped out by cholera while I sit around waiting. Besides, it's not far. If they come, Lollivar will send word in one of the plantation trucks, and I can be back in two hours."

He kissed her lightly and made as if to turn away, but she did not let him go. "Hold me close," she said. "Please. Just another moment—"

He held her, and she bent her head against his shoulder. "I'm afraid, Alec," she murmured.

"There's nothing to be afraid of. Even if things go badly, the troops won't touch the hospital."

"I don't mean the troops. I mean of—" She looked up into

his face. "Oh Alec, it's been so terrible. All this killing. All this hate and fear."

"Yes, it's been bad," he said. "But it's over now."

"Is it? Are you sure? Not just for the village, but for you too?" Her eyes were searching his. "You're so deep in it all, Alec; so much a part of it. As a doctor—yes, of course. But more than that. As a man. With your whole life. And sometimes—now, these last days—I have the feeling that I'm no part of you at all."

Windom's hand moved gently over her hair, her cheek. "No, Lee," he said. "You're wrong."

"You do love me? You do want me here?"

"What do you think?"

"I don't know what to think."

He smiled down at her. "Do you know what you sound like?" he asked. "A wife."

"That's what I am, Alec. That's what I want to be. A real wife. Not something apart from you—outside of you—just living here like some sort of stranger. You see what I mean, don't you, darling? I want really to *be* with you, share with you, help you. As if I were one of the people here; one of the nurses. As if I were—"

She didn't say it. Almost she did, but not quite. And suddenly Windom's lips were on hers, he was holding her tight, he was looking down at her again and smiling, and he said, "—as if you were my Lee, whom I love."

They stood together: not speaking, not moving.

Then she murmured: "I'm sorry, Alec."

"Sorry?"

"That I—that I—"

"That you nothing," he said.

They were silent again.

"All right?" he asked.

At last she smiled back at him. "Yes, all right."

But later that night she still knew that it wasn't, and she lay sleepless on her cot with her loneliness and her fear. After a while she got up and stood at the screened window, looking out. The rain had stopped a few hours before; the clouds had parted; the moon was bright. And though she could see no farther than the banyan trees across the compound, she knew that it was even brighter out in the darkness beyond—over the still shore and the bay and the headland and the silver beach. . . . Going back to the cots, she stood beside her husband's and looked down at him through the thin gauze of the mosquito netting. She was about to touch his shoulder, to whisper his name; but then, bending closer, she saw the deep lines of tiredness in his sleeping face; and she did neither. Instead, after a few moments, she went back and lay down on her own cot.

And in the morning, after breakfast, he drove off in the jeep.

The clouds returned. The rain beat down on the mud of the compound and the leaves of the banyan trees. It drummed, hour after hour, on the shingle of the bungalow's roof and seeped through ceilings and walls into puddles on the teakwood floors.

Kosti plodded boredly through the house with mop and pail, searching en route for the lairs of ants and roaches. He seldom found any, but as soon as he was off somewhere armies of them seemed to creep out from every corner and cranny. Waking toward late afternoon from a sweat-soaked doze, Lenore found a scorpion crawling leisurely across the foot of her cot. And when, soon after, she went into the bathroom two bats flew out, their flailing wings just missing her face. "Kosti, Kosti!" she called. But when the boy appeared there was no sign of them.

There was no sun. Only rain; only heat. The thermometer on the porch went from ninety to ninety-two and from ninety-two to ninety-five, and then Lenore covered it with a rag so that she wouldn't have to look at it. Toward evening the rain pounded down harder than ever, and, passing through the living room, she found a new puddle—this time not on the floor but on the couch. When a while later, she pressed the light-switch, nothing happened; in the kitchen, the refrigerator was as hot as the stove. For dinner she had one egg and three glasses of warm lime juice, and then, lighting a kerosene lamp, she read Manson on leeches and hill diarrhea. That should put me to sleep, she thought. But it didn't. After lying on her cot for an hour she got up and took a nembutal.

When she awoke in the morning, her mind felt drugged, her body soaked with moisture. It was like being drowned, she thought, and lying at the bottom of the sea. Except that at the bottom of the sea it wouldn't be raining. She lay still, with eyes closed, trying to suck air into her body and mind. But there seemed to be no air. And when at last she rose and went into the bathroom, the mirror was as fogged as if someone had been taking a hot bath.

During breakfast Lahana the cook burned her hand on the stove and went across to the hospital. Kosti made a lethargic round with mop and pail and disappeared into the rain. Left alone, Lenore puttered about the bedroom and closets, shaking and brushing the sodden linen and clothes; but soon she was drenched with sweat, her head spun, and she had to stop. Suddenly her body seemed to be burning with tiny pricks of fire, and, examining herself, she found a pink rash streaked across her flesh from throat to thighs.

Returning to the bathroom, she dabbed herself with lotion. Then, wiping the mirror, she looked at her reflection. Grimly, almost masochistically, she noted each feature in order: the puffed eyes, the shiny nose, the yellow strings of damp hair, the blotch on her cheeks where something must have bitten her while she slept. What you need, my girl, she told herself, is five fingers of brandy and a week at Elizabeth Arden's.

For a half-hour she busied herself with more lotions, powders, creams, applicators; for another with file and clipper on her stained and roughened nails. Then she looked for her nail polish, but couldn't find it, and wandering into the kitchen, found instead a can of paint that Kosti had been using around the house. "Why not?" she said aloud and daubed her nails bright green. Tomorrow she would put an ad in the *Papaan Gazette: Situation wanted: one green-nailed temple dancer.*

She began to laugh; then heard her laughter and stopped. Back in the bathroom she scraped the paint away with file and pumice.

How childish can you get? she thought angrily.

The rain had slackened to a drizzle. Putting on a dress and raincape, she crossed the compound to the hospital. Anna Vidal was not in evidence, but one of the student nurses was in Windom's office, sorting out a stack of filing cards, and when she saw Lenore she stared as if at an apparition.

"I came to see if I could be of any help," Lenore said.

"Thank you, my lady, but there is no need—"

"I'd like to, really. Anything."

"Thank you, my lady. But we have few patients now. There is nothing to be done."

As she turned to go she felt the girl's eyes following her curiously.

Leaving the hospital, she crossed toward the bungalow and then, on sudden impulse, changed her course and went through the gate and down the village street. It was good to be out of the compound, and she walked quickly, two blocks ahead, around a corner and then another block, and came presently to the bazaar. The drizzle continued, the mud was thick underfoot, and a hundred nameless stenches filled the air. But here, at least, there were people, life, movement, and for a few moments she was almost happy—until she was recognized and the stares began. They were neither rude nor hostile; merely curious, as the student nurse's stare had been curious; yet behind them, in the yellow-brown faces, in the dark opaque eyes, were thoughts unbridgeably alien and remote. She turned quickly into one of the shops; but the merchant behind the counter stared at her too, and almost instantly a little knot of passers-by was peering in through the doorway.

"May I see some of your materials?" she asked.

The merchant looked at her uncomprehendingly, and when at last he answered her she could not understand him either. She pointed to the bolts of cloth on the shelves, and he brought some down and she examined them. Meanwhile two women and a half-dozen children had appeared from the back of the shop and stood close beside her, watching. "Hello there," she said, smiling at the smallest of the children. But the button eyes looked back at her blankly.

The materials the shopkeeper was showing her were garish and sleazy. But I'll have to buy something, she thought.

She pointed. "I'll take some of this."

Then she realized that she had no money.

"Can charge, please? Me mem-doctor—hospital—yes?"

Even as she spoke she was annoyed at herself. If he can't understand English, she thought, what makes you think he can understand gibberish? . . . . But gibberish was all she could get out. . . . "No money, no. Charge please." She moved her hand as if writing out a bill. "Hospital—mem-doctor—you charge, send—yes?"

The man stared. The women and children stared. The

crowd in the doorway stared. And suddenly she turned and fled. She could feel the dark eyes following her out the door, around the corner, along the muddy streets.

Back in the bungalow she looked for a grammar or dictionary of the native language. He must have one, she thought. But there wasn't one. There was only *Manson's Tropical Diseases;* the *Journal of the American Medical Association,* for February, 1949, *Time,* for October 20, 1948. . . .

For fifteen minutes she read about *Thomas E. Dewey, Our Next President.*

Will he come back tonight? she thought. Will he come back tonight?

A while later there was a sound of commotion and shouting from the street beyond the compound, and she ran out to the porch in quick panic, sure that the government troops had arrived. But a moment later Kosti appeared with the announcement that it had been only a runaway bullock and an upset cart; and when she went back inside it was with a feeling almost of disappointment.

Rain again. Dusk again. Kerosene lamp. Egg and lime juice.

He's not coming, she thought. Not tonight. Not tomorrow. The troops aren't coming. Nobody is coming.

Then presently, through the rainbeat, she heard a knocking on the door, and, opening it, she found Anna Vidal.

"I hope you will forgive me, my lady," Anna said as she came onto the porch.

"Forgive you?"

"That I am so long in coming to see you. But with the doctor away, you see, I have been very busy in the hospital."

"Of course, I understand," said Lenore. She managed a smile. "What can I do for you?"

"No, you do not understand, my lady. It is I who have come to ask if there is anything I can do for you."

"Oh—thank you. But I don't think so."

"There is some help I could give, perhaps? Something I could bring?"

Lenore shook her head. Then she said. "But come in for a while, won't you?"

"Thank you, my lady. But I am sure you are busy."

"So busy that I need a little rest. Come in. Take off your cape."

Anna took off her raincape, put it on a chair and followed her shyly into the living room.

"Sit down," said Lenore. "No, there in the comfortable chair. What would you like to drink?"

"Truly, my lady, it is not necessary—"

"There's gin, rum, rice wine, a little whisky."

"No thank you, my lady. Rice wine I am fond of, but tonight, you see, I must go back on duty."

"Something plain, then."

"Well, a little lime juice, perhaps. That is, if you have—"

"Oh yes," said Lenore, "we have lime juice."

She went out into the kitchen, poured two glasses and, returning, handed one to Anna. Then she went to the sideboard and laced her own with an inch of gin. "Technical problem," she said. "Is this alone or not alone?"

"I beg your pardon, my lady?"

"Skip it." Lenore raised her glass and smiled. "Here's to the first weekly meeting of the Papaan Tuesday Evening Ladies' Club."

Anna looked uncertain. Then she smiled back, and her teeth flashed white in the yellow lamplight. She was wearing her uniform, and that of course was white too—spotless white and fresh and cool-looking, Lenore noted, against the golden brown of her face and throat. She was beautiful, she thought. As beautiful and fresh and cool as a spring flower.

Her own skin prickled with the heat. Sweat beaded her

lip and forehead. Three times that day she had pulled her hair tightly up onto the top of her head, but now several strands were awry again, falling damply across her cheeks.

"You must teach me, Anna," she said.

"Teach you, my lady?"

"How to look like that."

"Look like—?" Then she understood and lowered her eyes. "Perhaps it is only that I am used to the climate," she murmured. "Soon you will be used to it too."

"Maybe I will. But my skin and hair won't." Lenore sipped her drink and smiled again. "We couldn't arrange that, could we? To exchange skin and hair for a few months."

"Oh, my lady, you are joking—"

"And hands," said Lenore. "You have lovely hands, you know. I was watching them the other night, when you were dancing. And before that, in the hospital, when you were handling bandages and splints and syringes." She sat down and placed one of hers beside Anna's. "Look, it's hardly half the size of mine. . . . And it can do twice as much."

She removed her hand, picked up her glass and looked into it for a moment without speaking. Then she said, "I was going to be a nurse once, Anna. Many years ago, when I first met Dr. Windom. He never even knew it, but I had it all planned out. I was going to go to school and a hospital and get my R.N., and then I was going to spend my life working with him and helping him. . . . But it didn't quite work out that way, you see. I married him instead. . . . And do you know something I've learned, Anna? It's not easy to marry a man and help him at the same time."

She raised her glass again and drank, and the drink was warm, but the warmth was good.

"It's you who are helping him now, Anna," she said.

"Oh my lady—"

"Yes, he needs you."

"In little things, perhaps. But in the important ones it is the other way. It is we who need him."

"We?"

"All of us. Those who are sick and wounded. Those who want help or comfort."

"And those who work with him?"

"Yes, those who work with him, too."

"They love him, don't they?"

"Yes."

"And you, Anna: *you love him.*"

The girl started to speak—stopped—looked at Lenore for a moment as if she had not understood. Then she got to her feet. "My lady—please," she murmured. "What are you saying?"

"Nothing bad," said Lenore gently. "Nothing angry."

"Surely you cannot—you do not think—"

"I think that you're a very lovely girl, Anna. A very sweet and good girl." Lenore put a hand on her arm. "Come, sit down again. Here. Don't be afraid of me."

"Please, my lady. I must go now—please—to the hospital—"

"The hospital can wait a few minutes."

Anna sat down again, very slowly, like a person hypnotized. Her eyes never left Lenore's face.

"There. That's right," said Lenore. "It's lonely for me here, Anna. It means a lot to have someone to talk to."

Anna's lips moved, as if she were trying to speak. But no words came.

"Don't be afraid. Don't be shy," Lenore said. "We're not strangers any more. There's no East-is-East or Never-the-Twain or any of that between us." She paused and smiled. "I love him too, you see. We have a lot in common."

She raised her glass and saw that it was empty. Going to the sideboard, she mixed herself another drink.

FOURTEEN

THE JEEP LURCHED THROUGH THE MUD OF THE JUNGLE ROAD, and the wheel spun and quivered under Windom's hands. A half-hour before, when he had started on the return trip to Papaan, there had been merely a thin drizzle, but now it had swelled into a downpour. The drumming on the jeep's canvas top was so loud he could not hear the sound of the motor, and beyond the clacking squeegee on the windshield he could see only the bare outline of the road ahead. Not that it mattered, he thought, jockeying the wheel into submission. There was no traffic on the road, and one rut was as good or bad as another.

His visit to the down-coast village had ended in satisfying anticlimax; for what had been reported as cholera had proved to be merely an outbreak of garden-variety dysentery, and all that had been required was to dispense a few drugs and order the sealing up of a polluted well. In a few days he would send one of the student nurses down to make sure the well had not been sneaked open again. And that, with luck, would be the end of it.

Cholera or no, however, he had not been able to get away in less than three days. As always on his countryside rounds, the villagers had turned out with a complete catalogue of ailments, pains and problems, and hour after hour he had dealt with them as they came: from a liver abscess to an abandoned wife and from a skin cancer to a splinter in a small boy's bottom. A dozen times he had announced, "No more, I'm sorry. Next week I'll come again." But each time a wail of protest and pleading came from the long queue outside his makeshift dispensary. Dr. Windom, hell, he thought; Dr. Pushover was the name. Then he smiled to himself. All right, that was his name and he was content with it. He would rather see that little pile of copper coins on the table than all the gems from all the mines in southeast Asia.

Now, in the lurching jeep, his thoughts moved from the village behind to the village ahead. There had been no message from Papaan. Apparently nothing had happened, and he would be in time for . . . For what? he thought. For whatever was to come . . . And for that, he knew, Dr. Pushover must *not* be the name.

Presently he realized that the rain had stopped. The clouds were thinning. In five minutes they were gone entirely, and the afternoon sun appeared, huge and golden in the clear bowl of the sky. Its light fell on the red mud of the road, on the tall screens of the forest walls, on the leaves and fronds and ferns that rose above him, glittering emerald-and-diamond-bright with the globules of a million raindrops. Within the greenness, the blossoms of flowering shrubs flashed blue and red and yellow and disappeared. A brown knob-tailed hare bounced suddenly across the road. An unseen parakeet shrilled.

Now his thoughts moved back again: not in space but in time. It had been—how long?—seven years since the tides of war had first brought him to this jungle world, and everything in it, then, had been strange and alien. Even when he had returned two years ago, the forest itself had still been largely unknown to him—a place of shadows, secrets, hidden meanings. But now, after those two years, it was as familiar as the fenced fields of Wisconsin or the shopfronts of New York. There in the welter of greenery he recognized the straight slim bole of a dhak tree. Beyond it, a clump of tiberry bushes. Farther on, a stream well-known for its carp fishing. In a few moments he would come to the place where a trail branched off through the seemingly impenetrable brush to a small village of teak-cutters. And in the village was an old man with paralysis agitans whom he was overdue to visit.

He made a mental note: next trip.

Then the road twisted, the trees fell away, and he came out on the rim of a deep valley. Off to the west, now, he could see the ocean, placid and shining, and, to the north and west, range upon range of low wooded hills. His eyes counted: one, two, three, four. The highest point of the fourth range was Blue Mountain, where Jan and the others were waiting; but, seen across those miles of stillness, it gave no hint that it had been so much as visited since the beginning of time.

Instinctively he looked at the sky. . . . Empty . . . The valley below him was empty. Papaan was in the next valley, beyond the first hills, and it would be another half-hour before he came in view of it. As he drove down the winding road he hummed softly to himself:

"Going home, going home. . . ."

And it was true, he thought. It was home. More than any place he had ever lived, this tiny and remote corner of the earth was where he belonged. Not only as a doctor but as a man. Not only in terms of what he had brought to it, but of what it had given to him. Once again his mind went back to his first days there; to the trucks and ambulances of the field hospital moving through the village streets; the crowds lining the way, the dark faces watching. That was all they had been to him then: crowds, faces. When they spoke he could not understand them. Their thoughts, their emotions, their selves were as unknown to him as the jungle itself. . . . Whereas now . . . Now, after seven years, he knew them better than any human beings he had known in his life. Scarcely a patient came to the hospital whom he could not call by name. Scarcely a family lived in the whole valley who did not come to him when they were sick or troubled.

"You must be having quite a time out there," one of his friends had written him "—playing God to the little brown men."

"Yes, I'm having quite a time," he had answered. "but instead of God I'm playing something more interesting. The little brown men, I gather, have never seen a white man try it before, and they seem rather to like it."

He had liked it too. In his mind and in his heart. Here, as nowhere else, he had known that sense of service, of participation, which he so deeply needed in his life—both in the practice of his profession and in his relationship with other human beings. For he had soon discovered that it was not only the people of Papaan who needed him, but he who needed them. He needed their simplicity, their warmth, their gentleness. He needed their trust in him. Above all, he needed the consciousness they had given him of a world deeper and more real than that which he had come from; a world of earth and sea, of rain and sun, of planting and harvesting, of birth and death; a world with no beginning and no ending, that could never be destroyed.

It had not all been easy, of course. In such a country no doctor could hope to escape malaria and dysentery, and he had suffered his share of both. Also there had been the strangeness; there had been loneliness; and while the strangeness had quickly passed, loneliness had, to a degree at least, remained. Close as he had come to the people of Papaan, it was not the closeness of shared experience, shared language, shared blood. And it never could be. But he had lived long enough to know that every step in life is made at a price and that every reward carries with it its own penalty. He had made his choice, and he did not regret it. On the seat beside him lay a ripe pawpaw which one of his patients had anonymously placed there. The copper coins clinked in his pocket.

Looking up, he saw that the weather had changed again. The sun was receding, the clouds closing in; soon there would be more rain. The jeep had come down off the hillside and was moving along the valley floor, and close ahead now was the steeper rise that would carry him up and over the intervening ridge to Papaan.

"Going home, going home. . . ."

To the village. To the hospital.

And to Lee.

Yes, he thought—Lee was part of it too now, part of himself again. Part of home. During the three days of his absence he had thought about it almost constantly. But thinking and feeling were not the same thing, and he had not been able really to feel it. He could not quite feel it yet.

Because it was not that simple, he told himself. Lee was here, and a part of it, yet she was also, so to speak, still *there,* and a part of what she had come from. True, her life from this point on would be utterly different from what it had been before. But his life, by the very fact of her presence, would be different too. This time she had come to *his* world, to the life *he* had chosen, and he knew that she was struggling with all her might to adjust herself to it. But she was still Lee; he was still himself; and neither two years nor ten thousand miles had made them into different persons. From here on, theirs would be a marriage not only of a man and a woman, but of two worlds, two ways of living.

So far it had been better than he would have believed possible. Indeed, there had been only one really bad time—on that first night in the darkness of the bedroom when the years had risen like a wall around him. It was hopeless, he had thought then. Too much had happened; they were too far apart; it was all gone. But he had been wrong. For the very next day they had rowed out to the headland, and suddenly, miraculously, it was not gone at all. It was back again, strong as ever, deep as ever. They were back again where they once had been—together, the two of them.

The two of them—he mused. Perhaps that had always been the answer. When it was just the two of them they had invariably been all right. It was when things beyond them impinged that the trouble started. When they ceased being alone and faced the world of living and doing, of work and decision and responsibility. When he ceased being a husband and became a doctor.

Well, he was still a doctor. He would always be a doctor. The one great hope for them in what Lee had done was that at last she understood it and accepted it.

But there are things too, he told himself, that *you* must accept and understand. It's very strange for her here, and not easy, and you must help her. With the language, for one thing. With the people, the customs, the climate. And when things in the village quiet down a bit, you're going to work it out to spend more time with her. Perhaps you can at last make that trip to the capital—just you and she together—and when you come back it will be familiar to her. It must be her home as much as yours. Even more than yours, because she's a woman.

Woman, hell, he thought. Because she's Lee, your wife. And you love her.

It had begun to rain again—first in a violent downpour, then in a slow gray drizzle—and the jeep moved slowly up the steep twisting road. Now and then its progress stopped entirely, as its wheels spun holdless in the oozing mud. Once it slewed sideways until it was at right angles to its proper course. Each time, however, he managed to extricate it, and presently he had crossed the crest of the rise and was descending on the far side. Below him now was the valley of Papaan, but he could see nothing of it through the opacity of forest and rain.

Ten more minutes and at last the road leveled off. The forest thinned, receded, and in its place were open fields. He passed the first houses, a crossroads, the margin of one of the new rice paddies, and ahead of him now, dimly, he could make out the peaked roofs of the village. His eyes strained through the rain, but there was nothing else to see. No movement. No sign of trouble . . . And also, he suddenly realized, no people. . . . It was late afternoon, the time when traffic in and out of town was usually at its heaviest; but on the road stretching before him there was not a single human figure.

Then there were two figures. They came suddenly up from either side of the road and stopped in front of the jeep, facing him. They were wearing khaki tunics and steel helmets and in their hands they carried guns.

FIFTEEN

There were two sentries at the compound gate and another in the foyer of the hospital. The office door was closed, but, after a word with Windom's escort, the sentry knocked, and a voice said, "Come in."

Windom entered and found three men there. The first he saw—and the only one he recognized—was the mayor, Dai Lollivar, standing in the center of the room with his handkerchief in his hand. Beyond him, near the desk, stood a squat middle-aged man in the uniform of a colonel in the national army. And beyond the desk, in Windom's chair, was a younger, slighter man with gleaming black hair, in a gleaming white linen suit.

Lollivar started to speak, but thought better of it. For a moment the man behind the desk studied Windom with small flat eyes. Then he rose and said, "Ah, it is the doctor. We have been waiting for you."

"Have you?" said Windom.

The man dismissed the sentry with a nod and came around the desk. "Permit me to introduce myself," he said. "Tanit Belhedron, vice-commissioner for the Northern Provinces and at your service. This"—he indicated the man in uniform—"is Colonel Lupat, in command of troops."

Windom looked at Lollivar. "Why didn't you send for me," he said, "as I asked you?"

"I would have, my doctor. I wished to. But—"

"But it was not possible," said Belhedron. "Thanks to Colonel Lupat here, we managed to give our arrival a certain element of surprise. And once here, we felt it wiser, for security reasons, to permit no one to leave the village." He paused and added pleasantly: "Also, we learned where you were and did not wish to interrupt you in your important work. We knew you would be back presently."

"How long have you been here?" asked Windom.

"The troops since late yesterday. Myself and the others for only an hour or two."

"The others?"

"Yes, naturally you could not know yet. Your compatriot, Colonel Hasbrook, is with me. And also, of course, Mr. Schusterman."

"Where are they?"

"Mr. Schusterman has gone to inspect his plantation. Colonel Hasbrook is at the moment, I believe, paying his respects to your wife. Unfortunately I have not yet had the opportunity to pay my own, but I understand, if I may say so, that she is a most charming lady. In fact, she has been so gracious as to send us an invitation to dinner."

Windom nodded. "I'll see you later then. And now, if you'll excuse me, I too haven't seen my wife."

"Yes, of course, I understand; after your absence you are anxious to see her. But as long as you are here now, perhaps we can take a few moments—"

"Can't we take them at dinner?"

"I have always found it better," said Belhedron, "not to mix matters of social pleasure and professional duty. So if you will be good enough, doctor—" He started to go back behind the desk, stopped, and looked at Lollivar as if he were seeing him for the first time. "Oh you," he said. "You may go now."

"Yes, your excellency," said the mayor gratefully.

"You will wait outside. I may want you later."

"Yes, your excellency." As he went toward the door Lollivar turned to Windom. "I have explained, my doctor—I have made clear—"

Then he was outside.

"All he has made clear," said Belhedron, "is that he is a coward and a fool." He sat down again at the desk, rubbed his ruby ring against his lapel and looked up at Windom. "Well, doctor—"

Windom looked back at him.

"Comfortable?" he asked.

The commissioner looked puzzled. Then he smiled. "Ah yes, I see what you mean. We must apologize for moving in on you, but there was really no other place in the village that was at all suitable. Your hospital makes an excellent headquarters, you know. Walls, a gate, a compound, office space."

"And wards," said Windom. "And an operating room."

"I assure you, doctor, we shall in no way interfere with your work. Indeed, it was my thought that our presence might make you feel more secure."

"Secure? From what?"

"From our enemies, doctor. Yours and mine. Oh yes, the village is quiet now. There has been no resistance or disturbance. But surely you are not so naive as to think that many of these people are not friendly to the outlaws; that they are not waiting for the first chance to turn on us."

"Perhaps I should explain—"

"Yes, exactly—that is what we need now. Explanation. Clarification. And that, of course, is where you can be of the greatest help to us. . . . Do sit down, doctor. . . . No?

Well, as you say." The commissioner spread his hands on the desk. "In any case, this is the situation. We have liberated the village, but the village is obviously a hollow shell, for those whom we have come to get are gone. We understand that they have moved up into the hills. Colonel Lupat here, as a military man, is for quick action; for moving after them immediately—today. I, however, have counseled a slower approach: of securing all the information we can, rather than plunging ahead blindly. And I shall appreciate it, doctor, if you will tell me all you can about the strength, plans and whereabouts of these bandits."

"I know nothing," said Windom, "about any bandits."

"Strikers, then. Guerrillas. Partisans. Call them what you like."

"I call them the men of this village."

"*Formerly* of this village, you mean."

"No, not formerly. Still."

"They have left, haven't they?" said Colonel Lupat.

"Yes."

"For the hills."

"Yes."

"And why have they left?" asked Belhedron.

"Because they heard troops were coming."

"Exactly—because troops were coming. Because law and order were coming. They are outlaws, criminals; and they fled like criminals."

"And when they are caught," added the colonel, "they will be treated like criminals."

There was a pause. Then Windom said quietly:

"Commissioner—colonel—please listen to me. There have been reports in the capital, of course, as to what's happened here. But from what you say, these reports have been false; or at least so one-sided as to be the same as false. There has been trouble here—yes. There was a strike and violence. But that violence, I assure you, was caused much more by the police and the plantation management than by the villagers. These people aren't criminals or bandits. They're decent peaceable men. They had a just grievance, and if they answered bloodshed with bloodshed it was only because they were driven to it."

"I see," said Belhedron. "And if they are as innocent as you say, doctor, why should they now have left the village?"

"They had no intention of leaving the village. They went back to the plantation, to take care of the trees and rebuild what had been destroyed. Then your plane came and machine-gunned them."

Belhedron smiled slightly. "And they were afraid?"

"Not so much afraid as angry. It was *I*, chiefly, who was afraid."

"You, doctor? Of what, may I ask?"

"Of what would happen when you came here. Of more violence and bloodshed."

"You thought perhaps of leaving yourself?"

"I thought of it, but I didn't want to. Instead, I urged them to leave."

"You urged—?" Belhedron paused. Then he leaned forward slightly and his small eyes seemed to become still smaller. "Let me make sure that I understand you, doctor," he said. "You conferred with these men, is that right? You were their confidant, their adviser?"

"That is right."

"And you advised them to go?"

"Yes."

"You urged them to go?"

"Yes."

Before the commissioner could speak again, the door opened and a tall figure in khaki appeared.

"Well, the old doc himself!"

Colonel Hasbrook crossed to Windom and shook hands. "I've just been calling on the mem-doctor," he said. "She seems to be holding up fine. . . . And you?"

"Getting by," said Windom.

"Had quite a time of it, I gather."

"Yes," said Belhedron, "Dr. Windom seems to have had a most interesting time. He has just been telling us about it."

"We were doing some worrying about you," said Hasbrook, smiling. "Glad to see the buggers didn't bother you, though." He turned to Belhedron. "Looks as if they're not as tough as you thought, commissioner. Leaving the doctor alone. Clearing out without a fight."

"I am afraid you are not quite up to date, colonel. The reason they left, according to the doctor, is that he told them to."

"Told them to?"

"Precisely. He seems not only to be on excellent terms with them but also in charge of their strategy." Belhedron looked at Windom. "Isn't that about it, doctor?"

"I don't know if I would call it strategy," said Windom. "But I've been trying to help them—yes."

Belhedron nodded. "You were reluctant to believe Mr. Schusterman, were you not, colonel?"

Hasbrook's smile had faded. "You mean it's true?" he asked. "You've been mixed up with these Reds?"

"They are not Reds," said Windom.

"Of course they are Reds," said Belhedron. "They take their orders from Than-kar, who takes his from Peiping and Moscow. What do you take us for, doctor? Nincompoops? Fools?" With a quick catlike movement he was on his feet, leaning forward across the desk. "Has he been here?" he demanded.

"Has who been here?"

"Than-kar. Here in this valley. In this village."

"Of course not."

"They have gone to him, then?"

"No, they have not gone to him."

"They are on a picnic, I suppose? An outing to gather berries?"

"Steady. Steady," said Hasbrook, interposing himself. "Commissioner, sit down—please. Take it easy, doctor. There's no point wrangling among ourselves. After all, we're on the same side in this thing."

"Are we?" said Belhedron.

"Of course we are. Maybe there are different ways of looking at it. The doctor from up here; us from down at the capital. But what we want is the same: to get this trouble settled." Hasbrook looked at Windom. "Right?" he asked.

"That's what *I* want," said Windom.

"Good enough. Now let's go on from there."

"The only place to go on to," said Belhedron, "is to where these men are hiding. And that is what Dr. Windom seems unwilling to tell us."

"They're in the hills," said Hasbrook. "Aren't they?"

Windom nodded.

"Where in the hills?"

Windom didn't answer.

"You see," said Belhedron. "He is helping them. He will tell us nothing."

Colonel Lupat took a step forward. "If you will permit, commissioner," he said, "there are perhaps certain ways of—"

Belhedron gestured him back. His small eyes studied Windom intently. "You are an intelligent man, doctor," he said quietly. "A man of standing and attainment, and I am well aware of how much you have done for our country. Let me point out, however, that you have now been living in this valley for two years. As Colonel Hasbrook says, you perhaps see the situation only from the local point of view, and not in its wider implications. But the implications, I assure you, are very wide. And very serious."

"They are also serious," said Windom, "to these people here."

"These people? They are peasants. Coolies. What do they know or care about such things?"

"They know that they have to struggle for what they want."

"For communism, you mean? For banditry?"

"For their lives," said Windom. "For their homes, their rice crop."

"Ah yes—their rice crop. I have seen their new paddies." The commissioner leaned forward again. "Did you perhaps not know, doctor, that they have been forbidden to grow rice here?"

"Of course I know it. And that's where the whole trouble started. It's impossible to forbid such a thing."

"Impossible?" Belhedron smiled. "Tomorrow, I think, you may change your opinion." He looked at Lupat. "Your men have their orders, colonel?"

"Yes."

"A labor corps has been requisitioned?"

"Yes."

Belhedron nodded and turned back to Windom. "By tomorrow evening," he said, "there will be no more rice crop in Papaan."

There was a pause. Windom slowly opened and closed his hands.

"Unless, of course," Belhedron added, "you change your mind and decide to co-operate with us. In that case, perhaps . . ."

There was a knock on the door and a sentry appeared. "There is a nurse here," he announced, "who says she must—"

But before he could finish Anna Vidal had come in.

"Forgive me that I interrupt, my doctor," she said. "But I have just heard that you are here, and there is one of the malarias whose temperature is up to one hundred and six."

Windom nodded. "Coming," he said.

Anna glanced at the others, and Hasbrook smiled at her. "Miss Vidal," he said.

"My colonel."

She turned to go; but as she reached the door she was stopped by Belhedron's voice. "One moment, please," he said.

Anna looked back at him questioningly.

"If I understood correctly," he said, "your name is Miss Vidal?"

"Yes," said Anna.

"You are perhaps of the family of one Jan Vidal?"

"I am his sister."

"Ah, his sister. That is most interesting." The commissioner studied her for a moment. "By coincidence, Miss Vidal, we have just been speaking of your brother."

Anna looked at Windom.

"Miss Vidal knows nothing about her brother," he said.

"No?" said Belhedron. He came slowly around the desk and went up to Anna. "Nothing at all, Miss Vidal?"

"Nothing at all," said Windom. "She hasn't seen him in ten days."

"Ten days?" Belhedron nodded. "Well, now at last we are getting a little information. He has been gone ten days." He turned back to Anna. "I wonder if you would be good enough, Miss Vidal, to tell us *where* he has gone."

"I don't know," said Anna.

"You don't know? Your own brother leaves and does not even tell you where he is going? 'Goodbye, sister,' he says.

'Where are you going?' you ask. 'Nowhere,' he says. Yes, of course." Belhedron's voice was quiet. He seemed almost to be smiling. Then suddenly he reached out and seized Anna's arm.

"Where is he?" he demanded.

"I—I don't—"

Windom took a step forward. "Let go of her," he said.

"I shall let go of her," said Belhedron, "when she has answered my question."

"You'll let go of her now."

The two men faced each other, and Anna slipped her arm free. "I scarcely think, doctor," said Belhedron, "that you are in a position to give orders."

"And I scarcely think—"

"Gentlemen—gentlemen—" Hasbrook stepped quickly between them. "We can work things out better than this."

"Can we?" Belhedron said. "If the doctor persists in his attitude they may work out more drastically than he expects."

Windom turned away. "Come on, Anna," he said.

"Just a minute," said Belhedron. "We have not yet finished."

"I'm afraid we have, at least for now. You heard Miss Vidal say there's a patient waiting."

"This is more important than a patient."

"To you perhaps. Not to me."

Windom went toward the door and Anna followed him. Belhedron seemed on the point of stopping them, and then changed his mind.

"Very well," he said. "You may go. I would not want it thought that I lack respect for your profession."

"Thank you," said Windom.

The commissioner nodded. "But I shall see you again later, doctor. And you too, Miss Vidal."

Lenore, she said, had asked them for eight, but at seven-thirty there were footsteps on the bungalow porch. Going out, Windom found Hasbrook alone.

"I wanted to speak to you before the others came," he said.

"Good. Sit down. I'll get a drink."

"Later, thanks." Hasbrook's face had none of its usual placid joviality. "I was sorry we didn't have a chance to talk before you saw Belhedron."

"He snapped me up pretty quickly."

"Yes, I know." The colonel glanced down at his big hands. Then he raised his eyes to Windom's. "Look, doctor," he said (and Windom noted that it was no longer "doc.") "Suppose you give it to me straight."

"Give you what straight?"

"What's been going on up here."

"Just what I told the commissioner. The people want their own rice crop. When they were refused it, the plantation workers struck. And when they struck, the police arrested their leader, tortured him and killed him."

"And then the strikers killed back?"

"Yes."

"They burned the plantation?"

"Yes."

"And you helped them?"

"I certainly didn't help them with any killing or burning. I tried to stop them."

"But you couldn't."

"No."

"And so—"

"So what was done was done. I went on from there. I tried to help them and advise them."

"You let them know you were on their side."

"In most respects, yes."

Hasbrook's mouth was a thin line. "You've certainly let

this love affair of yours with the gooks foul up your judgment."

"On the contrary," said Windom, "I've thought about this thing as deeply as I've ever thought about anything in my life."

"And you've decided the gooks are right."

"Yes."

"In—"

"In wanting their rice. In striking for it."

"Rice! Who gives a damn about rice?" Hasbrook didn't wait for an answer. "The thing you don't seem to get, doctor, is that all this adds up to much more than one flea-bitten valley. It's not rice we're concerned with; it's rubber. It's this Than-kar up north. It's China and Russia and World War Three. You know as well as I what the Reds are trying to do here in southeast Asia. And we've got to keep a firm hand on these people."

"There are different sorts of firm hands," said Windom.

"No, there's one sort. Authority. Strength. Showing the Reds we can handle them."

"But these people aren't—"

"All right, they aren't Reds. They go to Sunday School. They're kind to their grandmothers. But they're going to be Reds damn soon, if we don't keep them in line."

Windom shook his head. "It strikes me just the opposite. That the one sure way to lose them is to keep on exploiting and repressing them, the way we always have." He paused briefly. "No, colonel," he said, "I'm no soldier and no politician, but I know a few things about people. Particularly these people. And I can't go along with that."

"I'm afraid you're going to have to," said Hasbrook.

"Because some pigheaded commissioner—"

"I'm not talking about commissioners, doctor." Hasbrook took a slip of paper from his pocket. "I'm talking about something like this, for one thing. It came for you a few days ago, but the wires to Papaan were down, so they delivered it to the American minister."

He handed Windom a telegram.

Deeply disturbed recent reports, it read. *Must insist you refrain political activity.* It was signed by the president of the International Medical Foundation.

Windom looked at it in silence.

"And for another thing," said Hasbrook, "I'm talking about the government. There've been a lot of rumors around the capital lately. Not only about the situation here—but about you. Even before he saw that wire the American minister called me in and asked what was going on. I told him I didn't think it was anything to worry about, but he wanted me to come up here again to see what the score was." Hasbrook paused, and his eyes were steady on Windom's face. "Now," he said, "I'm beginning to wonder about the score myself."

"You mean you think I'm a Communist?" said Windom.

"I'm damned if I know what to think."

"Well don't think that. Because it's fantastic."

"What are you then? What are you up to? . . . Look, doctor—" Hasbrook leaned forward and his voice was friendlier. "I'm not against you. I'm for you. It's because I'm for you that I'm trying to straighten you out on a few things, and if you don't get straightened out you're going to be headed for trouble. Not little trouble. Big trouble."

"I'm only—"

"Yes, I know. You're only a doctor. You're only trying to help these people. But there are ways that you can help them and ways that you can't, and one of the ways you can't is in anything that has to do with the political situation. That's why I've been sent here: to tell you that. Not by any gook commissioner. Not even by a gook prime minister. But by the government of the United States of America."

There was a pause. Windom got up and walked across the porch, and Hasbrook's eyes followed him.

"That's what you have to remember," the colonel said. "It's not just you out here. Not just this village. It's all of us that are going to stand or fall by what happens. Maybe these people are getting a bad break, as you say. God knows, their government's lousy and corrupt. That's too damn bad, but we're not here as reformers. We're here for just one reason and that's to hold the line against the Reds. Anything that helps it is good. Anything that hurts it is bad. In this man's world, Windom, you can't straddle the fence without getting splinters in your ass. You have to be on one side or the other."

He waited, but Windom said nothing. Then he rose and went to him. "Think what you're doing, man," he said quietly. "To your reputation. Your career. Your own country."

Windom looked down at the telegram that he still held in his hand. In the yellow light his face appeared lined and tired.

"What do you want me to do?" he asked.

"First of all, to co-operate with Belhedron."

"By betraying those who trust me?"

Hasbrook's patience snapped again. "God damn it, stop worrying about your gooks. Worry about your own people for a change. Try to realize what's going on in the world—and that the only importance of this country is its rubber and its strategic position."

Again Windom didn't answer.

"You don't believe that, doctor?"

"No."

"What *do* you believe, may I ask?"

"That the importance of any country is the people who live in it."

"That's your way of seeing things?"

"Yes, that's my way," said Windom.

Then he turned and went to the door, as a car pulled up at the bungalow steps.

SIXTEEN

RAIN WAS FALLING AGAIN; THE NIGHT WAS THICK AND STARless. But both seemed remote beyond the bright chintz curtains of the living room windows. With the curtains, a string rug, the shifting of a few chairs and lamps, Lenore had somehow succeeded in transforming the bungalow from a man's dormitory into a woman's home. The table at which the five of them were seated gleamed white and silver. Kosti padded in and out in a new white mess jacket, and the gimlets that he had served were in tall frosted glasses that Windom had never before seen.

Belhedron sat at Lenore's right, Schusterman at her left. But during most of the meal it had been Hasbrook who kept the conversation going.

Now he rattled the ice in his gimlet and took a long appreciative swallow. "Chirikiri's was never like this," he smiled at Lenore.

"Chirikiri's?" she repeated.

"The best café in the capital. East meets West. Boy meets girl. Twenty hostesses—twenty." Hasbrook raised his glass. "I prefer my one hostess—one."

Lenore smiled back at him. "The first floor show goes on at nine."

Then Belhedron took over.

She had not seen much of the capital, had she? That was too bad. There were the ballet and the museum of antiquities, which she must make a point of visiting the next time. And also the royal palace and the floating gardens. She would then realize that there was more to the country than jungles and villages, coolies and rubber trees.

"Just what I've seen has been fascinating," Lenore told him. "Right here in Papaan."

"Fascinating? Yes, perhaps." The commissioner smiled gallantly. "But you are an unusual woman, of course. Let me tell you of my wife's one experience in an up-country village. . . ."

He told his story—amusingly—and Lenore laughed. He had not seen her so gay or at ease, Windom thought, in the six weeks she had been in Papaan. Or so strikingly lovely, either. She was wearing a green strapless dress that showed off the soft whiteness of her throat and shoulders. Her face was fresh and animated. Her hair and eyes glowed in the lamplight. All she had needed was the smallest stimulus from the outside world—the world she belonged to—and her response had been instantaneous and magical.

Windom had only half-listened. To Lenore's laughter. To Belhedron's bland voice and Hasbrook's hearty one. To the clink of ice and silver. You're not in Papaan at all, he thought, but back at the Hôtel du Cap at Antibes, and when dinner is over we'll drive along the Corniche to Monte for an evening at the green tables. Village and hospital, rice and strikes, were remote. More remote than the night and the rain.

Only Schusterman took no part in the talk and laughter, but sat silently—waiting.

Dinner over, Kosti cleared the table and brought coffee, and Windom replenished the drinks.

"You are the best of hosts, doctor," said Belhedron. "I only hope we are not keeping you from your duties."

"I've none this evening," Windom said.

"Your fever patient is better?"

"Yes, his temperature is down."

"Good." Belhedron placed his fingertips together and looked at the ruby on his left hand. "Especially good when one realizes that if it were not for your hospital he would probably be dead."

"It's simply a matter of—"

"Of a great institution, doctor. Of a great service. It must be a deep satisfaction to do such work as yours."

Windom said nothing. Here it comes, he thought.

Then it came.

"And it would be a deep shame," said Belhedron, looking up from his ring, "if you had to abandon it."

"Go on," said Windom.

"Whether or not you have to abandon it, doctor, depends entirely on you."

There was a pause, and Windom could hear the rain drumming on the roof. The three men were watching him. Lenore was watching him, her face no longer smiling, but tense and troubled.

"Look, commissioner," he said, "I think you have some misconceptions about me."

"I sincerely hope so, doctor."

"One of them is that I'm a Communist."

"I see."

"I am not a Communist, I have never been a Communist, and I have no intention of becoming a Communist." Windom's voice became edged. "Would you care for me to put it in the form of an oath?"

"I scarcely think that will be necessary."

"What *is* necessary, then?"

"That you—"

"First of all," Schusterman interrupted, "that you explain your actions, doctor."

"What actions?"

"At the time of the strike. When you incited these people to riot."

"I incited no one to riot."

"The strikers came to you, didn't they?"

"Yes, they came to me."

"And you conferred with them?"

"Yes."

"You gave shelter to their leader when he was wanted by the police?"

"Yes."

"And you advised them to go on with the strike?"

"Yes. And I would advise it again. They were justified in striking. They had a real grievance and were entitled to a hearing."

"And to killing policemen?" asked Belhedron.

"They killed no one—they used no violence of any kind—until the police killed their leader."

"In the performance of their duty."

"In the performance of as cruel and unnecessary an act as I've ever heard of." Windom's eyes went back to Schusterman. "Tell him," he said. "Tell him how the old man Amyan was killed—and why."

Schusterman hesitated. "It was—"

"Tell him honestly. Was it necessary?"

"No," said Schusterman, "it was perhaps not altogether necessary. It was an error in judgment by the sergeant of police."

"Policemen have made errors before," said Belhedron, "and they will make them again. That is no excuse for rioting and insurrection."

"Or for burning the plantation."

"Do you concede that, doctor?" asked Belhedron. "That, whatever their grievance, these people went too far in the wanton destruction of the plantation?"

"Of course I concede it. They were striking back blindly, foolishly. They concede it themselves."

"Themselves?"

"Yes." Windom turned to Schusterman. "You were at the plantation today?"

Schusterman nodded.

"And it was half-rebuilt, wasn't it?" The manager started to speak, but Windom went on. "By whom?" he asked. "By your workers. Why? Because they knew they'd done wrong in destroying it." He looked back at Belhedron. "It would be all rebuilt by now if your plane hadn't come and machine-gunned them."

"Suppose we grant," Colonel Hasbrook put in, "that mistakes have been made on both sides. The job is to get things back in order again."

"Exactly," said Windom.

"If these men were rebuilding the plantation, commissioner, it doesn't sound as if they were whole-hog bandits. In fact, it sounds as if they were willing to go back to work," said Hasbrook.

"Of course, they're willing," said Windom.

"Also," Hasbrook went on, "I've been having a little talk with the doctor here, and I think he's willing to co-operate."

Belhedron looked steadily at Windom. "Are you?" he asked.

"Certainly. If you'll—"

"If I'll what?"

"If you'll believe the evidence Mr. Schusterman has just seen that these men are not bandits or Reds. If you'll meet them halfway with their grievances and troubles."

"If I agree to that, you'll tell us where they are?"

"I'll do more than that."

"More?"

"I'll call them back."

"Back? Here to the village?"

"Yes, here to the village."

"What makes you think they will come?"

"They'll come," said Windom, "because they trust me."

Belhedron nodded slowly, "I see," he murmured. "I see." Then in a different tone of voice: "And you will do this, you say, on the conditions you just mentioned?"

"In general, yes."

"And more specifically?"

"More specifically, that you evacuate your troops from the village; that you meet these men without prejudice and listen to their story; and that meanwhile you issue orders that no harm is to be done to their rice crop."

"That is all?"

"No, there is one other condition."

"And that is–?"

"That you leave the people of the village alone."

"I was not aware that the troops had–"

"I'm not speaking of the troops, commissioner. I'm referring to yourself."

"Myself? What have I–" Belhedron paused. "Oh, I see. You mean my questioning of the young woman in your office."

"Yes."

"You do not want her questioned any further."

"No."

"Because–"

"Because that is one of the conditions, commissioner," said Windom. "And if you agree to them I shall call back the men."

"At once?"

"Yes. Tomorrow."

"And when will they be here?"

"It's hard to tell exactly. I should say within three or four days."

"You will guarantee it?"

"Yes, I will guarantee it."

Belhedron was silent. His soft brown hand slowly turned the glass on the table before him.

"It's the best way, commissioner," said Hasbrook. "You could beat around in those hills for a year and never find them."

"Yes, get them back," Schusterman agreed. "That is the important thing: that they get back to work on the plantation."

Belhedron turned the glass.

"Will you agree?" Windom asked.

Belhedron didn't answer.

"I beg you to agree."

Belhedron looked up at him. "Beg me?"

"Yes, beg you."

"I am afraid I do not quite understand you, doctor. One moment you defy me and the next you plead with me."

"If I've seemed defiant," said Windom, "it's only because I want fair treatment for these people."

"And now that you are pleading?"

"It's for the same reason."

"With no other motive?"

"No."

"No political motive?"

"No."

There was another silence, and through the silence the drumming of rain on the roof.

"Very well," said Belhedron. "I agree."

"Good." Windom stood up and began collecting the empty glasses. "I've been neglectful, gentlemen," he apologized. "Time for a refill."

It rained all night, but in the morning it was partly clear. After breakfast Kosti brought a laden knapsack from the kitchen and set it down on the porch.

"It is not heavy, my doctor," he said. "I could carry it easily."

Windom was busy cleaning an old Enfield rifle.

"And I could carry the gun," the boy begged. "I would go ahead with the gun and shoot the wild animals, so there would be no danger."

"Next time," said Windom. "When we really go hunting."

"Please, my doctor—"

Windom shook his head, smiling. "Next time, Kosti."

The boy went disconsolately inside, and when Windom looked up Lenore was there.

"You're sure you've enough canned things?" she asked.

"Sure," he said.

"I had Lahana put in some condensed milk."

"Fine."

He worked the bolt of the rifle, applied some oil, and looked up again. Then he rose and went to her.

"Lee—don't—" he said.

She didn't answer him.

"I'm not going off to the wars. I'll be back in three or four days."

"Yes, of course," she said.

He put his hands on her shoulders and looked down into her face. All the lightness and animation of the previous night were gone. Her body, under his hands, was tense. Her eyes were lustreless and dull.

"I know it's a rotten break," he told her. "Just coming back and having to go again. But it has to be done, Lee. Someone has to get those men."

"But why does it have to be you?" she asked.

"Because I'm the only one they'll listen to. Because they trust me." Windom drew her to him. "Believe me, Lee, it's nothing. Two days there, two days back—at the most. And don't worry about the jungle. I've been in it dozens of times, and there's nothing that will bother you if you don't bother it first."

He smiled down at her, but Lenore didn't smile back. "It's not the jungle, Alec," she murmured. "It—it's all this thing you're mixed up in." Her face was raised, her arms held him. "Truly, darling. It isn't just your going away. That doesn't make me happy, of course—it will never make me happy—but I didn't come here to be that kind of a wife again. If you were going because someone were sick; because of your work—"

"This is my work too, Lee," said Windom.

"No, no, it isn't—that's the whole point. You're a doctor, Alec; a wonderful doctor. But not a politician. Not a—an agitator of some sort, getting mixed up in all these things that don't concern you."

Windom stepped back a little. "I see Hasbrook's been talking to you," he said.

"Of course he's been talking to me. He's worried about you. . . . And so am I."

"I promise you, Lee—there's nothing to worry about. In a few days I'll be back. In a week or two Belhedron and the troops will be gone. It will all be over."

"Will it? How do you know? How are you sure you won't go on getting dragged into everything—deeper and deeper?" Lenore's eyes held his. Her voice was strained and pleading. "Oh Alec, I've been here only a few weeks, I know that. But

I can see it. I can feel it. Better than you can—truly—because you're used to it. Maybe that's the trouble, can't you see? That you've been here so long; that you're so close to it all—"

"That's right," said Windom gently. "And that's what you have to understand, Lee. That I *have* been here a long time. That I *am* close to these people."

"All right, you're close to them. You want to help them. But can't you do it just as a doctor? Do you have to get involved in the whole mess—with their rice and their rubber and their strikes and their killings? . . . Do you know what it's like, Alec? It's as if you weren't even an American or a white man. As if you were a gook yourself."

"Lee—"

"Yes, I know—that's the word you hate. But I can't help it. That's what they are—gooks—and I hate them all!"

Her voice had become shrill. Her face was contorted. But now suddenly the tautness went out of her and she bent her head against his shoulder. "I'm sorry," she murmured. "Oh Alec, I'm sorry. But—but it's only you I'm thinking of. I swear to you—only you. . . ." When she raised her face again her eyes were filled with tears. "Won't you believe me—please? Won't you listen to me? Can't we get away from all this—just the two of us—together?"

"I've been thinking of that too, Lee," he said. "When I come back—when the trouble's over—maybe we can go down to the capital for a while and—"

"Why can't it be now?"

He shook his head.

"But now's when it's important. Not just for me, Alec. I mean for you. Just until this thing blows over—don't you see? Until you've had a chance to rest a little and see things clearly."

"You mean the way the colonel sees them?"

"It isn't just the colonel. What about the American minister? What about the Foundation and their cable? If you go on like this, it could mean the end of everything you've hoped and worked for."

Windom held her gently. But again he shook his head. "That's a chance I'll have to take," he told her.

"You won't leave?"

"I can't."

"Then won't you at least stay here?"

"I can't do that either."

Her tears had overflowed. Her face was stained with them.

"When I come back, Lee," he said. "We'll go then—like you say. For a few weeks; a month, even. Just the two of us—"

"Truly, Alec?" Her hands gripped his arms. Her eyes searched his, pleadingly. "You really mean it? You'll go? You promise?"

"Yes, I promise," he said.

Through the screen, out in the glare of the compound, he saw Anna Vidal approaching the bungalow.

It was a new admission—this time with food poisoning—but in twenty minutes he was in bed, examined and prescribed for.

"Watch for fever," Windom told Anna. "Only liquids today, then a soft diet for the next two. If the cramps continue give him plenty of atropine."

Leaving her in the ward, he went to his office and began packing his routine instruments into a small bag. But before he had finished Dai Lollivar came in.

"I see you have got back your office, my doctor," he said.

Windom nodded.

"And his excellency—?"

"His excellency has consented to move down the hall. To the quarantine room."

"The quarantine room. Ha ha!" (The mayor was the only person Windom had ever met who literally made the sound "ha ha" when he laughed.) "That is good, my doctor. Very good." Then he became serious. "But it is really good, too, I mean—yes? It means that things are now better?"

"A little."

"And I have heard that you will go now to the hills to bring back Vidal and the others?"

"Yes."

"That is good, too. It is excellent. Only—" Lollivar hesitated and his round face grew clouded. "Only in some ways, I have been thinking, it may perhaps also involve some—er—difficulties—"

Windom shook his head. "The trip shouldn't amount to much."

"I did not so much mean the trip, my doctor. I was thinking, rather, of when the men return to Papaan."

"When they return?"

Lollivar swallowed. Then he brought out his handkerchief and dabbed his forehead. "Yes, my doctor," he said. "You see—you see, I am afraid Vidal and his men do not yet clearly understand my position in these unfortunate matters that have happened. They may think perhaps that I have been against them and not understand that I have tried only to do my duty as mayor."

For the first time, Windom looked up from his packing. "Have you?" he asked quietly.

"But of course I have. That is *all* I have done. To try to promote the welfare of my village. To try to make peace where there is strife—"

"And perhaps to stay on the good side of the commissioner and Schusterman?"

"Yes, yes, to be sure: to stay on their good side. What sense would it be to antagonize them—to make them angry? That is the whole point." Lollivar was now plying the handkerchief at his throat, and his voice became tense and apprehensive. "But it is a point, my doctor, that I am afraid these rebellious ones will not see. That is why I have come to you now. To tell you this. And to ask what I should do?"

"Do?" said Windom.

"When they come back. When they are here again, but not in jail—and angry—because they do not understand what I have tried . . ." Lollivar broke off. Then he leaned forward, almost supplicatingly. "You see the difficulty, my doctor. How can I explain to them? What can I do?"

Windom walked around behind his desk and sat down. For a long moment he remained without speaking, his gray eyes cool and measuring on the mayor's face. Then he said:

"I can tell you what I *think* you should do, Lollivar."

"Yes, my doctor?"

"I think you should come with me."

"With you?" Lollivar's mouth fell open. "You mean now—today? Into the hills?"

"Yes, today. Into the hills."

"But—but—" For an instant the mayor was wordless. "But it is not possible, my doctor," he murmured. "I am a family man, you see—a merchant—with many responsibilities. And most of all, there are my duties as mayor—"

"It's *because* you're the mayor," said Windom, "that you should come."

"I—I do not understand you, my doctor."

"Because you owe it to the people."

"But if I am gone, who would then run the village?"

"I'm sure that for the few days you're away the commissioner will have no difficulty running the village." Windom paused, his eyes on the mayor's plump face, and when he spoke again his voice was quiet and earnest. "Look, Lollivar," he said, "how you became mayor of Papaan I don't know, but I do know that since I've been here, at least, you've done nothing to merit the job."

"But you—"

"Never mind me. What I think doesn't matter. But what your own people think, does. They've no respect for you, and you know it. And now you're either going to have to win their respect or move out."

"I have tried only to—"

"Yes, I know what you've tried. To steer clear of trouble. To keep in the middle. All right, that's exactly where you are now: in the middle. You and I both. In the middle, between the government and those men up in the hills, and it's up to us to bring them together."

"There is nothing that would give me more happiness, my doctor. During my years as mayor, all I have done—"

"—is to weasel back and forth, wherever you thought you could do yourself most good. Well, things have got beyond that now. The only way you can do yourself some good is by doing some good for your people."

"Yes, yes—of course. To help them—to lead them—here in the village—" Lollivar was almost in tears. "But this thing you suggest, my doctor. To go into the hills—the jungle—"

"—is the one way you can show them that you *want* to help them." Windom stood up. "I've some things to do now," he said. "If you decide to come, go home, get some things together and meet me in front of my bungalow in half an hour."

The mayor's lips moved, but no words came. Windom went through the door into his laboratory.

"Cheer up—you'll probably enjoy it," he called back. "Maybe we'll scare up a tiger."

He took some drugs and bandages from the shelves, and

when he returned to the office Lollivar was gone. Anna was now there, however, standing by the window, apparently waiting for him.

"Might as well be prepared," he said, putting the things into his bag. "They've probably got everything from snake-bite to measles up there in the bush."

Anna didn't answer, and he finished packing and closed the bag.

"Poisoning case all right?" he asked.

"Yes, my doctor."

"And the others?"

"Yes, my doctor."

"Good enough. Now while I'm away I want you to—" Suddenly he stopped and looked at her curiously. "Something wrong?" he asked.

The nurse said nothing.

"What is it, Anna?"

"My doctor, please—" She stammered and was silent.

"Please what?"

"Please—I have heard—there has been talk in the village—that you are going—"

"Of course I'm going. Now. In a few minutes."

"I do not mean now, my doctor. Not the trip to get Jan. I mean later, when you come back. They say you will go away then, again, and maybe you will not—"

She was too agitated to go on. Windom looked at her for another moment and then went up to her. "What's the matter, Anna?" he asked gently. "What are you talking about?"

"That you and the mem-doctor will soon leave Papaan."

"Yes, we may. For a while."

"They say not only for a while. They say for good. That the mem-doctor does not like it here, and that you will go with her to America and never come back."

"Nonsense. I'll be gone a few weeks at the most."

"You are sure, my doctor? It will not be for always? You tell me the truth?"

Her eyes were raised to his, dark and pleading. But suddenly Windom's eyes were smiling.

"Women—" he said.

"What, my doctor?"

"I said *women*. My wife's upset because I'm going up to the hills. Now you're upset because I may go to the capital. What was it Hamlet said?" The smile became a grin. " 'There are more things in a woman's head, Horatio, than are dreamt of in your gynecology.' "

Anna looked at him uncomprehendingly. "You make jokes, my doctor," she said. "But I am not joking. No—" Suddenly she seized his hand. "You have done so much here in Papaan. For my people. For myself. And if you go now —if you do not come back—"

"I've just told you—"

"If you do not come back, my doctor, I could not face it. I could not go on—"

Her voice broke. Her slim body was trembling. Windom moved his hands to her shoulders and gripped them tightly, as if he could stop the trembling by their pressure.

"Anna—"

Her head was bent; for another instant she remained motionless and rigid. Then her body went limp, and she swayed forward against him. "I cannot help it," she murmured. "I am so ashamed. It is so terrible. But I cannot help it—"

He held her close. No longer tightly, but tenderly. And in his eyes, where the smile had been, there was now something close to tears.

"Anna," he said. "Dear Anna."

There was a long silence in the room.

Then he said:

"Do you know what I've been thinking? I've been thinking that since the hospital's grown bigger there's too much work here for just you and me. We need someone else—another doctor. And I'll tell you what I'm going to do. When I go down to the capital I'm going to see if I can find one. A good doctor—young and intelligent—one of your own people. . . . Yes, it's a good idea. I'm sure of it. We'll talk about it before I go. . . ."

Anna said nothing; and when at last he stepped back, she covered her face with her hands.

He glanced at the clock, went behind the desk and picked up a slip of paper. "There are a couple of last-minute things," he said. "First, the algid malaria in the South Ward. He's to have glucose intravenously twice a day. The three dysenteries—" He looked up. "Are you listening, Anna?"

"Yes, my doctor."

"—the three dysenteries need only routine medication, but watch their temperatures closely—"

"Yes, my doctor."

"—and in case one of them goes into coma . . ."

SEVENTEEN

NOW HE WAS IN THE JEEP AGAIN, BUT THIS TIME NOT ALONE. Beside him sat Dai Lollivar, and on the seat behind were two packs with their gear and food.

Windom was dressed in khaki—long-sleeved and trousered to keep out insects—stout G.I. boots and a fatigue cap; but his companion wore his usual white linen, pointed shoes and broad-brimmed straw hat.

"No old clothes?" Windom had asked.

"I do not have old clothes, my doctor," Lollivar had replied with dignity. And when Windom had suggested finding some, he declined. "It is as mayor of Papaan that I go," he announced, "and it is as mayor that I shall appear."

Windom shrugged and let it go. When they left the jeep they would take to muleback, so the shoes didn't greatly matter. For the rest, it would be most of the time under a raincape, and that, at least, Lollivar possessed.

Apparently word of their mission had already got around, for the village streets were lined with people, waving and cheering. In a moment the mayor's depression had vanished. He waved back. Beaming, he nodded to right and left.

All that's missing, thought Windom, is the ticker tape.

Then the village was behind them. On their left was

the river—no longer a chain of stagnant pools but a broad smooth-flowing stream. And on their right, the rice paddies. Here and there a coolie or bullock cart moved along the mud ramps that bounded them. But nothing else. No troops. No labor corps.

So far, so good.

Beyond the paddies they came to a fork in the road. The right-hand branch led to the plantation, but they bore to the left, along the river, and followed its course up the narrowing valley. Gradually the slopes on either side steepened into hills, and behind them appeared the outlines of higher, more distant hills.

Windom's thoughts moved forward. . . . Then back. . . . Back to the compound and Belhedron standing on the hospital steps.

"A pleasant journey, doctor," he had said.

"Thank you."

"And a successful one."

"That will depend less on me than on you."

They had shaken hands. Then Hasbrook shook hands. At the bungalow door Lenore raised her face and he kissed her.

"Easy does it," he said.

"Alec, you're sure—you won't be longer—"

"—than four days."

"And when you come back—"

"Then we'll go down to the capital."

He kissed her again, and for an instant she clung to him. Then he got into the jeep. Two of the student nurses waved from a hospital window. But Anna did not appear.

Ahead the valley narrowed. The road twisted.

"My doctor—" said Lollivar.

"Yes?"

"I have been thinking of the people in the streets, as we

left. Of their faces. Their voices." He was silent a moment. Then he added:

"I am glad I have come with you, my doctor."

"Good," said Windom.

It took them an hour to the village at the head of the valley. There they left the jeep in a shed and rented two mules.

Had anything been seen of the men in the hills? Windom asked.

No.

Or heard of them?

No. . . . But there were three villagers who were sick with the fever, and if the doctor would be good enough—

"On the way back," Windom promised.

"But one is *very* sick—"

"Well, all right; the very sick one."

And that was another half-hour.

Then the village was behind them. The valley was behind them. The trail wound up a low hill, descended on its far slope, and the forest closed about them in a green tide. Windom rode ahead, with Lollivar a few yards behind, and the only sounds were the creaking of their saddles and the plop of the mules' hooves in the mud of the path.

They crossed a second valley, climbed again, descended again. Though the trail twisted and meandered, its general direction held to the north, and in the absence of forks or cross-trails there was no danger of losing the way. Toward midafternoon it began to rain, but they were aware of it only as a pattering on the treetops high above. Scarcely a drop penetrated through the layers of leaf and branch into the deep twilit tunnel through which they rode.

Windom held the old Enfield balanced across his saddle. The chances of running into trouble were small—but not quite so small as he had indicated to Lenore—and he was well aware that a month before two teak-cutters had been mangled almost to death when they stumbled upon a mother tiger and her suckling cubs. Fighting off the drowsiness of heat and shadow, he kept his eyes sharp on the path ahead.

After a few miles they forded a shallow stream, and Lollivar drew abreast of him. "I will go ahead now, my doctor," he said.

"No need," Windom told him.

"Yes—please. I wish to do my share."

Taking the gun, he moved into the lead, and now ahead of Windom, instead of empty trail, was a rumpled pudgy figure swaying precariously above a mule's behind. . . . Windom grinned. . . . With Lollivar too: so far, so good. In fact a great deal better than he had dared hope. Whether it had been the sendoff of the crowd or some inner resolve, or a combination of both, he didn't know; but, whatever the cause, the mayor was putting up a fair show. He was afraid —yes. It showed in the stiff line of his shoulders, in his hand grasping the gun, in the quick jerking of his head when a bird or insect shrilled from the forest. But his fear made his performance the more admirable.

"I wish to do my share. . . ."

If he keeps it up, thought Windom, I might almost begin to respect him. More important, even his people might.

From the head of the valley to Blue Mountain was twelve miles on the map, but something more than twice that, he had estimated, along the twists and dips of the trail. By nightfall, as nearly as he could judge, they had gone about half the distance, which meant that at the same pace, and with an early start, they should reach their destination the next day around noon. They made camp, such as it was, on a bank of moss beside a small stream, coaxed a fire out of damp brushwood, and ate supper. Then, wrapping themselves in their raincapes and mosquito netting, they lay down close to the fire and slept.

Toward the middle of the night Windom was awakened by a sudden yell and, starting up, found Lollivar, rigid with terror, staring off into the shadows. But it was soon discovered that all he had heard was the snapping of a branch broken from a tree by one of the tethered mules.

"Forgive me that I disturbed you, my doctor," said Lollivar. "But in such a place we must take no chances."

Windom nodded and lay down again.

"And on such a mission," the mayor added. "It is not ourselves who are important, but only that we get through to help our people."

In the morning, when Windom awoke, Lollivar was already heating water for their tea over the replenished fire. In spite of raincape and netting, his clothes were covered with mud and his face with insect bites; but his manner was cheerful and his eyes bright with anticipation.

"In a few hours now we shall be there," he said. "Then no more can they say that their mayor does nothing for them. No more can old Mamarta Vidal make loud with her insults, or I will have the police put her in jail.

"—when we again have police," he added as an afterthought.

By six they were on the march. The way led up. The way led down. For perhaps an hour the trail clung to the pitch of a steep hillside, and they looked out over a green sweep of treetops. Then it leveled off again, they crossed still another valley bottom, and the mules sank almost to their knees in a red paste of mud. Now and then there was a flash of color in the foliage or the sudden sharp cawing of a bird. Once a slender brown-and-yellow snake darted across the path before them. But of larger animals there was no sign.

They moved in a stench of sweat—the mules' and their own—and it was only with a conscious effort that Windom seemed able to draw air down into his lungs. No rain fell, but the patches of sky above them were gray and sunless. No faintest shred of breeze touched the sodden web of the forest.

Lollivar's mule slipped, caught itself and plodded on.

Clop. Clop.

Windom looked at his watch. Nine-thirty. Ordinarily he would be just finishing the morning rounds and going to his office to arrange the rest of the day's schedule with Anna.

Anna . . .

He had tried to keep her out of his mind. Or, rather, his mind had automatically kept her out, focusing itself down to the next hour, the next mile, the job at hand. Windom the Focuser, he thought. He should have been a photographer, not a doctor. Is there something undesirable? Change the focus. Something troublesome? Reduce the lens opening. It might spoil the composition. In the living of his life there were two things that he had prized and sought above all others: simplicity and purpose.

Nice work if you could do it.

At the time of Anna's outburst he would have said that his single reaction was that of astonishment. But now he knew it had not been that simple. He had been astonished, yes—at the outburst itself, at the girl's sudden loss of control—but not at what lay behind it. For he had known that all along. Ignored it all along. "The nurse never lived," a colleague had said to him long ago, "who didn't either hate her doctor or love him." An exaggeration, of course; but not a great one. It made a neat entry for the miscellaneous file—until you reached into the file and caught your fingers in the drawer.

Anna. Anna . . . The unhappy lovely damnfoolish girl.

But why now? he thought. Why had it had to wait until now to come out into the open? With the "trouble" heavy over the valley. With Lenore there. Precisely, he knew, *because* of the "trouble." *Because* of Lenore. They had been what brought it out—the catalysts—the added strain that made the situation unendurable.

Poor Anna—

Poor Anna, hell, he told himself. . . . Poor Lee . . . It was Lee, not Anna, who had walked all unsuspecting into the mess; who wanted only to be with him and had been with him scarcely at all; who needed all the thought and consideration and understanding that he could give her. Lee, his wife. Lee, whom he loved.

And if, with Anna, only time would help, for Lee, at least, there were things that could be done. Hasbrook had been right—if not with his motive, with his answer. They would go down to the capital. As soon as the strikers were back and the trouble was over they would go off, the two of them alone, for a life of their own. They would stay a few weeks—a month—maybe more. He would stop being a doctor and be a husband. And when they came back . . . When you come back, he told himself, you're going to do just what you said to Anna. You're going to bring an assistant. A young native doctor from the capital. He can handle the outer villages. He can help with the clinic, with the routine treatments. You'll have some time for Lee.

And perhaps the young doctor and Anna. . . .

Clop. Clop.

His own mule stumbled and plodded on. When he next glanced at his watch it was past eleven.

And now at last, he saw, the forest had begun to change. The way was no longer up-and-down, but steadily up; the foliage was less dense, the air easier to breathe. They had reached the lower slopes of Blue Mountain, and the path climbed in switchbacks, higher and higher.

At one of the turns he paused and pointed, and there above them was a shoulder of rock, jutting bare and bold from the hillside.

"It is where they will be?" asked Lollivar.

"It's where they should be. At least their lookouts."

From below, the shoulder appeared close, but a half-hour later they were still zigzagging up between forest walls. Then abruptly the trees fell away, there was the gray gleam of stone, and the path twisted up onto an open level platform.

Windom stopped. Behind him Lollivar stopped, and Windom could hear the sound of his breathing.

There was no one there.

His eyes moved over the clearing, over the boulders and moss, to where the path led on upward into the trees on the far side. He called out—waited—called again.

Lollivar pulled up beside him.

"Do you think—"

"Maybe there's another open place. Up higher."

He guided his mule across the platform to where the path continued. It appeared no different from what it had been below.

"Best to keep going," he said.

He rode on, with Lollivar close behind. The path twisted, straightened for a few yards, twisted again—and the mule stopped. In the path, beyond the second turn, stood three men with rifles.

"Well—" said Windom.

The three looked at him without speaking. Then they looked past him at Lollivar. The one in the center was Lansang, who had been assistant foreman at the plantation. On the right was a young rubber-gatherer named Dolyan, but the one on the left Windom didn't know. They were dressed alike in soiled work-clothes, with knives in their belts and bandoliers over their shoulders.

"There are more of you?" asked Lansang.

"No," said Windom.

"Only you two?"

"Only us two."

Lansang jerked his head at Dolyan, and the latter moved past the mules and around the bend of the trail.

"You don't believe me?" said Windom.

Instead of answering, Lansang came closer. "You will give me your gun, doctor," he said.

Windom looked at him uncomprehendingly.

"Your gun." Holding his own gun in his left hand, Lansang extended his right.

"What are you talking about?"

Before Windom could tighten his grip the hand grasped the gun and snatched it away. "You will dismount now," said Lansang.

Windom didn't move.

"I said you will dismount, doctor." Handing Windom's gun to the other man, Lansang half-raised his own. "At once, please."

Windom got down and stood facing him. At a gesture from Lansang, Lollivar also dismounted.

"What is this?" said Windom quietly. "What do you think you're doing?"

"It is an outrage," protested Lollivar. "You may not act so to the doctor—"

"Quiet, fat-ass."

"—and when we return to Papaan I shall see that—"

Lansang swung his gun butt, and Lollivar fell. Windom's fists clenched and he took a step forward; but the gun was up again, muzzle pointing.

"Playing soldier?" he said.

"We are not playing anything, doctor. We are very serious."

"Where's Jan Vidal?"

"In our camp."

"Take us to him."

"We are about to."

Lollivar had regained his feet. His moon-face was almost white, except where a stream of blood flowed down from a gash on his cheekbone.

"When the authorities hear of this—" he began.

"—they will be glad," said Lansang, "that they didn't come with you." He looked past them as Dolyan came back up the path. "No one else?" he asked.

Dolyan shook his head.

"Good."

Windom took his medical bag from his pack, and from the bag a bottle of antiseptic, a gauze pad and tape. Lansang made as if to stop him, then changed his mind and waited while he cleaned and covered Lollivar's wound.

"The bone's not broken," he told him.

"I am glad, my doctor."

"Give some men a little power—" Windom shook his head. "Well, let's get to Jan."

"Yes, my doctor."

When Windom turned, Lansang was holding two lengths of rag in his hand.

"What now? Blindfolding?"

Lansang didn't bother to answer. While his two companions stood by with their guns he tied the rags tightly around their heads.

"Now march," he ordered.

"On foot?"

"Yes, on foot."

"But the mayor—"

Something hard prodded him from behind. "March," said Lansang.

He marched.

Or, more accurately, he stumbled. Through the mud. Over roots. Against the branches and vines that walled the twisting path. But each time his pace slackened there was another prod from behind.

"It can't be far," he said to Lollivar.

There was no answer. Apparently Lollivar wasn't there.

And then he was there. There was a sound of something falling and another that was half cry, half groan. Windom ripped off his blindfold and saw the mayor sprawled on the path ahead, while the man called Dolyan tried to kick him to his feet.

"Damn you—"

But before Windom could move he was pinioned tightly from behind, and in the next instant the blind was back over his eyes. "I would not do that again, doctor," said Lansang's voice.

"At least let him ride," said Windom. "He has no strength. And no boots."

Lansang said nothing.

They marched on.

"It can't be far," he had said. But it seemed far. They moved on for what seemed an hour—two hours—three—until his body ached with tiredness and he could scarcely lift his feet over the muck and roots of the path. If this goes on much longer, he thought, I'm simply going to sit down in the path, and to hell with them.

But he didn't sit down. . . .

And presently there was no longer a path. As far as he could judge, they had turned off of it into the forest itself, and a hand on his arm was guiding him in a twisting course between tree trunks, branches and brush.

"Where are you taking us?"

No answer.

"How far to your camp?"

No answer..

Then at last there was another change. More light came through his blindfold; the ground was level and open; he knew they were in a clearing. And although he could not see, nor hear any voices, he knew, too, that there were other people present—and that they were watching him.

Again he raised a hand to his blind, but it was knocked roughly away.

"Jan!" he called. "Jan!"

But again there was no answer.

A few moments later the light became dimmer. He surmised they had come into some sort of shelter. Then the rag was suddenly ripped from his eyes, and he saw that they were in a small bare hut built of thatch and wattles. Lollivar stood beside him, swaying slightly, while one of the men unbound his eyes. And in the next instant he collapsed like a half-filled sack on the earthen floor.

The three men went to the door.

"Where is Jan Vidal?" Windom demanded.

"He is here," said Lansang.

"Tell him I want to see him."

"You will see him when he is ready."

Lansang went out, and the other two followed him. Windom sat down beside Lollivar.

EIGHTEEN

IT RAINED. IT STOPPED RAINING. IT RAINED AGAIN. KOSTI HAD set pans about the bungalow to catch the leakage from the ceilings, and in each room there was a clicking and plopping, as if from a tiny metronome.

Lenore read Manson on infectious jaundice.

Toward midafternoon a soldier appeared with a small box. Inside was a spray of wild orchids and a card reading: *To a most charming hostess. Tanit Belhedron.* She took them to the kitchen and put them in the refrigerator; then changed her mind and took them out again. Going to the bedroom, she slipped off the print housedress she had been wearing and put on one of the three dinner gowns that hung in the closet. Then she made up her face carefully, arranged her hair, and pinned the orchids to her shoulder.

Back in the living room the drops of water fell click-click into the pans.

"The samba?" she said. "Why, yes—I *adore* the samba."

She smiled, held out her arms and danced. She danced until her head spun and sweat covered her body, and then she knocked against one of the pans of water.

"Steady, girl," she said. "Steady."

Returning to the bedroom, she took off the gown. Then

she bathed and put on the housedress again, and when she came out Colonel Hasbrook was waiting on the porch.

"I thought you might like to have dinner," he said.

She hesitated.

"There's a little Chinese place on the main street that doesn't look too bad."

I'd love to, she meant to say. But what she said was "I'm sorry—"

Hasbrook looked disappointed.

"I'm tired," she explained.

And she *was* tired. After Hasbrook left she sat for an hour almost without moving. When Kosti brought her supper she could scarcely eat it, and later she simply sat again: limp, drained, doing nothing. Not until she went to bed did the tiredness leave her, and then—as she had known would happen—she lay in the darkness tense and sleepless. Click-plop went the drops of water. Her bones ached and her flesh crawled with itching. Toward midnight she got a nembutal from the bathroom and washed it down with a tumbler of gin.

The next day at breakfast she spoke sternly to Kosti. "You promised a week ago you'd find someone to fix the leaks in the roof."

"Yes, my lady," said the boy. "But—"

"But nothing. You go to the village right now and bring a man back with you."

"Yes, my lady."

When he had gone, she called Lahana and announced that they would spend the morning housecleaning.

"But there is no need for the lady—"

"That's where you're wrong," she said. "There's plenty of need."

From nine to ten, with the cook's reluctant help, she thoroughly mopped and dusted the house. Between ten and eleven she rearranged the kitchen shelves, polished the tableware and hung clothes out behind the bungalow to air. At eleven-thirty it began to rain again and she brought the clothes back in. And at about noon Kosti reappeared—alone.

"Where's the man?" she asked.

"He will come, my lady."

"When?"

"Soon, my lady."

"How soon?"

"As soon as the rainy season is over, he says. He says the roof it must be dry before he can do good work on it."

It was one o'clock.

Then it was three.

He must be there by now, she thought. There and talking to them. Perhaps already on the way back. . . . Or had something gone wrong? . . . Had he missed the way? Were he and Lollivar, at this very moment, floundering blindly through trackless jungle: hungry, exhausted, lost?

Stop it, she told herself.

He will be back tomorrow. The day after, at the latest. For God's sake, why are you fretting about a day or two when you were separated for two years? . . . He will be back, and the trouble will be over. The loneliness and fear will be over. . . . Two days, that's all. Two days are nothing.

But the nights . . .

Stop it. Stop it.

It rained all afternoon. At intervals groups of soldiers crossed the compound; occasionally an out-patient or student nurse. Once Anna Vidal descended the hospital steps and seemed to be coming toward the bungalow, but she merely moved past it obliquely and went out through the compound gate.

A two-inch cockroach emerged from under the sideboard, waved exploratory feelers and beat a strategic retreat. Lenore got the D.D.T. gun from the kitchen and sprayed all the rooms. Then she got a brush and a can of white paint and covered up the chips in the bathroom cabinet.

It was four o'clock.

And then four-thirty.

A while later a new sound became audible behind the beat of rain, and she realized it was the droning of a plane. But when she looked from the window she could see only the gray emptiness of rain and cloud.

Then, toward evening, Hasbrook appeared again.

"I'll be leaving in the morning," he told her.

"Leaving?"

"They've sent a plane for me. Some three-star general and a State Department fellow have shown up in the capital, and they want me to brief them."

"You mean about—"

Hasbrook shook his head. "Don't worry," he said, "it's the big picture they'll be interested in. Than-kar—the Reds—all of that. They'll ask some questions about your husband, of course, but it will be a side issue. As a matter of fact, I can tell them it's no issue at all any more"—Hasbrook smiled—"since he's decided to be reasonable."

"You *will* explain to them—"

"Sure I'll explain." Hasbrook looked at her quizzically. "Unless, of course, you'd like to do some of it yourself."

"I—I don't understand."

"I mean if you'd like to come with me."

"Come with you?"

"Why not? You flew up with me once. Now you could fly back."

"Oh no, I couldn't." Lenore's eyes were wide. "Not possibly."

"Repeat: why not?"

"Because of Alec, of course. I must wait for him."

"You could wait for him in the capital," said Hasbrook. "He'll be a few days more in the bush; another week, say, straightening things out here. Then he could come down and join you. We'd send a plane for him."

Lenore shook her head. "We'll come down together—when he's ready."

"What makes you so sure he'll ever be ready? That he won't get so caught up in his work that it's impossible? If you're already there, though, he'll have to go." Hasbrook smiled again. "It would be a little old-fashioned strategy."

She hesitated.

"Write him a note tonight, and I'll pick you up after breakfast. You'll be in the capital for lunch. And in the evening—Chirikiri's!" His smile broadened into a grin. Then he saw from her expression that he was on the wrong tack and quickly changed it. "I don't mean a party, Lee," he said. "I mean a change, a rest. I mean getting away from here."

"I don't want to get away," she said quietly.

"Yes, you do. You know you do. And what's more, you need to." He took a half-step toward her. "Look, Lee—don't get it wrong. You're a damned attractive woman, and I'd be less than a man if I weren't aware of it. But that isn't what this is about at all. And it will never be what it's about, because I've got too much respect for your husband. And for you. But there's nothing in Army Regulations or anywhere else that says because I respect you I can't like you—and I like you too damn much to be happy about what's happening to you."

"Happening to me?"

"Your life here. This mess you're involved in. The strain you're under."

"It isn't I who's under the strain."

"Yes, I know. It's he you're thinking about. You want to

help him. But this isn't helping him, don't you see that? It's just wearing yourself down."

Lenore didn't answer.

"He's not in any danger. He's simply got a job to do. Let him do it; finish it. Then he'll come to you—after a while the two of you will come back here—and it will be different."

Lenore shook her head again. "No," she murmured. "No, I can't."

"*Why* can't you?"

"Because I love him."

"Of course you love him."

"Because I have to be with him—be part of him—part of his life."

"But this thing that is going on now—"

"—is part of him too. And so it's part of me. Oh, I know I can't really help him the way I'd like to. As if I could really *do* anything. As if I were—a nurse. But I've got to do what I can. Even if it's only standing by. . . . Oh, don't you see? That's why I'm here. The whole reason. To stand by him. Beside him. To be a wife to him. And if I went now . . ."

Her voice caught. Her hands were pressed tight against her sides. But as she raised her head and looked at Hasbrook her eyes were steady and clear.

"Do you understand?" she said.

For a long moment Hasbrook looked back at her. Then he nodded slowly. "The telegraph's working again," he said, taking his cap from a chair. "When the two of you are ready shoot us the word, and we'll send a plane for you."

"Thank you, George."

He came close to her again. "Make it soon, Lee."

"Yes, we will."

"And take it easy."

"Yes."

He extended his hand and touched her arm lightly. Then he put on his cap and crossed the porch.

At the door he turned, straightened and saluted.

"I meant that one," he said.

And he went out.

While at breakfast the next day she again heard the sound of a plane's engine, but again, when she looked from the window, there was only the grayness of cloud and rain. Then the sound faded. In its place was the drumming on the roof and the click-plop on the floor.

The morning passed.

Toward noon the rain slackened and there was sudden activity in the compound. A detachment of troops marched in through the gate, and presently a short thick-set man in a colonel's uniform appeared on the hospital steps and spoke to them. Then the troops marched off, and it was quiet again. After lunch she went into the bedroom, looked through her dresses and selected those she would take when they went down to the capital. Then she turned to Windom's clothes and, after a search, found a total of two suits that could conceivably be worn in a city: one a seersucker, one a worsted, both spotted and moldy. She did what she could with them and hung them up neatly. . . . Item: one new white linen for Chirikiri's . . . She smiled and for a few minutes was almost happy.

When she finished with the clothes it was after four. Manson on pock diseases carried her through until nearly five. Here's one little item that's *not* going in the suitcase, she thought, as she put the book down.

Then there was a step on the porch, and, going out, she found Belhedron.

"Forgive me that I disturb you," the commissioner said, "but I came only to pay my compliments."

"Thank you," she said.

"Everything is all right?"

"Yes, quite all right."

"With your husband away, it is dull and lonely for you, I am sure. But he will be back soon now."

"Tomorrow, do you think?"

Belhedron shrugged. "Tomorrow—the next day: it is hard to tell. But it will be soon."

"And then everything will be settled—"

"Yes, everything will be settled."

"—the way it was agreed?"

"I am afraid I do not understand."

"It was part of the agreement, I thought, that the troops would leave the village. But this morning I saw—"

"Oh yes, the troops." Belhedron's voice was reassuring. "They were called in for a final inspection, but have left again. And now, my lady"—he bowed and smiled—"if there is nothing I can do for you—"

She watched him as he crossed the compound and went up the hospital steps.

A while later the sun came out, almost startlingly, and in its slanting rays, beyond the banyan trees, she could see the faint outline of distant hills.

Tomorrow—she thought. Or the day after . . .

No. Tomorrow. It *had* to be tomorrow.

Soon the sun receded and it began to rain again. Mist closed in. The walls themselves seemed to close in.

Click. Plop.

Kosti brought in tea, left it, and went back to the kitchen.

Click. Plop.

Take it easy, George Hasbrook had said.

All right. *Take it easy.*

Then, suddenly, she realized that someone had come into the room. This time there had been neither knock nor footsteps, but when she looked up Anna Vidal was standing before her. She had a raincape thrown over her uniform, but her head was bare and streaming with water; and her breath came in deep labored gasps.

Lenore got to her feet.

"Forgive me, my lady," said Anna. "But I must come to you. I must see you."

"What is it? What's the matter?"

"It is a terrible thing. So terrible!" The girl seemed unable to go on. For a moment she looked around, almost wildly; then suddenly down at the floor. "Excuse me that I make it wet," she murmured dully.

Lenore unfastened the cape and slipped it off her. "Sit down," she said.

"No—there is no time."

"Sit down."

Anna sat down. Her hands, on the chair arms, were trembling. It was hard to believe that this was the same girl who, in most of her life, went armed in the composure of a professional nurse.

"Cigarette?" Lenore asked.

She shook her head.

"A drink, then?"

She shook it again, but Lenore overruled her. "Yes, that's what we both need—a drink."

Going to the sideboard, she mixed two gin-and-limes, then brought them back and set one beside Anna. The girl had gained at least outward control of herself, and her hands were now quiet. But there was no quietness in her dark eyes. Only anguish and fear.

"Drink it," said Lenore.

Anna sipped from her glass and set it down.

"Now tell me. What is it?"

"It is all a lie," said Anna.

"What's a lie?"

"What is happening. What they have promised and what they are going to do."

"What *who* is going to do?"

"This Belhedron. And his troops. Before the doctor goes there is an agreement, yes? The doctor will get Jan and the others from the hills. And when he brings them there will be no trouble—no punishments. Only talking and agreements."

Lenore nodded.

"What they will do is not that at all," said Anna. "Instead, they will kill them."

"Kill them?"

"Yes. Jan and Lansang, who are the leaders. The others they will force back to work. With no land—no rice—but like slaves again at the plantation."

"Who told you all this?"

"I have heard it just now from the young girl Aminya. She is one of those who cleans in the hospital, and this afternoon she is in the lavatory beside the office of Belhedron. He is talking to the colonel of the troops. He is telling that he has had orders from the capital that there must be strong action. That an example must be made. With no compromise. No pity."

Lenore was on her feet. "But he promised my husband—"

"Yes—he promised. And the doctor promised Jan. But that is not how it will be. They will arrest Jan. They will shoot him. Aminya heard him say it."

"How do you know she is telling the truth?"

"Why should she lie to me? She is a good girl and intelligent. . . . And also there is another thing. You saw the soldiers who came here this morning?"

"Yes."

"Now we know why they came."

"The commissioner said they had gone again."

"That is what he said, perhaps. But they have not gone. They are hidden in a warehouse behind the hospital."

"You're sure of that?"

"Yes, I am sure of it."

There was a pause. The only sound in the room was that of Anna's breathing.

"Who else knows about this?" Lenore asked.

"No one," said Anna.

"Only you and this girl?"

"Yes. I made her promise to tell no one. If it is known in the village what they plan to do, I cannot think what awful things will happen."

There was another pause.

"I'm going to the commissioner," said Lenore.

Anna shook her head. "It will do no good. He will say it is not his decision but that of the government."

"But—"

"And also, if he knows that we know, there is no telling what he might do here in the village."

Lenore walked distractedly across the room and looked out the window across the empty compound. When she turned back, Anna, too, was standing.

"There is only one thing to do," said the girl.

"What?"

"To go to Jan and the others before they come. To warn them not to."

"But who can—"

"*I* can," said Anna.

"You?"

"Yes. It will soon be night, and I can leave the village without being seen. On the road I will find a mule or ox-cart, and by morning I will be at the head of the valley."

"But you can't go into the jungle—"

"I will not have to go into the jungle. At the village up the valley we have friends. I will wait there until the men come, and then I will tell them."

"Can't someone else go? A man?"

"All the real men are with Jan. Those who are left here I would not trust." Lenore started to speak, but Anna went on: "No, my lady, it is the only way. It is an hour now since Aminya has told me these things, and I have thought and thought, and it is the only way."

The last trace of hysteria was gone now. Her voice was quiet. Her dark eyes were straight and level on Lenore's face.

"It is not only for my brother that I must go," she said. "It is for the whole village. And for the doctor . . . That is why I have come to tell you, my lady. Because the doctor is part of it too, you see. It is as bad a thing for him as for the rest of us."

"For the doctor—yes—of course—" Lenore's voice was barely audible, and for a moment her thoughts seemed blurred and disjointed. Then, suddenly, she was staring at the girl and her body went rigid. "Oh God, what will happen?" she said. "What will he do now?"

"I do not know, my lady. Perhaps he will feel that his place is with the men. Or more likely, I think, he will come back alone to defend them."

"Defend them?"

"To speak to the commissioner. To argue—to ask explanation—"

"But he's already done that. He's worn himself out doing it. And now, if the orders are from the government—"

"Yes, I know," said Anna. "It will be hard. Even harder for him than anyone else. But what can he do? Bring them back to be killed or made slaves? Abandon them when they are helpless and hunted?"

Lenore said nothing.

"Other men would do it—yes. But not he. He is a good man, my lady. He is a great man. And it will be hard, against the commissioner and the government—it will be long and bitter—but in the end he will convince them."

"In the end—"

"Yes, I am sure. I know it. He is kind, but strong. He is gentle, but a fighter. No soldier has fought so hard as he has: against sickness, against poverty and ignorance, against injustice. . . . And now he will fight again. He will fight for what is right and true and decent, and in the end he will win."

Again Lenore said nothing. Anna looked out the window at the rain and the fading light.

"But now I must go," she said. "If I do not stop Jan and his men, it will all be too late." She went to the chair where her raincape lay. "It is almost dark. I will get a few things—change my clothes—"

Lenore's eyes followed her.

"I'll go too," she said suddenly.

Anna shook her head. "No, my lady, it is not possible. I will wear peasant clothes. No one will notice me. But you they would see at once. A sentry. A coolie. And word would get back. . . ."

She threw the cape over her shoulders. Then she crossed to the door.

"Anna—wait. Listen."

"There is no time, my lady."

"There must be some other way—"

"No, there is no other."

"But—"

"Goodbye, my lady."

Then she was gone.

Lenore ran after her, across the porch, and flung open the screen door. The rain beat at her.

"Anna!" she called. "Anna!"

Click. Plop.

"Kosti!" she called.

But there was no answer.

"Lahana!"

No answer.

She sat down. After a few moments she reached for the glass beside her, but found it empty. The other glass, however, beside the chair where Anna had sat, was still almost full, and presently she went over and got it. Sitting down again, she sipped it slowly.

Tomorrow, she thought—

The tomorrow you've been waiting for. When he would come back: when the trouble would be over. Only now not over. Only now worse than ever.

She looked at the wall, and a fly walked down it.

In the end, the girl had said.

The end is the end is the end.

Courtesy G. Stein.

The fly went back up the wall. . . . Click plop . . . The pans on the floor were almost full, but now both glasses were empty. When the fly starts down again, she told herself, it will be time for a refill.

She waited.

Thank you.

Going to the sideboard, she poured a drink. There was no more lime, but it didn't matter. Nothing mattered, she thought. Except tomorrow. Except the tomorrow that was no longer tomorrow. That would be the same as before. Worse than before.

She was sitting again.

You are coming back, she thought. You are coming back, and it was going to be different. The trouble was going to be over. We were going to be together. We were going to the capital.

And now . . .

It was getting darker.

Dear God— No, not dear God; dear Alec. Dear Alec, I want to be a good wife to you. So much. So much . . . But to make a wife there must be a husband. To make me there must be you.

I can be a doctor's wife, Alec. Yes, I can. I can. But this is something else, that I don't understand. And it frightens me. It frightens me more than it does the little brown girl. . . . Who loves you too.

The fly was gone. So was the drink.

She went to the sideboard and poured another.

Yes, she loves you, Alec. And in a way, too—I know—you love her. You need her. You have gone so far from the world we knew; so deep into another; so deep into these people and their lives. You have gone where I cannot follow you. . . .

And I must get you back.

How? How?

Where is she now? In the hospital? At her home? Changing her clothes; no longer a nurse but a peasant; a coolie woman setting out for the next village. Tomorrow she will see him. She will tell him what has happened, and the men will stay in the hills, and he will come back alone. Back to the village; back to the commissioner; back to the trouble. But not to me.

Not tomorrow for me. *In the end* for me.

The room was heavy with dusk. Rising, she went toward the light switch, tripped over one of the drip-pans and almost fell. Then she reached the switch and snapped it on. She saw that the pan had spilled and the floor was covered with water.

All right, the floor was covered with water.

Click. Plop. Or was it plop click?

With slow measured steps she moved around the room, overturning the other pans with her toe. Now, on the floor, it was plop plop.

Unmistakably.

You must stop her, she thought. If you stop her, they will all come. The men will come too, and they will be arrested, and the trouble will be over. . . . Not only for you, but for him . . . All this craziness with land and rice and strikes will be settled—finished. He will be a doctor again, and only a doctor, with no more riots, no more troops, no more killing, no more fear. With no more American army colonels investigating him. With no telegrams warning him . . .

You see—it's not of yourself you're thinking. It's of him. For *your* sake this mustn't happen, Alec. For *your* sake this thing must stop.

Not in the end. But now.

The glass was empty again. Then it was full again.

The trouble will be over, she thought. And we will fly down to the capital. We will go to the place called Chirikiri's, and you will wear a new white linen suit, and we will dance a samba together, like we used to at the Hôtel du Cap d'Antibes. Then we will come back here. Not to trouble, but to peace. You will heal the sick and I will stand beside you. I will be your nurse, your helper, and you will need no other. And when the day's work is done, the rain will stop, the sun will shine, and we will row out across the bay to the bright beach, the deep blue water. . . .

She stood up again. Not restlessly now, but deliberately. Straight and cool. Straight and clear. She took her glass and set it down on the sideboard. She went to the closet and put on her raincoat. Then she crossed the porch, went out the door, crossed the compound and went up the steps of the hospital.

"I wish to see the commissioner," she told the sentry in the foyer.

NINETEEN

They sat in the bare hut, waiting.

Waiting for what? Windom thought.

Rain pattered on the thatch roof. Then it stopped. But the moisture still seeped up through the earthen floor, and his bones ached with stiffness and fatigue. He tried lying down, sitting, squatting, standing. But one was no better than another. The stale air of the hut seemed almost impossible to breathe, and his body was covered with a glaze of sweat.

Hunched in a corner, Lollivar had not moved for half an hour.

"All right?" Windom asked him.

"Yes, my doctor." Then after a pause: "What will we do, my doctor?"

"Wait. Jan will come soon."

But he didn't come. No one came. Instead, after a while, their two packs were suddenly thrown in through the doorway. They had been opened and rifled, and Windom's knife was gone; but their small food supply had not been touched, and he spread the soggy mess before them on one of the flattened packs.

"Eat something," he told Lollivar.

"I am not hungry, my doctor."

"Eat anyhow. You need it."

They forced down some of the food, and Windom put the rest back in the packs. As they sat waiting again it began to grow dark.

Suddenly Windom rose, went to the doorway and stepped outside. Instantly two guns pressed against his ribs, one from either side.

The guards were unknown to him.

"Where is Jan Vidal?" he said.

"Get inside," ordered one of the guards.

"I demand to be taken to Jan Vidal."

"Get inside."

The guns pressed harder. He went back into the hut. He had been outside only a few seconds, but they had been enough for a quick glance around him, and now he was more puzzled than ever. The hut was one of many, as he had expected. They were in a clearing, as he had expected. But the size of the clearing and the number of huts took him wholly by surprise. It seemed a village rather than a camp; a community of many hundreds rather than the hundred and twenty who had set out, a few weeks before, from Papaan.

They had joined up with others: that was obvious. But with whom? And how? And why? In his brief moment outside he had seen many figures—mostly men, a few women and children—moving about the clearing or squatting around scattered cook-fires; but they had been too distant, and the light too dim, for him to recognize anyone. When he called out Jan's name there had been no answer.

In the hut, now, it was rapidly getting darker. Opening the packs, he groped for their flashlights, but found that they too had been taken. Lollivar seemed to be asleep. He sat down beside him. When it's full night, he thought, there may be something we can do. Make a dash past the guards in the forest. Or pry a way out through the rear wall.

And then what?

He sat waiting. He felt his tiredness enveloping him in a dark numbing tide. . . .

And when he awoke it was morning.

In the gray light he rose and moved about the hut, trying to stretch the damp stiffness from his body.

"Move around too," he told Lollivar, who was awake and watching him. But when the mayor tried to rise he stumbled and fell back again, and Windom had to help him to his feet.

"My doctor—"

"Yes?"

"It is not good, my doctor."

Windom felt his forehead and pulse, and there was no fever. But that was all that could be said for him. His body sagged on his stubby legs, his eyes were glazed, and he was covered from head to foot with thick half-dried mud. Dirtiest of all was the bandage on his cheek, which had become half-loosened during the night; and removing it, Windom saw that the wound was dirty too, and angrily swollen.

"Guard!" he called.

And presently a strange face appeared in the doorway.

"We need water."

The man grunted something and disappeared, and a while later a partly filled bucket was shoved in through the entrance. Windom washed the wound, applied antiseptic and rebandaged it. Then, taking their food from the packs, he ate again and made Lollivar do likewise.

"It can't be much longer now," he said.

They sat in silence. Windom looked at his watch, and it was a quarter of eight. . . . I'll wait for an hour, he thought. I'll wait for exactly an hour, on the minute, on the second, and then I'm going to get up and walk out that entrance, and they can do any damn thing they like.

When he next looked at the watch it was eight fifteen. When he looked again it was eight thirty-two.

Then there were footsteps outside, and, one by one, five men entered the hut. The first and last were apparently guards, for they immediately stopped on either side of the doorway with their rifles at the ready. The other three also had rifles, but they were slung on straps over their shoulders and they came straight forward until they stood in the center of the hut. The one in the center was Lansang. The two who flanked him Windom did not recognize.

He arose and faced them.

Lansang looked at Lollivar. "Get up," he said.

The mayor got slowly to his feet. Then he swayed a little.

"Stand still."

The mayor stood still.

"He has no strength," said Windom. "He's sick."

"His sickness," replied Lansang, "will not bother him long." He took a slip of paper from his pocket and handed it to the man on his right. "Read it," he said.

The man unfolded the paper and read in a high singsong:

"The Provincial Court of the People's Republic makes announcement as follows. One. That one Dai Lollivar, merchant and politician, of the Municipality of Papaan, Province of Papaan, has this day been brought before it for trial. Two. That the charges against him are as follows: a—malfeasance in his office of mayor; b—corruption in his office as mayor; c—complicity in the exploitation and enslavement of the people of Papaan; d—complicity in the wanton slaughter of the people of Papaan; e—the giving of aid and comfort to the enemies of the People's Republic. Three. That after due process of law the court has found him guilty as charged. Four. That the sentence of the court is death."

Refolding the paper, the man handed it back to Lansang, and Lansang put it in his pocket. There was a moment's silence. Lollivar swayed again. His lips moved, but he made no sound. His eyes were fixed, as if he were hypnotized or in a coma.

"In the name of God—"

Windom took a step forward but was stopped by the guns of the guards. His gray eyes blazed at Lansang.

"What sort of farce is this?"

"It is scarcely a farce, doctor," said Lansang. "As the criminal will soon discover."

"You're going to shoot him?"

"Most certainly we are going to shoot him. This morning. Now."

"You can't—"

"I am afraid you will find that we can."

"Then it will be you who are the criminals. The murderers."

"In your opinion."

"In all men's opinions. And under the law."

"Your law and ours," said Lansang, "are not the same."

There was another pause. Again Lollivar's lips moved, and this time a few words came out.

"I ask—I beg—"

Lansang gestured to the guards to take him out. But Windom stepped forward again. His hands were tight and rigid at his sides, and sweat rolled down his forehead into his eyes.

"What are you saying about law?" he demanded. "You haven't tried him."

"Of course we have tried him," said Lansang. "And sentence has been passed."

"Without giving him a chance to defend himself?"

"What purpose would there be in that? He would only lie."

"Give me a chance, then. Let me talk to your court."

"I am afraid, doctor, that you would lie too."

Again Lansang gestured, and the two guards moved up on either side of Lollivar. As they did so, his knees buckled, and they had to hold him under the arms to keep him from falling. His ridiculous pointed shoes dragged in the dirt as they moved toward the entrance.

This time it was not a step that Windom took, but a leap. He stood with his back to the door, facing the others.

"Let him go," he commanded.

The guards looked at him impassively.

"You will step aside, doctor," said Lansang.

"Let him go."

No one moved.

"I am afraid," said Lansang, "that you are in no position to give orders. In the new People's Republic white men give no orders at all."

"I'm not talking as a white man."

"As what, then?"

"A human being."

Lansang seemed about to answer, changed his mind, and nodded briefly to the guards. Letting go of Lollivar, the one on the left reversed his gun and smashed the butt into Windom's side.

Windom fell.

"We have wasted enough time," said Lansang.

The two guards dragged Lollivar out, and the other men followed. Windom pulled himself to his feet and stumbled after them.

"How about me?" he called. "No trial for me? No murder for me?"

He reached the entrance and stepped out.

"Jan!" he called. "Jan Vidal! Jan!"

The two other guards were still outside. Another gun butt

swung. He crawled back inside and sat with his face in his hands.

It began to rain.

After a while it stopped raining.

It is my fault, he thought. It was I who urged him, taunted him, made him come. I who would make a man of him.

A dead man.

His side ached and throbbed. Opening his shirt, he saw a large purplish mark extending from his right nipple down across the ribs. He felt the ribs lightly but could not tell if any were broken.

He rebuttoned his shirt and for a long time sat motionless in the gray stillness of the hut. He listened, straining, for the sound of a shot. But there was no sound.

It began to rain again.

Then, a while later, one of the guards from outside appeared in the doorway.

"Stand up," he ordered.

Windom didn't move.

"Stand up. You're to come with us."

"Come where?"

Without answering the guard prodded him to his feet. As he rose, there was a quick spasm of pain in his side, but then he no longer noticed it. Outside, the second guard fell in beside them, and they marched diagonally across the clearing. As on the previous night, there were many people about —men, women and children—and now he could distinguish them as individuals. There were a few he knew, more he didn't know; but none paid any attention to his passing.

At the far side of the clearing they stopped in front of a hut, indistinguishable from the one he had just left. One of the guards went inside, reappeared, and beckoned him in. The interior of the hut, too, was the same as the other: with wattled walls, thatch roof, earthen floor. The only difference was that a rough table stood at its center; on either side of it two boxes, as chairs. And on the farther box sat Jan Vidal.

The guards withdrew. Jan stood up. Windom looked at him without speaking.

"Sit down, my doctor," said Jan.

Windom remained where he was.

"Very well. As you wish." Jan resumed his own seat. When he spoke again his voice was quiet and not unfriendly.

"I am sorry," he said, "that we meet in such circumstances."

Windom still looked at him in silence. It had been—what? —some three weeks since he had last seen Jan Vidal, but now it seemed more like three months. Or three years . . . Had there been physical change? Yes—some. His black hair, once long and habitually rumpled, was now cropped close to his skull, giving a square flat-planed cast to his head and features. He was wearing a khaki shirt and heavy boots that lent him a vaguely military air. . . . But there was more than this, something more essential and more subtle; and suddenly Windom knew what it was. On all previous occasions when he had seen him, it had been he, the doctor, the white man, who had been behind the desk or table, with Jan Vidal in front of it. Now their positions were reversed.

"We mean you no harm," said Jan.

"No?"

"You are thinking of Lansang. Lansang is hard and bitter, and with good cause. You do not remember, perhaps, that one of his brothers was killed by Bilko's police and another by the plane at the plantation?"

Windom said nothing.

"But he knows, as do I," said Jan, "that these things were not your fault. And we mean you no harm."

"And Lollivar?"

"With Lollivar it is a different matter."

"It wasn't his fault that—"

"He was a coward and a fool." Jan's voice grew hard. "He was a traitor to his people; a tool of their exploiters. And it is necessary that we make an example of him."

"An example of what? Your own barbarity? That you can outdo Bilko?" Windom came forward and spread his hands on the table. "Jan, we're old friends. You're not that sort of man; I know you're not. Stop. Think what you're doing. Don't take out your grievances and hates on one poor defenseless individual."

"We are not concerned with individuals," said Jan. He stood up abruptly. "And besides, it is a waste of time to talk further of this Lollivar."

"You won't listen to me?"

"There is nothing to listen to. It is too late."

"He's dead?"

"Yes, he is dead."

"I didn't hear any shot."

"There are other forms of execution than shooting. We have not so many bullets that we waste them on such as he."

There was silence. Windom's body went tight, and he felt an anger that was close to sickness rising inside of him. For a moment he closed his eyes. Then he sat down on the nearer of the wooden boxes and looked at the ground.

Jan watched him. Then he resumed his own seat. "But it is not with these past things that we are now concerned," he said. "It is with the present—the future. . . . How are things in Papaan?"

Windom didn't answer.

"My sister Anna—she is all right?"

"Yes, she's all right."

"I have been afraid it might go badly for her with the enemy in the village. When we left, I wanted her to come with us. I argued with her. I begged her. But no, she would not. She said, my doctor, that her place was with you."

A smile touched Jan's lips.

"No," he said, "instead of my sister it is my mother who comes. You do not have a mother, perhaps? Well—sometimes it is a good thing, and sometimes it is difficult. Especially when she is such a one as mine. Half the time I am not sure who is the leader here—she or I."

He paused, waiting for a smile in return. But none came. When at last Windom raised his head the eyes were cold and bleak.

"The leader of what, Jan?" he asked.

The two men faced each other across the table. Jan's smile faded.

"Do you not know, my doctor?" he asked.

"I think I do. But I want you to tell me."

"Leader," said Jan, "of the Fourth Volunteer Field Group of the People's Republican Army."

There was another silence.

"How did it happen?" Windom asked quietly.

"Most simply, my doctor. We came to these hills, as you advised us. We made our camp and waited and struggled to live. We thought we were alone. But we were not alone."

"Than-kar's men were here."

"Yes."

"And you joined them."

"Yes."

Windom got to his feet. With all the strength that was in him he was struggling for control; but when he spoke again his voice was tense and strained.

"Why?" he asked. "For God's sake, Jan—why?"

"In the beginning," Jan said, "it was not wholly a matter of choice."

"They forced you to?"

"They came to us. They said we could either join them or be their enemies."

"That was when you first came here?"

"Yes."

"And now?"

"Now we are part of them."

"But if you find a way—"

Jan shook his head. "No," he said, "we are not looking for a way. *This* is our way."

"With the Reds?"

"With the People's Republic."

A sentry appeared in the doorway. "There is a messenger—" he announced.

Jan nodded, and after a moment a second man came and handed him a note. Then he stood by while Jan read it.

"Tell the commander," said Jan, "that it shall be done."

The man saluted and went out. Jan put the message under a stone weight on the table.

"The commander," said Windom, "being Than-kar."

Jan nodded.

"He's here?"

"In this camp—no. We have dozens of camps, my doctor, across the width of the Northern Provinces. This is only one of them, of which the commander has put me in charge."

"You've met him, then?"

"Yes, I have met him."

"And—"

"And since I have met him," said Jan quietly, "I have begun a new life. Soon all of us will begin new lives."

"As bandits?"

"No, not as bandits. As patriots. As liberators of our country."

"You believe that, Jan?"

"It is not a question of believing, but of knowing. Of

seeing the truth at last, after being blinded by a lifetime of capitalist, imperialist lies."

"They've taught you the lingo quickly, haven't they?"

"Lingo? I do not know what that is. . . . But they have taught me—yes. . . . Of course I have much yet to learn. Our commander studied five years in China, in Russia, before he was ready to return here to lead us; and I know that what I have learned in a few weeks is as nothing. . . . But at least my eyes are now open. I see who our friends are, and our enemies. Who it is who only talk while they exploit and enslave us, and who gives us the power to strike and to conquer." Jan paused and looked steadily at Windom across the width of the table. "Before, my doctor, we could only beg for our rights. Now we shall fight for them—with steel and blood."

Windom looked back at him. Then, slowly, he shook his head.

"Well, my doctor?"

Windom didn't answer.

"What are you thinking?"

"I am thinking," said Windom, "of a man called Amyan."

Did Jan flinch? He wasn't sure. For an instant the dark eyes seemed to move past him. The big hands closed tight over the edge of the table.

"Well?" he said.

"Amyan would not have done this."

Jan said nothing.

"He had no use for steel and blood."

"No," said Jan. "And that was why things happened as they did. He was a good man, but weak. A leader, but helpless."

"You thought he was a saint."

"All right, he was a saint. And what came of it? The

world is not made for saints, but for fighters." Jan rose suddenly to his feet. "And that is what we are going to do. Fight," he said. "For our lives, our homes, our freedom."

"Jan, listen to me—"

"No, my doctor. For two years I have listened to you, and now for a change it is you who will listen to me. . . . You think we are fools, do you not? A crowd of helpless coolies hiding in the forest, waiting for an army to come and kill us. . . . But we are not. We are an army too."

He ripped the recently received message from under the stone where he had placed it. "Do you see this? Do you know what it is? It is an order from our commander that in four days we shall move down from these hills and take the valley of Papaan."

Windom stared at him.

"Have you lost your mind, Jan? There are troops in the village. A whole regiment."

"We know exactly what is in the village. Do you think we do not have reports from there? We know exactly what we face, and I promise you that five days from now Papaan will be ours."

"They have machine guns; grenades."

"As have we."

"And they can bring up reinforcements."

"No, that is precisely what they cannot do. In these rains, on the jungle roads, it would take them two weeks to bring in a platoon." Jan smiled thinly. "Do not worry about us, my doctor," he said. "It is your friends down there you should be concerned about."

"My friends?"

"The commissioner, with his bloody hands. Your fellow-American, who does not care for gooks. Your charming wife, with her gowns and perfumes."

"Careful, Jan—"

"No, it is you who must be careful, my doctor. Here, for the first time, I may speak as I like."

"Yes, of course," said Windom. "Just as you like. Provided the Party likes it too." Anger, quick and hot, had risen inside of him. But now, suddenly, it was gone, and in its place was something deeper than anger. "Oh, Jan, Jan—can't you see what you're doing? This isn't freedom you're finding. It's a worse slavery than you've ever known. . . ."

Jan tried to interrupt, but he didn't let him. Rising, he leaned across the table and spoke with tense, passionate emotion. "We're friends, Jan. You and I. Your people and I. For two years now I've lived with you, worked with you, tried to help you, and I can't stand by now and watch you throw away every chance of a decent life. All right, I'm an outsider—an American—from a different world. And my world wants no part of communism. But that isn't what I'm thinking about now. Not myself, not my country, not my world, not any of it. I'm thinking of *you,* Jan. I know the kind of man you are; what's in your heart; what you want for your people. And I beg you—don't ruin it all. Don't sell yourself and your people for cheap revenge and a taste of power."

He paused. He tried to catch and hold the eyes that seemed to be looking past him at something beyond.

"Come back, Jan," he pleaded. "The others will follow you. That is the way it was agreed, and the way it must be. I've been talking to the government people, and they're reasonable. They'll meet you halfway. Come back and fight it out: not as some crummy little warlord, but as a civilized decent man. Come back, and we'll fight it out—you and I together—for what we believe in."

He paused again. Again he struggled to reach the eyes

that stared beyond him. He raised his arm, held it out . . . held it . . .

And then dropped it.

"So they've really got you," he said quietly.

Jan put the message back under the stone on the table. Then, with a stub of pencil, he began making notes on a pad.

"I will go then," said Windom.

Jan looked up. "Go?"

"Back to Papaan. Alone."

"I am afraid that will not be possible, my doctor."

"What do you mean?"

"You know too much about me. And our plans. You will have to stay here until we go down to Papaan ourselves."

"As a prisoner?"

"Whether as prisoner or guest depends on you." Jan put down the pad and pencil and looked at Windom squarely. "On whether you are willing to co-operate with us," he said.

Windom was silent.

"Let me point out something to you," Jan went on. "Your coming here was not, of course, a surprise. We knew you were coming, and while we waited we discussed what should be done. There are those here who do not know you. To them you are simply a white man—therefore an enemy—and they were for dealing with you as such."

"As you dealt with Lollivar, for instance."

"Exactly . . . But I told them—all of us from Papaan told them—that your case and the mayor's were quite different. That you had been our friend. That we owe you a debt of gratitude."

Windom smiled thinly. "And that you need the hospital, perhaps?"

Jan ignored the interruption. "I told them," he continued, "that you were politically unreliable. That you were weak.

A bourgeois straddler and compromiser. But not evil, as the others are evil. I told them that, at the worst, we should hold you as prisoner. That, under certain conditions, it might even be possible to give you your freedom."

"Under what conditions?"

"As I said before—that you co-operate."

"How?"

"By acting as doctor to us. By helping the sick and wounded."

"I will always do that. For any men."

"And that you give your word," said Jan, "that you will not try to escape."

There was a pause.

"Will you?" said Jan.

Another moment passed before Windom spoke. Then he said: "If I gave my word, how do you know I would keep it?"

"Because I know you, my doctor."

Windom smiled again. "And my weak bourgeois scruples?"

"Will you do it?" asked Jan.

"No," said Windom.

"You refuse?"

"Yes, I refuse."

"Because—"

"Because I am a peculiar man, Jan," Windom said quietly. "And I value some things more than my freedom."

Jan sat looking at him across the table. He seemed about to speak, but changed his mind. Then he shrugged and stood up.

"Guard!" he called.

One of the sentries appeared.

"You will take the doctor back to his hut."

The sentry stood aside for Windom to precede him. "Perhaps after a while," said Jan, "you will change your mind."

Windom didn't answer. Outside the door a second guard fell in beside him, and he walked across the clearing in the rain.

TWENTY

TOWARD NOON, A MAN HE HAD NOT SEEN BEFORE CAME INTO the hut.

"I am sent by Jan Vidal," he said. "He asks if you have something to say to him."

"No," said Windom. "I have nothing to say."

"You have not changed your mind?"

Windom shook his head, and the man left. Perhaps an hour later a bowl of food and a pan of water were pushed in through the entrance. It stopped raining, and then began again. No one else came.

He sat with his back against the wattled wall, his knees raised, his head bent onto his folded arms. Behind his closed lids he saw the five men entering the tent . . . standing there. . . . Lollivar standing there. He saw them drag him out; the limp white shape sagging between them; the pointed shoes trailing along the ground.

He tried to shut it out. Then deliberately, bitterly, he called it back. You will never shut it out, he thought. It was you who did it. You who are responsible.

He thought of Lollivar.

He thought of Jan.

Again he saw the tall square figure behind the board

table; the square immobile face; the dark eyes looking, not at him, but beyond him. It is like a disease, he thought. A rigidity—a paralysis—of the face, the eyes, the mind. And there is no medicine that can help it; no surgery that can cut through the iron wall. "Jan—listen," he had pleaded. "Jan—see. Jan—think." But it was no use. It was no longer Jan who was there, but someone else. No longer a friend, but a stranger and an enemy.

Jan, whom he had trusted. Jan, whom he had loved.

His ribs ached. Opening his shirt, he pressed his hand against them, and the pain grew worse. Better that pain than the other, he thought. A bruised—even a broken—rib was a thing that healed.

A while later there was the sound, outside, of men marching in step. They are coming for me, he thought. But the steps moved on past. And presently there was a shouted command and a thud of rifles being grounded.

They are drilling, he told himself. For three more days now they will drill and prepare and plan, and then on the fourth day they will move down toward the valley. In four days, across four hundred miles of the Northern Provinces, armed bands would be moving down from the hills into the valleys—burning, plundering, killing.

Windom turned to the wall behind him. His fingers probed the wattle and thatch. . . . Then abruptly he stopped. . . . Even if he could claw his way through, he would be seen the moment he was outside. The one chance was to wait for darkness.

He waited.

He sat motionless against the wall, and the hours passed, and at last the light in the hut began to fade. One more hour, he thought. And in that hour it became night. Through the entrance he could see the gleam of scattered campfires, but beyond the rear wall, in which he had now made a thin crack, there was no light at all, and the forest was no more than fifty yards away.

He began to widen the crack. But the fibers of the walls were thick and tough, and the work went slowly. Every few minutes he stopped, looked toward the entrance and listened, but there was no sound from the guards outside. He worked on. The pain in his ribs swelled until it became almost unendurable, and his fingers were raw and bleeding. I can't go on with it, he thought despairingly. . . .

And then, turning again, he saw that there was not even the hope of going on. For a figure had appeared in the doorway.

He rose silently, waiting for the guard to speak. But in the next instant he realized that it was not a guard. It was too small for a guard. As small as a child . . . Then the figure came toward him, and in the darkness he could see a seamed face and sharp watering eyes.

"Mamarta–" he said.

The old woman approached until she was close beside him. "You are all right, my doctor?" she asked.

"I'm alive," he said.

"You can walk? You can run?"

"Yes. But–"

"Then you will listen to me," she interrupted. "And you will do what I say." She was peering at him. Her voice was low and hoarse. "It is not necessary that you make this hole. You will go out the door with me. We will walk to the right –fifteen paces, twenty–until we come to the edge of the forest. Then you will step quietly into the forest and go back to Papaan."

Windom stared at her without speaking.

"You do not wish to go?" she asked.

"Yes, of course."

"Then do not stand there like a fool. Come. You have a pack, yes? A rain-covering? Some food?"

But still Windom stood motionless. "I don't understand, Mamarta," he said.

"Understand? What is there to understand?" she snapped. "Is it not enough that I help you to go?"

"But how can you do it? What about Jan?"

"Jan!" She spat out the word as if it offended her mouth. "He is no longer a son of mine. No longer anything." Windom started to speak but she went on with harsh bitterness. "No, you do not need to ask why. You know. You have seen why. What he has done to Lollivar—you have seen that. All last night, my doctor, I talk to him, I plead with him. I say yes, this Lollivar is a fool, a weakling, he must no longer be mayor of Papaan. But he is not evil, not a criminal. You must not do this thing. . . . I beg. I cry. But it is no use. He is not my son any more, but a stranger. He spits on God and the Virgin. He is as hard and evil as Bilko, the policeman."

Her clawlike hand grasped Windom's wrist. "And do you know what they will do next?" she said. "When they go down into the valley they will have lists of those they say are against them. Not only of the soldiers and police, but of the people of the village—women and old men and friends—and they will say they are enemies of the revolution and bring them out in the streets and shoot them."

Her voice broke. She bent her head against Windom's hand. "It is a terrible thing that I have seen, my doctor. Like a darkness of the heart, a poison in the blood. I have pleaded with Jan. I have prayed to God and the Virgin. But it is hopeless. Then I hope and pray that I might return to Papaan—to tell the people, to warn them. But that is hopeless too. I am too old, too weak, to go on foot through the jungle."

Windom put out his hand to touch her head. But suddenly she raised it. And in the darkness the old eyes glittered. "But this much I can do," she said, almost fiercely. "To come to you, my doctor. To help you. Of all that Jan has done, this is the worst—that he should cheat and betray you. But I shall not let it happen. I have not forgotten what you have done for me and my people. And I shall never forget. . . ."

She turned and glanced at the entrance. "I am an old woman," she said, "who talks too much. Come now—we must go."

"But the guards—" Windom began.

"You need not worry about the guards. Tonight there are new guards and they are your friends." She called softly and two figures appeared in the entrance. "You remember Bandor, yes? You remember Dastil? . . . And they remember you, my doctor. They remember when they were hurt and beaten by the police, and how you helped them—and now they will help you."

Windom looked at the shadows in the doorway, then back at the old woman. There was a sudden tightness in his throat, and when he spoke again his voice did not sound like his own.

"What about Jan?" he said. "When he finds out—"

"I will take care of Jan," said Mamarta. "Do you think that after thirty years I am afraid of him?" She picked up Windom's pack and shoved it into his hands. "Here—take it. Now we go."

She all but shoved him to the doorway. Bandor and Dastil stepped aside.

"They will make a large hole in the back wall," said Mamarta, "and say you escaped in the night."

Windom stopped and looked at the two men in the darkness. Silently he grasped each of them by the hand.

"Come," said Mamarta impatiently.

Then they were outside. Across the clearing a few campfires still glowed, and he could see figures squatting around them. But on their own side there was no light or movement, and they passed unseen through the shadows.

In a few seconds the jungle wall loomed before them. The old woman stopped. "The trail is to the left," she whispered. "But there are sentries a half-mile out, so do not use it until you are beyond them."

"Mamarta—"

"Go now," she commanded. "A safe journey, my doctor. And tell my Anna—tell her—"

The old voice cracked. Windom bent and kissed the seamed and withered face.

Then the forest enveloped him.

For perhaps an hour he crept through tangled darkness. He had neither light nor knife. Branches lashed his face, thorns tore at his clothing, and his feet slipped and stumbled in the dark ooze of the jungle floor. But it was not of these things that he was thinking. It was not even of wild animals or of the possibility that he was being followed, but only that he must not get lost. Whenever there seemed a choice of route he bore left, and still farther left, and at last, with a great surge of relief, he came out onto the thin lifeline of the trail.

A half-mile, he knew, was already well behind him. No light or sound broke the dark stillness. For a few minutes he rested, patting his torn face with what was left of his handkerchief, drawing in deep breaths of the damp fetid air. Then he rose and moved on.

He would continue all night, he had decided. He would go on without stopping until daylight and then rest during the morning. But even on the path the going was hard and treacherous. He tripped and fell over roots; the mud sucked at his boots; in another hour his legs were heavy as iron and his body trembled with fatigue.

Keep going, he thought—

Then he fell again. This time he struck against something hard, and his side ached as if the ribs had been shattered into fragments. Dragging himself into the brush, he sat on a patch of moss with his back against a tree trunk. He would rest for ten minutes, he thought, closing his eyes.

And when he reopened them it was morning.

His first sensation was that of fear; but when he crept out onto the trail there was nothing to be seen, and when he listened he heard no sound. Back under the tree he opened his pack, found a moldy half-loaf of bread and forced himself to eat it. Then, rising again, he slung on the pack, but in the next moment realized it was empty and took it off again.

Steady, he thought. Steady.

Looking down at himself, he saw that his clothes were ragged and filthy—filthier even than Lollivar's had been when they had dragged him off to his death. Not only his ribs ached now, but his whole body, and the exposed parts of his flesh were covered with cuts and welts. He had fallen asleep without taking his boots off, and his feet looked—and felt—like bloated clubs.

He smiled grimly. "Physician, cure thyself. . . ."

Then he was on the trail again: stumbling, lurching, picking his way endlessly among the roots and stumps and muckholes. It had begun to rain again—and apparently he had left his raincape with the empty pack—but it did not matter. Even before the rain, his clothes and body could not have been more soaked if he had been swimming a river.

As he moved on, the river-image grew. He *was* swimming, it almost seemed to him: not across a river, but against it.

The trail was a river, twisting, churning, flowing—flowing always toward him, always against him—a swaying, dizzying brown tide between the green banks of the forest.

Five miles? Ten? . . . Then he was resting beside the path. He was sitting with his finger to his pulse, then with his palm to his forehead but he could not tell if the heat that enveloped him came from outside or within.

He moved on again.

Steady . . .

But a few minutes later he was brought up with a jolt. He had descended a steep pitch in the trail, rounded a turn, and now suddenly came out on an open level place, overlooking a valley. It was near here, he realized instantly, where he and Lollivar had been intercepted on their way up, and he stopped in his tracks, filled with momentary panic. This time, however, there was no one there. Hillside and valley spread empty to the horizon. Hurrying on, he passed the open place and re-entered the forest on its downhill side.

You were lucky, he thought. You were a fool, and you were lucky.

At the bottom of the slope he stopped and rested again. This time he rested for a long while, closing his eyes and drawing slow deliberate breaths, and when he arose his legs felt a little stronger, his head a little clearer. . . . Then on again . . . And now his pace, too, was slower and more deliberate. He counted his steps: to a hundred, five hundred, a thousand. Then he began over again. Not once in two thousand steps did he slip or stumble, and not once did he look back over his shoulder. The beat of his heart was almost normal. For the first time he knew that he was going to make it.

And for the first time, too, his thoughts moved ahead. With luck, it would be—when?—the next day around noon that he would reach the head of the valley. Then another two hours in the jeep to Papaan. Would they still be expecting him to arrive with Jan and his men? Or had word somehow filtered through of what had happened? . . . Of what was *going* to happen. . . . In three days the Reds would be moving along this same trail. In four they would be in the valley. And before that . . .

Before that—what?

He was driving into the compound, and Anna was standing on the hospital steps. She was running toward him, seizing his hand, asking about Jan. . . . "Tell my Anna—" old Mamarta had said. . . . All right, tell her. Jan is a Red, Anna. He is an enemy. Your brother is our enemy.

Tell Belhedron. You were right. I was wrong. I told you the truth, but the truth was a lie. I backed the wrong horse, and now I am bankrupt. My faith and judgment are bankrupt. My work is bankrupt.

Tell Lenore. I was wrong. I left you; I came halfway around the world; I rooted up my life, and yours, because I believed there was a job here that I must do. And I was wrong. I was not up to the job. The job is bankrupt.

Tell them all, he thought. Tell them excuse it please. And then get out. I am not a Communist, ladies and gentlemen. I am only a fool. I am only a juggler of pills and forceps, and now that I have tried to be something else, you have seen what has happened.

I am sorry, Lee. Sorry, Anna. Sorry, commissioner.

I am sorry, Dai Lollivar.

Tiredness flowed in a dark wave through his body and mind. Sitting down by the path, he closed his eyes. And when he opened them again a figure was standing beside him.

"My doctor—"

"Kosti!"

"I have found you, my doctor—"

The boy stood in the trail, looking down at him, his small body almost trembling with excitement. He was wearing heavy boots and carried a pack on his back, and his clothes, like Windom's, were plastered with jungle mud.

"Since the sun rose I have been following the trail," he said. "And I thought I had missed you." His quick eyes flicked along the path. "The others, my doctor—where are they?"

"The others?" said Windom dully.

"Jan and the men. They are not with you?"

"No, they aren't with me."

"They are not ahead of you? By another trail, maybe—already in the valley?" Windom shook his head, and the boy showed his relief. "That is good, my doctor. It is why I have come, you see. To tell them they must not go. That they must stay away. You do not know yet, my doctor, but since you have gone from Papaan there are evil things that have happened."

Suddenly Kosti did something Windom had never seen him do. He began to cry. At first he half-turned away, struggling for control; but then it went beyond control, and with a muffled sob he flung himself down and hid his face against Windom's shoulder.

"Kosti—Kosti—"

The boy's sobs grew deeper. Windom held him tightly, as they swelled to a racking paroxysm, and then at last they subsided and Kosti raised a twisted tear-stained face. "I am sorry, my doctor," he murmured. "It is for girls to cry so; not a man. But it was so terrible—so terrible. . . ."

"What was so terrible?" Windom asked gently.

"What they would do to Jan. What they have done to Anna."

Windom's body stiffened. His hand gripped the boy's

shoulder. "Anna?" he said. "What do you mean—Anna?"

"I will tell you, my doctor." Kosti's lips were quivering; his voice broke, but he did not cry again. "Two nights ago I am outside the bungalow and I see a coolie woman climbing over the wall of the compound. I run after her and ask what she is doing, and then I see it is not a coolie woman but Nurse Anna, wearing old clothes like for work in the rice paddies. What is she doing, I ask again, and at first she will not tell me, and then she does—that she is going into the hills to find you and Jan. She says the people from the government have changed their minds. That they will no longer talk with Jan and the men when they come back, but will shoot and kill them. And that she must find them and stop them before it is too late."

The boy paused and drew a slow trembling breath.

"Go on," said Windom.

"I say that I will go with her, but she says no. Then I say please—please; I beg; I say such a trip a woman cannot make unless there is a man too. And at last she says yes. I get my boots and some food, and we climb over the wall and go through the back streets, and soon we find a farmer who is going back late in his ox-cart, up the valley, and he says he will take us, and we get in."

Windom's hand was still on Kosti's shoulder no longer grasping it, but flat and nerveless. Inside him now there seemed no longer blood and bone, but only hollowness, and, within the hollowness, a deep, measured pounding.

Get it done, he thought. For God's sake, boy—get it done.

"So we ride out of the village," the boy continued. "We are on the road along the river, and it is dark, and we think we are all right. But then ahead we see a whole line of soldiers across the road, and they say stop, they are looking for someone, and they come nearer, with lights and guns, and they see Anna. . . . Then we are running. . . . Before they can hold us we are away from the cart and across the road and into the long grass that grows beside it, and quick, we are out of sight—yes, I turn and look while we run and they can no longer see us—and then the shots come wild through the grass, and I think no, they cannot see us, we are safe—but then we stop and look and there comes one more shot and Nurse Anna falls, and when I bend down there is blood all over her throat, and—"

"She was dead?"

"Yes, she was dead. For a few minutes I wait beside her, to make sure. Then I hear the soldiers coming and I move. They go left and I go right, and then I come to a paddy where is water and I . . ."

The thin, low voice went on. Windom sat as he was: not speaking, not moving.

TWENTY-ONE

THE NEXT MORNING THEY PICKED UP THE JEEP AT THE HEAD of the valley. The rain had stopped, and around them, as they drove down toward Papaan, the hills rose green and glittering into the cloudless air.

There was no traffic on the road. Not an ox-cart, not a mule, not a person—nothing.

"I have never seen such a thing," said Kosti. "I think now they have stopped everyone from going in and out of the village."

Windom didn't answer, and they drove on in silence. The only sounds were the humming of the jeep's motor and the sucking of the tires in the red mud of the road.

After an hour the valley began to broaden. The ground fell away steeply before them, and, rounding a sharp turn on a hillside, they could see in the distance the blue miles of the ocean. A little later they passed the point where the plantation road forked off into the forest, and then they were on open level ground beside the brown flow of the river.

"Oh, look, my doctor—"

Kosti was pointing to the left, away from the river, across the flat acres of the rice paddies. Or, rather, at what had been the paddies a few days before; for now the water had been drained from them, the earth was cracked and bare, and the slender rice shoots stood withering under the flaming sun.

Windom looked briefly and turned his eyes away.

Then, after a few minutes, the boy spoke again. "Here is where the soldiers were," he said. "You see the long grass? No, on this side: between here and the river. That is where we ran to and where Nurse Anna—"

Windom's eyes remained fixed ahead. There was a farmhouse, a clump of trees, a curve—and beyond the curve, suddenly, a military truck standing broadside across the road. As the jeep slowed and stopped, a half-dozen armed soldiers came out from behind the truck, followed a moment later, by what was apparently the officer in charge. Approaching, he stopped beside the jeep. His narrowed eyes looked first at Windom, then at Kosti, then back at Windom.

"You are the doctor?" he asked.

"Yes," said Windom.

The officer looked off down the road. "You are alone?" he asked.

"Yes."

"There are no others behind you?"

"No."

The officer was silent for a moment; then he spoke a few words to his men. One of them got into the truck and pulled it to the side of the road, and two others climbed into the back seat of the jeep. The officer nodded. Windom put the jeep in gear and moved on past the truck.

Behind it, two machine guns had been set up, one on either side of the road. Their crews squatted on the grass beside them, and, further on, were still more troops—two ragged rows of small expressionless men, in faded khaki, sitting along the roadside with their rifles on their knees.

They moved through another empty stretch. Then they passed a second road-block and entered the village. Here at last there were a few civilians in evidence: men standing in doorways, women watching from their windows, scattered children playing in the streets and alleyways. But all normal activity seemed to be suspended. Most of the shops were shut. No vehicle or animals moved through the streets, and at every corner were two sentries with bayonets fixed to their rifles. Once there was a shrill cry—"Doctor—doctor!"—and a woman waved at him from a window. A man here and there gestured silently. But most of the villagers simply watched with impassive faces, their eyes fixed, not on Windom, but on the two guards in the back of the jeep.

Then they passed through the gate into the hospital compound, and Windom drove toward the bungalow. One of the guards tapped his shoulder and pointed to the hospital building, but he paid no attention.

"To the hospital," the soldier said. "To the commissioner."

"First," said Windom, "I am going to see my wife."

He stopped the jeep in front of the bungalow and got out, followed by Kosti. The two guards made as if to stop him, but he ignored them and went up the steps onto the porch. The porch was empty. So was the living room. Crossing it, he entered the bedroom.

The curtains were drawn and the light was dim. Lenore lay on her cot—motionless, face down—and at first he thought she was asleep. But as he came closer and stood looking down at her, she turned slightly and her hand went out to him. Taking it, he sat down beside her.

"I'm back, Lee."

She didn't answer, and for a moment simply lay as she was, while her hand tightened on his. Then she turned the whole way and looked at him, and with a shock he saw her face. It seemed at the same time swollen and strangely shrunken. Her eyes were blurred and lustreless, her lips twisted, as if with pain.

"You're sick—" he said.

She shook her head.

"You're feverish."

"No."

Getting up, he went into the bathroom and took a thermometer from the cabinet. When he returned with it she had pulled herself to a sitting position and was slowly pressing her hands back over her face and hair.

"Come on," he said. "Doctor's orders."

She shook her head again.

"Lee, behave!"

"Yes—behave. . . ." Her dull eyes stared at him and suddenly the twisted lips seemed to be smiling. "Love, honor and behave—that's it," she said. "And I have, Alec. Look and see. . . . The perfect doctor's wife, that's me. No need for a thermometer; no need for a diagnosis. Because I've made it for you. I've saved it for you. Look and see—" She pointed. "All nice and neat beside the bed."

Windom went around to the far side of the cot. There on the floor were five empty gin bottles.

"Good God, Lee—"

"Aren't they pretty?" she said. "All in a row. So nice and shiny."

"How could you—"

"Yes, of course: how could I? That's what you used to say: how could I? . . . All right, I'll give the old answer. I don't know how I could. But I did."

Windom didn't look at her. He looked at the bottles and then away at the bare floor, and then he closed his eyes and for an instant thought he was going to be sick.

"Alec—" her voice said.

"Yes?"

"Alec—" Her voice was different now. The awful flippancy was gone. It was so low that he could scarcely hear it. "Why don't you kill me, Alec?" she said. "With some medicine—a gun—any way. Why don't you—please, for the love of God—kill me?"

"Stop it, Lee."

He sat down on the cot again. But now she was covering her face with her hands, and the sobs had begun, deep and wrenching.

"Stop it—do you hear me?"

Her sobbing increased.

"All right, you were drinking," he said gently. "It's not the end of the world."

He reached out and tried to draw her hands from her face; but she held them there, tight and rigid. Her crying swelled to a climax and at last subsided.

"No, not of the world," she whispered. "Just of me. Just of us."

"Lee—"

She dropped her hands. For a moment she lay still, with her eyes closed; then opened them and looked at him dully.

"You're back," she said.

"Yes, I'm back."

"You're back. I've waited so long for it—prayed so hard for it. And now you're back and—" Her voice broke. She turned her eyes away. "Oh God, Alec—how can I tell you? How can I—"

He put his hand on hers.

"Tell me later, Lee."

"No, no—now. I have to." Suddenly she sat bolt upright. Her lips were twisted again, and when she spoke her voice was strained and harsh. "Now you're back, and that's what I've been waiting for. To tell you a story. Such a pretty story—"

Before she could go on, Kosti appeared in the doorway.

"Excuse me, my doctor," he said. "But the soldiers are on the porch, and they say that the commissioner—"

Windom got up. "Tell them I'm coming."

The boy disappeared. Lenore had turned her face away. Windom looked down at her and said, "Rest a while, Lee. Then get yourself together."

Lenore murmured something that he couldn't hear. Going out, he joined the two guards who were waiting for him on the porch.

The compound, as they crossed it, was full of activity. Troops were everywhere. Piles of equipment stood against the walls. Trucks moved in and out the gate. Ascending the hospital steps, they passed Windom's empty office and went down the hall to the room Belhedron used as headquarters. There was a sentry at the door, but he stepped aside, and Windom went in. Belhedron was behind the desk, talking to Colonel Lupat, who stood before it.

"Ah, the ambassador—" he said, looking up.

"You want to see me?" said Windom.

"Yes, doctor, I do. And I am glad to have the chance. In the circumstances, I was not so certain that I would."

He turned back to Lupat.

"It is understood then?" he said. "All troops to be withdrawn beyond the river by noon tomorrow."

"By noon," said the colonel.

"Then the bridge will be blown."

"Then the bridge."

Belhedron nodded and looked at his watch. "I shall see you at four—before I leave for the airfield. Any final matters can be discussed then."

Lupat nodded and went out.

"My apologies, doctor," said the commissioner. "We were concluding a conference." He indicated a chair. "Sit down. . . . Yes, do—please. You must be tired." He smiled slightly. "I can see you have had a hard journey."

For the first time Windom became aware that he had not yet washed or changed his clothes. His hands and arms were almost black, his khakis torn and smeared with dried jungle mud.

"Yes," he said quietly, "it was a hard journey."

"Your friends the Reds were not good hosts?"

Windom looked at him steadily.

"You know, then?" he said.

"Oh yes," said Belhedron. "We know. We have had our reports. Perhaps my government is not altogether perfect, doctor, but it is also not quite so imbecilic as some people seem to believe."

Windom said nothing.

"I am surprised," the commissioner went on, "that your friends let you go."

"They didn't," said Windom. "I escaped."

"Oh."

"And they killed Dai Lollivar."

Belhedron nodded. "I am not surprised. It is no great loss, to be sure, but still another crime on their record." He paused and glanced down at his ruby ring. "Well, in any case," he added, "the time for reckoning is not far off."

"So you know that too," said Windom.

"That they are going to attack? Certainly. And not only in this valley, doctor, but across the whole of the Northern Provinces."

"What will you do?"

"We shall fight them, of course. And we shall destroy them."

"Here in Papaan?"

"Yes, here. And everywhere."

"But you haven't enough—"

"Yes, I know—at the moment we haven't enough troops. They are coming to Papaan in force, and temporarily we shall have to withdraw. Perhaps you heard the end of my talk with Colonel Lupat. Tomorrow our troops will leave the village, cross the river and demolish the bridge. Then they will establish themselves in the near-by hills, from which they can harass the enemy while awaiting reinforcements."

"And you?"

"I have received orders to return to the capital and help there in organizing the campaign. A plane landed here a few hours ago and will fly out this afternoon at five. Mr. Schusterman, the plantation manager, will leave with me. And there will be room, also, for Mrs. Windom and yourself."

Windom was silent.

"Unless, of course," Belhedron went on blandly, "you prefer to stay here and greet your friends."

There was another pause.

"Do you, doctor?"

"There is no need," said Windom quietly, "to keep calling them my friends."

"Ah—you have renounced them, you mean? You are no longer a Red?"

"I have never been a Red, and you know it."

"No longer a sympathizer, then. No longer an apologist for this Vidal and his bandits."

"No."

"You have seen what has happened?"

"Yes."

"And you were wrong about them?"

Windom hesitated.

"Yes," he said.

The commissioner nodded. "Good. We all make mistakes, doctor. You have recognized yours. And I am sure that, in view of your long service here, the authorities in the capital will incline toward leniency." He glanced at his watch. . . . "Well—I shall not keep you longer. The plane will leave at five o'clock, which gives you an hour and a half for your preparations."

He bent to the papers on his desk, but looked up again as Windom stood motionless.

"There is something else, doctor?" he asked.

"Yes," said Windom.

"What else?"

"There is Anna Vidal."

"Oh." Belhedron put his fingertips together and looked again at his ring. "The matter of the young nurse, you mean. It was an unfortunate business."

"Yes—unfortunate." For another moment Windom looked down at him. Then his control broke; his body went rigid. Leaning forward, he gripped the edge of the desk until his knuckles showed white. "Why did you do it?" he demanded. "Why in the name of God did you do it?"

"I assure you I did not shoot the girl myself."

"You gave the orders."

"Of course I gave the orders. That she be stopped." Belhedron paused and went on quietly. "As I say, it was unfortunate. Especially so, since as things turned out, it was unnecessary. A few hours after she was dead we received the information that her brother had joined Than-kar; and it all became—academic."

"Academic?"

"Meaningless, doctor. Perhaps you do not yet know the whole story, but soon after you left I received certain instructions from the capital that in effect voided your mission. Somehow this young woman learned of these instructions and decided that she must warn her brother. Obviously, if she had known what we all knew soon after—that he was not coming back with you; that he had joined the Reds—there would have been no reason for her to go. But she did not know this. She made her plans to go. And when your wife came to me and—"

"My wife?" said Windom.

"Yes. It was your wife we had to thank for finding out. The girl went to her and told her what she was going to do. And when the girl had left she came to me and said she felt it was her duty . . ." The commissioner paused and looked at Windom questioningly. "Are you listening, doctor?"

"Yes," said Windom.

". . . her duty to tell me, which of course it was. And we took the necessary steps. As I say, it is unfortunate. You no doubt feel badly about it. But she was working against us. She was our enemy. And this is war."

The commissioner paused. His eyes were still fixed on Windom. "You understand that now, do you not, doctor?" he said evenly. "This is not some sort of game we are involved in. It is war."

Windom said nothing. He was still standing with his hands on the desk, but the hands no longer gripped it, and he was no longer looking at Belhedron. If he heard what he was saying he gave no indication of it.

The commissioner stood up.

"And now if you will excuse me," he apologized, "I have several things yet to do. I shall see you at the plane at five."

Windom straightened and turned and went to the door.

"You are worn out from your trip," said Belhedron. "You are tired and discouraged. But after a few days in the capital you will be a new man."

Windom went out. He walked slowly down the corridor and through the foyer and down the steps and across the compound. The afternoon sun was blazing. Soldiers and vehicles were still moving about, but the equipment that had been stacked along the walls was almost gone. Windom reached the bungalow and went in. It was cooler inside, and quiet, and for a few moments he sat alone in the living room. He put his hands to his face, feeling the five-day stubble of beard and the sunken flesh under his cheekbones. He held them to his eyes, feeling the tiredness behind them; the emptiness, deep and desolate. . . .

Then he got up and went into the bedroom. The curtains were still drawn, but Lenore was sitting, half-dressed, on the edge of her cot.

"A plane has come," he said. "It will be leaving in an hour."

She nodded dully. "Yes, I know. Belhedron sent a message."

"You'll have to get ready quickly."

"Yes—quickly," she murmured.

But she didn't move. In the dim light her face was white as chalk. Her eyes, fixed on Windom, seemed no longer blue, but dark and sunken.

"Did he tell you?" she asked.

"Yes, he told me."

"So now—"

"Now you should pack, Lee," he said. "There isn't much time."

He came toward her, hands extended to help her up; but when she took them, instead of rising, she pulled him toward her and gripped them with all her strength.

"I was drunk, Alec," she said desperately. "I was alone and afraid and began drinking—"

"Don't, Lee."

"And I was jealous," she said. "Oh, I know there was nothing between you. Even when I was blind crazy drunk I knew that. She may have loved you—yes, she did love you—but not that way. And I know you'd never touched her. . . .

It wasn't that, Alec. It was worse than that; deeper than that. . . . It was knowing how much a part of your life she was. How much you needed her—and that you didn't need me. . . ."

She paused. The tears were close now and she fought them back. "But even that isn't why I did it. Believe me—please believe me—I didn't mean her any harm. All I cared about was you, Alec. And us. And I thought, if I told them and they stopped her, that then the men would come back to the village—they'd be arrested—the trouble would be over. All the awful mess would be over, and you'd be just a doctor again, and we could . . ."

The tears came. Her face contorted. "I never thought—" she whispered. "I never dreamed . . ." Still holding his hands she bent her head against them. "But then the next morning Lahana came. She told me what had happened. And oh God, it was so terrible—so terrible—and I couldn't face what I'd done—and I began drinking again. . . ."

He let her cry, his hands gentle on hers, feeling the trembling of her body as she pressed against him. And then at last he said quietly:

"The plane, Lee. You have to get dressed and packed."

But she would not raise her head. "Yes, of course—" she murmured—"the plane. The plane I've waited and prayed for. Now it's here—now *you*'re here—and we can leave this awful place. I've got what I wanted, haven't I?" Her sobs convulsed her. The words jerked out as if they were pieces of her flesh. "Oh dear God, yes: I've—got—everything—I—wanted. . . ."

The seconds passed. Perhaps the minutes.

Then she stood up.

"I'll get ready," she said.

She went into the bathroom, and Windom sat on the edge of the cot. He looked at the row of bottles. He looked at a *moki* spider crawling down the wall. Then he heard the sound of voices outside and, going onto the porch, found Kosti arguing with one of the student nurses.

". . . because the lady is not well," the boy was saying, "and he is with her. When he is through, then I will tell him."

"What is it, Ti-san?" asked Windom.

The girl was very young and so nervous she could hardly speak. "Forgive me, my doctor," she stammered. "But there is a new patient—a little boy—and he is sick with fever and spasms, and we do not know—"

Windom glanced at his watch.

"All right. Come on," he said. At the door he turned back to Kosti. "Mrs. Windom is packing," he told him. "See if you and Lahana can help her."

With Ti-san, he went back across the compound, up the hospital steps, down the corridor. In the first bed in the North Ward lay a boy of perhaps seven, his eyes glazed with fever, his thin body writhing in convulsions. Two other student nurses were standing beside him, and they looked at Windom with dark anxious eyes.

"You've taken his temperature?" he asked.

"Yes, my doctor," said Ti-san. "It is a hundred and five."

"Pulse?"

"A hundred and forty."

"We'd better give him an intravenous. Prepare a hypo of sodium amytal, two cc's."

"Yes, my doctor."

He stood looking down at the boy; then noticed the dirt that still caked his hands and turned to go to the washroom. Just then, however, Ti-san came back with the syringe, and he changed his mind and stopped.

"You do it," he said to her.

"I, my doctor?" The girl looked terrified. "But I have never done it into the vein. Nurse Anna always—"

"Yes, I know: Nurse Anna always did it. But she isn't here any more, and you'll have to learn." He got a length of rubber tube and handed it to one of the other nurses. "Make a tourniquet around the bicep," he told her; "and hold the arm still." Then to Ti-san, pointing. "In the crook of the elbow—there—you see it? Don't jab, like for the other kind. Go in slowly and then pull back on the plunger to make sure you have the vein."

Ti-san's hand trembled; she bent close over the boy's arm. Then suddenly her hand was still. She pushed gently, and the needle went in, and presently a trickle of blood appeared in the syringe. She looked at Windom, and he nodded. Then she pushed down on the plunger. The boy's body stiffened; his legs thrashed; but the other two nurses held the arm tightly. Ti-san pulled out the needle and swabbed the drop of blood that it left behind.

"Good," said Windom.

Again he stood looking down at the boy, and after a few minutes the writhing stopped and he lay still.

Windom turned away.

"He should be all right," he said. "The fever will break soon."

"Is there anything else we should do?" asked Ti-san.

"Not for a while. Just let him sleep."

"And you will be back later?"

Windom seemed not to have heard.

"You will be back, my doctor?" the girl repeated.

"Yes," he said. "I'll be back."

He walked slowly across the compound. When he reached the bungalow it was four-thirty, and Kosti was carrying suitcases from the porch out to the jeep. Lenore was in the living room, closing her overnight case, and she was wearing the blue-and-white print dress that she had worn on the day of her arrival. Her face was composed, her hair combed, her lips red. Only her eyes, as she looked up, told of the hours and days just past.

"I'm ready, Alec," she said.

He nodded. "Let's go then."

As they came out, Kosti was lifting the luggage into the rear seat of the jeep. There were four pieces, including the overnight case, and suddenly Lenore was staring at them.

"But there aren't any of—"

She broke off. Now she was looking at Windom. And as if for the first time, she saw his tattered clothes—his grimed hands—his bearded face.

"You're not— You're not—"

She couldn't say it.

"No, Lee," he said.

For another instant she remained motionless. Then her hand moved. It groped for the side of the jeep, found it, held it tightly.

"I can't go, Lee."

"Can't?"

"My work is here."

"Yes, of course—your work." Her voice was barely audible. "But now—with the Reds coming. They'll capture you—kill you—"

"No, they won't kill me," he said.

"How do you know?"

"They had me before and they didn't. Some of them may have wanted to, but not Jan. Jan wouldn't let them. And he still won't."

"You still believe that—after all that's happened?"

"Yes, I still believe it." Windom paused a moment. "If I didn't believe that, Lee," he said, "I couldn't believe anything in the world."

Lenore stood motionless. Her face was pleading, despairing. "But you'll be here alone, Alec. All the others are going—"

"The *people* aren't going," he said.

"You can come back to them, then. Later. When things are all right. But now—"

"Now they'll need me most of all." He paused. "And then there's another thing," he said. "A strange thing. I need them."

She started to speak, stopped, and stood looking at him. She looked at the thin, bearded, mud-stained face. She looked at the gray, quiet eyes and what lay behind them.

"I've made my mistakes, Lee," he said. "I've done some foolish things. But there's one thing I can't and won't do, and that's to run away."

Suddenly her hand went out to him. "Then I'll stay too," she said.

But he shook his head.

"Yes. Please—please."

"No, Lee. It wouldn't work."

"Because of the Reds, you mean?"

"Partly. And also—"

She waited.

"Also what, Alec?" she said.

He didn't answer.

"Also because we're finished. Is that it?" For an instant she closed her eyes, and when she spoke again her voice was toneless and dead. "Don't be afraid to say it. I deserve it."

"It's not a question of deserving, Lee," he said. "Only of what's best for us both."

They stood silently. Kosti was staring at them. An army truck rumbled by, its wheels raising a veil of red dust.

"We'd better go," he said.

Lenore hesitated; then got into the jeep. Windom went around, climbed behind the wheel and started the motor.

"Goodbye, my lady," said Kosti.

Then they were driving across the compound, through the gate, along the streets of the village. Sentries still stood at the corners, and a few villagers watched from doorways and windows. They drove in silence. At the edge of the village they came to a road-block, stopped, and were passed through. A half-mile farther on they passed through a second. Then there was only the road, the river, the ruined paddies.

"Alec—" she said.

"Yes?"

"Don't hate me. Please don't hate me."

"I don't, Lee," he said.

"And you believe me—that I didn't know—I didn't mean—"

"Of course I believe you."

They drove in silence again.

"But it's still no good, is it?" she said.

He didn't answer.

"You can't come with me. That's no good. And I can't stay, because that's no good either. I'm no good to you, Alec, am I? Here or anywhere."

"Stop, Lee," he said.

"No. In a minute I'll stop. I'll stop for keeps. But not quite yet." Her eyes were fixed straight ahead, on the road, and she seemed to be speaking less to him than to herself. "You're right," she said. "You belong here. I couldn't believe that at first. I don't want to believe it even now. But it's true, and I know it. All our lives together, I've tried to make you into something that you're not; into something that you could never be. But it hasn't worked, has it? . . . You belonged in that little town in Wisconsin, Alec. Now you belong here. . . . And I—well—I belong somewhere else. Somewhere where things are easier, I suppose. Where the lights are bright; where people are laughing and wearing nice clothes; where there's nothing to do tomorrow except have breakfast and go down to the beach. . . ."

She paused and looked at him and then away again.

"The beach—" she murmured. "We've had our beaches, haven't we, Alec? . . . The beach at Nassau, the beach at Antibes, the beach at Rio. Then the beach at Papaan. . . . That's the real hell of it, isn't it? That it's never been any good, but sometimes so damned wonderful. . . ."

They reached the fork in the road and bore right, away from the river. Up to the left he could see the narrowing valley and the climbing ridges of the hills.

But now, ahead, was the open grass of the airstrip.

"Alec—" she said.

"Yes?"

"Couldn't we—isn't there just a chance—that we could make it wonderful again? If I wait in the capital. If I come back later—or you come down—when the trouble is over. . . ."

Windom shook his head. "That's the whole point, Lee. Don't you see it?" he said. "Trouble is never over."

They drove onto the strip, and there was the plane, bright in the sunlight. A few soldiers were standing beside it, and through the cabin window, as they came closer, he could see Belhedron and Schusterman seated behind the pilot. He stopped, and two of the soldiers carried the bags into the plane.

Then he helped Lenore from the jeep.

"Goodbye, Lee," he said.

She turned her face away. "I can't, Alec—" she whispered. "I can't do it—"

"Yes you can."

"I'm going to—"

"You're going to have a good rest in the plane and a good bath in the hotel." He smiled at her. "And then you're going to put on your best dress and pin an orchid on the shoulder and go out to Chirikiri's with George Hasbrook."

"Hasbrook? . . . Oh no, I couldn't. How could I face him? What would I tell him?" Suddenly she glanced at the plane. "What will I tell the commissioner?"

"Tell them the truth, Lee. That we swung and we missed." He smiled again, gently. But within the smile was something deeper than gentleness. Beneath the softness of his voice was something strong and hard and pure. "And tell them too," he said, "that when they send up their reinforcements they needn't bother about medical units. Because the Papaan General Hospital will still be open for business."

For a long moment Lenore looked up into his face; then turned and went slowly up the steps into the plane. Windom got back in the jeep. As he started off, Belhedron appeared in the plane door and gestured at him, but he drove straight on, across the field and out of sight.

TWENTY-TWO

HE SAT AT HIS DESK IN THE OFFICE. THERE WAS THE SMELL OF formaldehyde and, beyond the window, the buzzing of insects.

After a while the girl Ti-san appeared in the door. "Forgive me that I disturb you, my doctor," she said shyly, "but here are the reports for the last few days."

Windom nodded and took them.

"The small one with the cramps," she asked—"he is better this morning?"

"Yes, a little." Windom glanced through the papers. "Nothing else serious, apparently."

"No, my doctor."

"Good." He looked up at her. "But soon, Ti-san," he said, "I'm afraid there may be many that are serious. Tell all the nurses that I would like to see them here in an hour."

"Yes, my doctor." The girl turned to go, but at the door she paused and looked back at him. "My doctor—"

"Yes?"

"We wish to tell you—" She hesitated, then went on. "We cannot do what Nurse Anna could. We do not know so much; we cannot help so much. But we will do all we can."

"Thank you, Ti-san."

She went out. Windom sat alone. It had rained heavily during the night, but now it was clear again, and beyond the window the compound lay in a hot glare of sunlight. The stacks of equipment were gone. The trucks and squads of soldiers were gone. All that was left were two sentries at the gate and a jeep with a driver standing before the hospital steps.

Then there were steps in the hall, and Colonel Lupat stood in the doorway.

"We are going now," he said.

Windom nodded.

"You are still determined to stay?"

"Yes."

"I remind you again that you do so at your own risk."

"That's right. At my own risk."

"And I also remind you that if you give aid to the enemy—"

"Those I give aid to," said Windom, "are the sick and the wounded."

The colonel turned and left, and a moment later Windom saw him going down the steps and entering the jeep. At the compound gate the jeep stopped and the two sentries got into the rear seat. Then it disappeared and the compound was empty.

A half-hour passed.

Then, suddenly, Windom became aware of the sound of a crowd in the street beyond the gate. There was the tramp of feet—scattered shouts—cheering. Going out onto the steps, he saw a procession of villagers marching past, led by two boys with a red banner.

On the steps beside him were two patients from the dispensary. One was a young man on crutches, the other an old woman.

"They are going to meet Jan Vidal!" the young man cried. "To meet our saviors—our liberators!"

"No," said the old woman, "it is bandits they are going to meet—the fools. And the bandits will kill them and then come here and kill us."

"It is the day of freedom!" shouted the man.

"It is the day of death," said the woman.

Windom went back into his office. A few minutes later he heard the old woman crying, as she crossed the hall to the dispensary. But she is not the one you're sorrier for, he thought.

He looked at the jade and ivory box that stood on his desk. Then he picked it up, and held it in his hands.

"My sister Anna—she is all right?" Jan had said.

"Yes," he had answered, "she's all right."

That was then. This was now. When Jan learned of Anna's death, what would he do? The new Jan. The strong Jan . . .

Windom put the box down gently.

A little later the student nurses came in. There were eleven of them, and they filled the little room. Sitting on the edge of the desk, he spoke to them quietly.

"Some of you," he said, "have been here many months, some only a short time. But you have all done good work. If you had not—quite frankly—you would not still be here."

He paused.

"Now," he said, "we shall probably have harder work than we have ever had before. The government troops are withdrawing to the south. The Reds are coming from the north. Papaan lies between them and will almost certainly be a battleground. How bad it will be, and how long it will last, we don't know. But it will not be easy. There will be many wounded; the hospital will be full; you will have great responsibilities. And you will have to carry them without the help and guidance of Anna Vidal. I think I can count on you to do it in a way that would make her proud of you.

"There is only one other thing. The most difficult thing. This is civil war. The government troops are your own people; the Reds are your own people; and you are caught in the middle, between them. The government is not in all ways a good government. There have been abuses and injustice and suffering, and I know that as well as you. But I hope you are not foolish enough to think that what the others are bringing with them is 'liberation.' What they are bringing, I promise you, are more abuses, more injustice, more suffering. The government may not have had enough respect for the rights of human beings, but the Reds do not even admit that human beings exist.

"All right, we are in the middle. We are not soldiers, not politicians. We are doctor and nurses. Bullets may fly in the streets, shells may fall on the hospital: it will not be your function to strike back, but only to help those who are hurt. Your first duty is to the people of this village; your second to the wounded of both sides. And those are your only duties. Whatever you think, whatever you feel, must wait—because you too are now soldiers. There are many ways in which soldiers can fight. But this is your way. Our way."

When they had gone he sat for a while alone at his desk. It was hot and still. Leaving the office, he walked down the corridor and looked in at the North Ward. The boy in the first bed was sleeping quietly.

"I'll be back in a few hours," he told the nurse on duty.

Then he went out and crossed the compound toward the bungalow; but, instead of going in, he got into the jeep and drove through the gate. There were no soldiers to be seen, and no celebrants. A few shops were now open, a few pedestrians and carts moved through the streets. But an uneasy stillness hung over the village. When he reached the warehouses he left the jeep, walked out onto the dock and climbed down into the skiff.

Facing the land as he rowed, he could see the hills to the south, but there was no hint of the government convoy that he knew was moving through them along a twisting road. Then his eyes moved to the north—to the higher, more distant hills—but there was nothing to be seen there either. Between its long ramparts the valley lay in green, gleaming peace.

There was the headland, the sand, the sea. Beaching the skiff, he took off his clothes and swam out to the reef, and for a long time he sat there, as he had so many times before. It is the same, he thought. Everything else has changed. The valley and the village have changed, and Jan has changed, and Lollivar is gone and Anna is gone and Lee has come and gone. . . . But this remains.

It remains, he thought—but it is a lie. Its beauty and comfort are a lie. In the green peace of the hills men are waiting to spring at one another's throats. On the glittering beach lies the wreckage of a marriage. Somewhere under the red valley earth lies the body of a girl.

In your life, he thought, two women have loved you. And what has happened to them? . . . In your life you have tried above all else to help, to serve. And what has come of it?

He looked at the sea. Blue, serene, crystalline. Was it, too, a lie? Beneath the surface was the deep, beneath the sunlight the dark; and now he was leaning forward—he was staring down—and yes, there it was: the shine, the clearness, the quick gleam, and, beyond the gleam, the waiting shadow, the darkness. Was the darkness the only truth? He thought. The reality beyond every illusion. The end of every way . . .

No.

He sat motionless.

No.

The darkness was there: always there. But so, too, was the gleam. It receded, faded, vanished; but always it returned again; always it reappeared out of the depths, out of the shadow—never lost, never quenched—the deep gleam, faint and flickering, following its dark way forever through the waste of the sea.

He raised his eyes.

"This is our way," he had said to the nurses. All right, it is your way. And if it is often dark, often lonely, often bitter, so is every way that is worth the traveling. . . . Lee is gone. Anna is gone. What is left? . . . The village is left, and its people, and their need of you. Sickness is left; suffering is left; the struggle is left. And you are needed. . . . What can you give to this need? . . . The skill of your hands. The knowledge of your craft. Perhaps a faint gleam from the waste of the sea.

Jan is left. He is coming back. Perhaps there is something you can give to him: something that will make him Jan again, a human being again. If not, there is Kosti, the generation beyond Jan. There are the girls, the student nurses. Perhaps one of them, someday, will be a woman like Anna Vidal.

He stood up. His eyes moved across the bay. The way home lay broad and gleaming under the sun.

He was halfway back when he heard the sound. At first he thought it was thunder, but the sky above was still blue and flawless. Then, turning at the oars, he saw the black plume of smoke rising over Papaan.

A little later he could see a gesticulating figure on the dock. And as he pulled in alongside, Kosti stood above him.

"It is the bridge," the boy said excitedly. "They have blown up the bridge, and some of the people did not know and were standing there, and—"

"How many were hurt?" said Windom.

"I do not know exactly, my doctor. But there were many—many. And now they are bringing them to the hospital, and I came at once here to—"

Then they were in the jeep: threading the streets, entering the hospital gate. Villagers crowded the compound and steps, and through them moved a column of men with laden stretchers.

In the foyer Windom found three of the student nurses, trying to cope with the confusion.

"Valya," he said, "you will stay here and separate the badly wounded from the others. Bhama, take another girl, go to the laboratory and get the morphine and glucose saline. Ti-san, take two others and prepare the O.R."

"My doctor—"

A hand plucked at his sleeve, and, turning, he faced a tiny woman, barefoot and wearing a peasant's shawl.

"My little boy—" she said. "He who has the pains. You will not forget him, my doctor? Now that there are all the others, you will not forget him?"

"Don't worry, mother." Windom smiled at her. "We won't forget him."

He went down the corridor to the washroom and began to scrub up. Beyond the window the glare was fading from the compound. The leaves of the banyan trees stirred gently and drops of rain fell on the yellow dust.